THE HOUSE LOST AT SEA

R.J. BLAIN

THE HOUSE LOST AT SEA
THE TALES OF CATALINA DE LA CORONA BOOK ONE
BY R.J. BLAIN

Cursed by the lover of her former captain, Catalina de la Corona, the Pirate Princess of the Seven Seas, has lived an unnaturally long life and longs for the day she can find eternal peace. Hiding in plain sight as an investment banker, she waits for the end of eternity and the death she has rightfully earned.

When a rich client's fascination with her captain and her lover threatens to exhume the watery grave of Catalina's past, she must take up arms against friends and enemies alike to protect her captain's legacy. Should the Calico's sunken ruins be discovered, Catalina's one true treasure, the House Lost at Sea will be plundered, exposing the secret of Catalina's immortality, and guaranteeing she'll lose the only thing she has left: her freedom.

Cover Design by Daqri Bernardo of Covers by Combs.

ONE

Was my first offer not good enough?

INSTEAD OF ACCEPTING my generous offer to get into the water-filled bag and come home with me, the octopus sprayed ink in my face. Leaning over the tank's wall, I reached for his tentacles, waiting for the moment he cooperated and wrapped them around me. If he didn't want to go into the bag willingly, I'd carry him around until he stopped fighting me, and then I'd stuff him in anyway.

"You'll like it better with me," I promised through clenched teeth, struggling to get a good hold on his slippery, slimy hide. "It'll be fun. I'll take you out to sea when you've been good, and we'll have ourselves a great time."

How many times could an octopus spray ink? More than twice, apparently. Spitting salty, black fluid out of my mouth, I made another grab for the newest love of my life. I expected my admiration for my unwilling companion would last however long it took the octopus to escape my clutches. Such interludes rarely lasted, but I would enjoy it while I could.

I gave it a few days—maybe longer if he accepted I'd transformed my entire dingy living room into a palace for him. Like me, he deserved better than being locked in a small tank and put on display for the world to see.

If anyone found out just how the sea had cursed me, my fellow humans would do exactly that, too. They'd lock me away and study me, and I'd never see the light of day ever again.

"Was my first offer not good enough? How about rations on me? A daily cap o' rum? How about gold? I can do gold."

I could, too. If the meager stash I kept hidden in my closet wasn't enough to satisfy the cephalopod, I'd have to venture out to sea to raid my true hoard. I'd consider it a small price to pay for tolerable company.

Grunting from the effort of keeping a grip on my new friend, I hauled him from his tank and shoved him into the sack, sloshing water all over the floor. Tying shut a bag full of writhing octopus and water took a bit of work, but at least the thick, durable material protected me from another spraying.

We really needed to sit down and have a long talk about his inking habit.

With the main objective of my heist achieved, I needed to haul ass out of the area with my prize without getting caught. For some reason, the marine studies aquarium really didn't appreciate when I liberated my friends from their prisons. One day, maybe one of them would stick around after their rescue, but until the octopus escaped from me, I'd make the most of the situation. The bronze placard adhered to his tank informed me his name was Maximus.

He seemed more like a Ricardo to me. I'd known a smart, clever Ricardo some one or two hundred years ago, and just like Maximus, he had hated getting in the sack, too.

Why couldn't men and women understand the simplest truths of life? Pirates plundered, and once a pirate, always a pirate. So what if a few hundred years separated me from sailing the seas in search of wealth, glory, fame, and a good fight?

I missed the days when I could take whatever—and whomever—I wanted without it making a single lick of difference in the grand scheme of things.

Damn it, despite the long years, I still missed Ricardo. He'd been the best of my conquests, and I'd left the good parts of my heart with him in a past I couldn't forget. I tried, at times, to fill in the gaping wounds, but time hadn't done me any good on that front.

I refused to forget his fire, his flare, his resentment of my capturing of his person, and everything that had made us work so well together. After a few weeks of my company, his resentment had become a reckless passion.

He'd been my sea.

I'd been his stars.

Then fate had bit me in the ass, and he'd been retrieved by his damned crew, dumping me into one hell of a mess. My captain hadn't been pleased by my dalliances with a rival pirate, but how could she blame me? I'd taken a treasure right out from under a captain's nose, and I'd kept him for an entire six months while waiting to return to the ocean.

Those had been the best six months of my life, and I wanted them back.

The real reason annoyed me. My captain had fancied women and had seen zero use for my Ricardo. Worse, she'd resented I'd paid someone other than her any attention at all.

Sometimes, there was only one force stronger than my love for my old captain, and that'd been my hatred for her ruining what might have been with Ricardo.

Maximus protested his captivity through ramming the thick bag, reminding me I had more important things to do than grieve what might have been had things just been a little different.

"First they'll see the ink you sprayed everywhere," I complained, dragging the unwieldy sack across the slick floors on route to the pier stretching out into the ocean. "Then they'll call the cops, because heaven forbid someone liberate an octopus from his glass prison. After that? The cops will start sniffing around, causing me trouble *again*. Why is it they always blame me first? Just because I showed a lot of interest in that other octopus last year doesn't mean I'm the culprit. It's not my fault you all are so devilishly smart. Maybe if you weren't so smart, I wouldn't have to liberate you from their filthy clutches."

Without fail, whenever I witnessed someone—or something—do something deviously clever, I got involved. Humans took work to approach, and for some reason, they didn't appreciate my open advances, especially if they were women, too. They didn't even care if I just wanted to be their friend. At least animals, especially cephalopods, made delightful companions. One day, I'd find one willing to stick around for more than a few minutes.

The instant I opened his bag, he'd be long gone, probably chasing down some octopus hussy so they could make lots of little babies together.

I sighed and dragged Maximus outside to the pier. It'd taken me at least twenty minutes longer than I liked to bust him out of the joint; the sirens of approaching police cars warned me of trouble headed my way. Too bad for them, I'd come prepared. Maybe one day the aquarium would learn to install a security system worth writing home about. Until then, I'd walk in and out of the place like I owned it.

Working my foot under the sloshing bag, I shoved it into the ocean. The waxed, waterproofed material caught on a nail, and before I could do more than sigh my resignation over my cursed luck, the sack tore open just enough to dump my squirming, tentacled bounty into the sea. "Well, shit."

At least I didn't end up with another stream of ink in my face, although the moonlit water darkened, evidence of Maximus's displeasure. "Ungrateful wretch!"

Maximus didn't stick around, leaving me to fend for myself and make my own escape. The sirens drew closer, and I heaved a sigh before jumping into the ink-stained sea.

~

THE SHORT SWIM along the coast to my motorcycle allowed me to dodge the cops. Within thirty minutes of losing my bounty to the sea, my bike roared while I skirted the coast of mainland Connecticut before cutting into New York to my house tucked deep in the woods. The tires crunched on gravel, reminding me I needed to get around to paving the driveway. I pulled up to the stone sidewalk, killed the engine, and grimaced at my home's decrepit state.

Forget the driveway; if I didn't do something about the roof or the siding, the next stiff wind would knock the whole thing down around my ears, and it'd serve me right. I could handle multi-million dollar accounts, but the instant I needed to buckle down and act like a landlubber, bad things happened.

Usually to my house.

Damn it, damn it, damn it.

Without an octopus to keep me company, I wouldn't need the aquarium I'd set up in my living room. I stomped my way to the front door and stormed my way inside, wincing at the creak of abused wood and rusting metal. I really, really needed to do something about my house, soon.

Maybe I needed to give up masquerading as a human and make one last trip to the ocean, living out the rest of my life as a shark. Sharks had it easy. Humans expected sharks to eat them, so I'd be appropriately feared. A few pirates still existed, but they were mere shadows of the past and lacked proper pride and dignity. Most people hated them, and the so-called successful pirates didn't last long before the various governments around the world dealt with them.

They were weak, and it shamed me that they polluted the seas.

Gone were the days a clever pirate could

strike fear into the hearts of men around the world. Gone were the days when one good ship and a better crew could face off against the navy with a hope of victory. Gone were the days of gold, spice, and treasures hidden away on distant shores for another day.

I missed those times.

All thinking about that did was remind me that those I cared for most were gone, especially my fiery Ricardo.

Muttering curses my captain would've cleaned my mouth out over, I squeezed my way around the massive tank, already regretting the removal of my couch and coffee table. Getting the glass and metal monstrosity of an aquarium inside, piece by piece, had cost me a fortune, as had filling it with the absolute perfect water for my new octopus, who had made his grand escape out to sea. The filters and pumps mimicking the ocean purred, and a fortune in handpicked corals swayed in the artificial currents.

With so many of the sea's corals dying, it'd taken a great deal of work to find good livestock. Any aquarium in the world would want my corals, each chosen to transform the huge tank into a reef worth praise.

There was even a nice flat rock for me to lounge on in the tank. I'd indulge, too, as soon as I got the ink off me. I headed to the bathroom, yanking off my clothes and dumping them in the hamper. From past experience, a lot of scrubbing would eventually get the black mess off.

I might not have any skin when I finished, but I couldn't afford to show up to work dusky skinned or splotched. At least my hair escaped unscathed; octopus ink couldn't dye black hair darker. My Spanish heritage gave me a bronzed skin tone, so if I scrubbed enough, no one would notice my run-in with Maximus.

If push came to shove, I could always take my motorcycle out on a ride and eat gravel; it took more than a crash to do more than inconvenience me, and if I had enough cuts and scrapes, no one would notice something as insignificant as a few ink stains.

One shower and half a bottle of body wash later, I decided I could model for a domestic violence magazine without working at it. The ink stains resembled bruises, and red ringed my eyes as a memento of Maximus's very short time with me.

"Well screw me with a plank," I muttered. Tomorrow, I'd have a lot of questions to answer unless I managed to figure out how to apply makeup without looking like a cheap whore. Sometimes, I enjoyed spending time with a cheap but smart whore, but modern society didn't appreciate them the way us pirates had. Modern society also didn't like when men whored themselves out for pay. I'd never understand the preference for female prostitutes.

A pity, that.

A soak would help, and since I'd gone through all the trouble of setting up a miniature sea in my living room, I'd enjoy the damned thing, with or without an octopus to keep me company. I made it halfway across my house before the phone rang. Sighing, I pivoted and stormed into my bedroom, eyeing the wretched device.

It rang again.

On days like today, I wanted to introduce myself as Catalina de la Corona Something-or-Other, Pirate Princess of the Seven Seas, First Mate of the Pirate Queen Louisa de la Something-or-Other, the Shark Tamer, along with some other string of titles I couldn't remember. I'm pretty sure some idiot had dubbed her 'the Shark Tamer' after I'd gotten tossed overboard during a battle and spent the rest of the fight eating the enemy in my cursed form. I may or may not have eaten everyone tossed overboard, friend or foe, but I'd gotten a little better at controlling the blood frenzy since then.

I hadn't eaten anyone in a long, long time.

Over three hundred years ago, the long chain of gibberish would have impressed someone, but now? Now I went by Cathy, and I couldn't even remember how to speak

Spanish anymore. I sighed, snatched the phone off its hook, and spat, "Cathy."

"Girl, you need to lighten up."

Of all the people who could have bothered me, Benny wasn't too bad for a human. While he was a little dumb, his buckets of sweetness made up for it, which was why I tolerated him around when I would have kicked any other human to the curb. It didn't hurt the middle-aged man was handsome enough for a landlubber. "Long day. You don't call unless you want something. What can I do for you?"

"Remember that cute little getup you wore last Halloween?"

"Yes. Why?" I arched a brow, glancing towards my locked armoire, which contained every last bit of my pirate apparel. Over the centuries, I had been forced to replace bits and pieces of it, upgrading the leathers and choosing silk over the rough linen meant to withstand life at sea. A few frills turned one of my shirts into something a bit closer to what a captain showing off would wear, and I tolerated the suffocating corsets Captain Louisa had favored when we made land and went on the prowl for a good time.

More often than not, she had done the prowling and I had done the kidnapping, which suited me.

She had been the looks, I had been the brawn, and together, we should have ruled the high seas. Then another pirate queen had come along and stolen Captain Louisa's affections away from me. That damned pirate queen had been Ricardo's captain, too, the kicker of the entire shitty situation. Their ill-fated love had ruined everything, and my captain and crew rested at the bottom of the sea while I suffered through the ocean's curse alone.

My captain had charted a new course in her hopes of ruling the high seas with a woman who had, in the end, cost us everything. Somewhere far away, the other queen's ship rested on the ocean floor, too.

Ricardo rested with her, and I'd hate the bitch for all of eternity for that.

On bad days, like today, I remembered her name was Maritza, and she had hailed from Italy. At the bitter end, Captain Maritza had jumped ship to join the British, leading the Royal Navy straight to the *Calico*.

My memories, renewed heartbreak over a past I couldn't change, and Benny's silence annoyed me into snapping, "Why are you asking me this?"

"There's a museum exhibit opening tomorrow evening. Could you come dressed up like that tavern wench?"

My cheek twitched. "Pirate, Benny. I was dressed like a pirate."

"But you didn't have a hat or a bandana."

Closing my eyes, I sucked in a deep breath through clenched teeth. "I wasn't a pirate captain. Just part of the crew. I didn't have to wear a hat or a bandana." Last year, the wind would've whipped a hat or bandana right off my frizzy head anyway. "Why am I going to dress like a pirate?"

"Because I'm asking you nicely? Please? I'll take you out for a beer afterward."

I missed grog. I missed good ale. I missed a jigger of rum on the rolling seas. Beer, however, could talk me into a lot of things, and Benny knew me far too well. "Make it three and a nip of something to eat, and I'm in." I paused, drumming my fingers on my phone. "However, ye best be dressin' up like ye be on the high seas too, me hearty."

"Aye-aye, Captain!"

"I didn't say I was coming as a captain."

"Please come as a captain. You can, can't you? I'll make it four beers, and I'll bring cookies."

Ah, cookies. The bane of my existence, the delight of my tongue, and expander of my waistline. I'd have to spend a lot of time swimming if I wanted to undo the damage Benny's cookies would surely inflict on my self-restraint, not that I had much self-restraint to begin with. "They better be chocolate."

"With hazelnuts," he promised. "Meet me at the pier-side science museum in Norwalk."

I came to a full stop, stunned into momentary silence. I'd just come from Norwalk's aquarium. Had my curse of bad luck and misfortune worked its way on shore to haunt me yet again? "Norwalk? You mean in Connecticut?"

"Yeah, they built that new science museum not far from the aquarium. You need directions?"

I sighed. "I can figure it out." As I'd just come back from successfully robbing Norwalk's aquarium, I was at no risk of getting lost. Maybe I'd find something worthy of stealing from the museum. I could go all in and become Norwalk's most notorious criminal. Considering the town's population—or lack thereof—I wouldn't have to work very hard at it. "What time?"

"Eight."

I did the math; it'd take me an hour to get home from work and another to get dressed and geared up. That'd leave me with half an hour to spare if I wanted to get to the museum on time. "They better be damned good cookies." I hung up on him, cursed my inability to tell the dumb, sweet man no, and headed for my living room.

If lounging in an artificial coral reef paradise couldn't cool my jets, nothing short of a swim in the sea and allowing the ocean's curse to take hold would.

TWO

I would spend the rest of my cursed days grumpy, miserable, and refusing to settle for less.

WHY HAD I decided working as a banker was a good idea?

Worse, not only was I a banker, I was an ethical one. Since when did someone like me adhere to the contrived ethics of society? Instead of gaming the system to build my wealth like a good little pirate, I played the game fair and square, hunting fortune for the sake of those who scraped their pennies together in hopes of finding a dollar.

Anyone could be a sleaze and win the money game. Overcoming the system and its corruption without cheating was the real challenge, and I needed a challenge, or I'd go insane.

I bulldozed my way through the Monday slog, turning a lot of lost pennies into what might become a dollar if I played the market just right. Sometimes I won, sometimes I lost, but I liked winning far more than I did losing, so I worked to make certain I came out on top more often than not.

Maybe my evening outing with Benny to a museum would help restore my sense of normality. Then again, not much about me was normal. If I worked on that, would I have an easier time forming a long-term relationship with someone?

No, it wouldn't. I abandoned the idea, as I couldn't view another man without thinking about Ricardo and finding my new interest lacking in some way or another. Ricardo hadn't been perfect.

He'd just been perfect for me, and I hadn't found anyone who could compare.

As such, I would spend the rest of my cursed days grumpy, miserable, and refusing to settle for less, because that's what I did. I refused to settle and stayed miserable.

Maybe one day, I would grow tired of being alone and miserable and start settling for something a little less than perfect for me. Considering my stubborn streak, it would take another few hundred years. By that time, humans might be inhabiting space, I might live somewhere without an ocean to bother me, and my life would be an alien existence.

Hell, who was I kidding? Several hundred years had dumped me into an alien existence, and I often found myself less than impressed with the modern world and its trappings.

Five minutes after five, I abandoned the office and almost made it to my motorcycle when my cell rang. I dug the device out of my pocket and considered slamming it onto the asphalt to rid the Earth of it. My boss didn't like the rate I broke phones, and if she learned I destroyed the damned things on purpose, she'd make me walk the plank.

Since it was my business phone, I was stuck answering with a politer greeting than I used at home. "Corona speaking."

"Cathy," my boss purred in my ear, her voice seductive and smoky, able to entrap men foolish enough to listen to her for too long. "Did you expand the Bensen account like I asked you to earlier?"

I pulled my phone from my ear and checked the time on my watch. At six after five, I should have been on my motorcycle, roaring my way towards home to get dressed to go to a museum rather than discussing an idiot billionaire who needed me to scrape his pennies together because he had less common sense than the average bilge rat.

Damn it, I liked the old man almost as much as I liked Benny. I'd lost my edge, lowering myself to the shallow comradeship of men who sometimes even appreciated the work I did with their money.

I sighed softly enough my boss wouldn't hear me. "Yes, ma'am. I submitted the proposal to Mr. Bensen this afternoon."

"Has he replied yet?"

"Not as of five minutes ago, ma'am."

"You're not in your office. Why not?"

Benny had no idea his sudden need for a pirate had saved my ass from a long night of waiting for my office phone to ring, and while my boss had her flaws, she liked Benny, too. Benny earned her a lot of money. "I am going to the opening of a museum exhibit this evening, ma'am."

"A museum exhibit. The Bensen account could expand by five hundred million tonight, and you're going to a museum exhibit?"

"Mr. Allen invited me to attend with him, ma'am."

"Benjamin Allen? Our client?"

"The same."

"Why would he invite you anywhere?"

I marched my way through the bank's underground parking to my motorcycle, snatching my helmet from the seat. Several deep breaths and a few reminders I couldn't afford to break my phone again kept my temper in check. "He asked a favor, ma'am."

"What could you possibly have that he could possibly want? Surely not your bike. You really should get around to replacing that antique, Cathy. I can put in a good word for you at a dealership. I know a guy."

All right, so maybe my motorcycle had been old before my boss had been born, but I liked my 1936 Harley-Davidson Knucklehead. It wasn't my fault she couldn't understand the bike's worth—or that it really didn't matter my house was worth less than a hundred thousand if I ever got around to fixing the place up. Maybe my home was poised to fall down around my ears, but I treasured my antique bike. I even kept her the same teak red and black she'd been painted the day I had liberated her from an idiot who couldn't hold his liquor or his cash—or play cards worth a damn.

"You would have to ask Mr. Allen that, ma'am. I—"

My boss hung up on me. I lowered my cell and stared at the display, which informed me the call had ended. Weighing the pros and cons of throwing the device across the garage, I bounced the phone in my palm. "Why me?"

I tucked my helmet under my arm and straddled my bike, settling on the seat to give my boss the five minutes it would take her to verify I wasn't lying through my teeth. Would the idle-brained bilge sucking landlubber ever figure out I wouldn't lie about something so easy to confirm?

Four minutes and thirty-seven seconds after hanging up on me, my boss called back.

"Corona speaking." I deserved an extra cookie for keeping my voice pleasant when I wanted to snap curses at my boss for wasting my time.

I only had thirty minutes in my schedule to waste on idiocy.

"When will you be finished with this exhibit?"

"I don't know, ma'am. Mr. Allen didn't specify a time." If my boss came between me and my cookies, I'd teach her a thing or two about how to make crew—or co-workers—miserable. "I assumed it would be a late evening affair."

"What about the Bensen account?" My boss's tone grew shrill, and I held my phone away from my ear.

Had she been asleep through the entire proposal process? I closed my eyes and thought about the rolling of a ship on storm-tossed seas, the creaking of the masts when wayward winds caught the sails, and the whipping hiss of rain-soaked ropes.

I had braved the ocean's fury, and I had emerged safe from its wrath time and time again. I could handle anything my boss threw at me without smashing my phone to teeny tiny bits. "Ma'am, Mr. Bensen has over a hundred pages of proposal to explore. I do not expect a response from him until tomorrow afternoon at the earliest."

"But what if he has questions?"

While tempted to tell her Mr. Bensen was a reasonable human being, he really wasn't.

He was more of a shark than I was, and that was saying a lot. He was intelligent for a modern human, too, uglier than sin, older than respectable for any man, and when he was in a mood, he had a mouth so foul I sometimes thought he was a bit like me, someone who had lived before the world had gone completely mad.

I considered my pirate outfit and decided I could find a spot for my cell somewhere. "I'll have my phone with me."

"Fine." My boss hung up.

I stashed my phone in my leather jacket, stuffed my helmet over my hair, and kick-started the engine. At least some quality time on my bike would soothe my temper before I had to endure an evening of reliving a life long lost.

~

MY BOSS CALLED me five times in the span of an hour, and by the time I got dressed, buckled my belts in place, fluffed my frills just right, wiggled my way into my corset, polished my boots, and otherwise turned time back to 1690 or so, I considered loading my old flintlock with live ammunition and sparing a few minutes to take a whetting stone to my cutlass. I used my home phone to call Benny. While it rang, I twitched my hand over my pistol and thought about shooting my cell, so the wretched device would never bother me again.

"What can I do you for, darlin'?" Benny drawled.

"Can you either gag my boss, put her on a leash, or find some way to get her off my back?"

"I told her you were coming with me tonight for an event. She called."

"You still pals with Bensen?"

"Ask him yourself. He'll be at the museum."

My day went from bad to worse, and I locked my glare on the ammunition box in my armoire. "Isn't Norwalk a dinky little blink-and-miss-it town? Why in blazes would Bensen be going there?"

"It's a really unique exhibit."

I thought about cookies, chocolate chip ones with hazelnuts. "I'm going to need five cookies for this, Benny."

"It's a good thing I made you an entire batch, then. You are getting twenty-four cookies all for your enjoyment. Will you make it on time?"

"Maybe if my boss stops calling me!"

"I'll take care of it. There will be a valet at the museum. What will you be driving?"

"I was planning on riding my motorcycle."

"Do you have a car? It's supposed to rain. Wouldn't want you to wreck your wench outfit."

I did have a car, but I only brought it out when absolutely necessary; I preferred to get wet over joining modern society. I loved my car, but it was more of a vehicle Ricardo would have appreciated, had he survived to the modern era. He hadn't, so all my prized car did was remind me of the past and make me miserable while making me like it. I was truly my worst enemy, and I needed to stop being such a bitch to myself. "I do have a car…"

"Bring it," he ordered.

Damn it all to the darkest, deepest trench of the seven seas. "It's rain. All it's going to do is get me wet."

"Just humor me this once."

I was proud of myself. Despite the urge, I didn't scream my frustration or fling my phone at the wall. "Fine. I'll bring my car."

"Just tell the valet you're with me when you arrive. They'll make sure your vehicle is parked somewhere safe. Anyway, you wouldn't want to leave your motorcycle with kids who wouldn't know how to start it. I'll see you soon." Benny hung up without giving me a chance to protest.

Somehow, I resisted the urge to sharpen my sword and load my flintlock.

~

I MADE it to the museum with five minutes to

spare. Thanks to my less-than-legal exploits in the town, I knew my way around, although I had made a point of parking near the coast and approaching the aquarium from the ocean during my thefts. Museum patrons clogged the narrow, picturesque streets, and when I finally did reach the valet, I wanted to grab a pair of landlubbers and bash their heads together.

Why had Benny made me drive my car? I had a love-hate relationship with the damned thing; the Rolls-Royce Silver Cloud turned heads and, like my motorcycle, was painted red. Self-conscious me, a pirate, drove a luxury vehicle some collector would love to have in his garage. Worse, I'd picked it with a long-dead lover in mind. I got out of my car and tossed the keys to the young man waiting at the curb. "I'm with Benny Allen." I gave my car a long look to communicate there would be death and mayhem if I got it back with a single scratch.

The valet gulped, and I left him gaping at my vehicle.

"You even wore a hat," Benny cooed, striding through the museum's front doors to join me.

When I had sailed the seas, few fleets had worn actual uniforms; captains picked their own attire until 1770 or so. British captains often chose blue overcoats with gold trim to represent their nation.

Benny wore a British captain's coat well, and he'd almost gotten the costume perfect, right down to his white leggings and black shoes with gold buckles. I narrowed my eyes, squared my shoulders, and examined him from head to toe. "British bilge scum."

"Lady pirate," he countered, dipping into a bow, tipping off his tricorne hat and swishing it with excessive gusto. Under his hat, he wore one of the ridiculous white wigs the British had enjoyed inflicting on everyone, another thing he'd gotten right about his attire. "We meet again."

"My lucky day."

At least I wasn't alone in wearing a costume. Several other pirates made their way into the museum, although all of them looked like they'd gone to some cheap costume store. The men wore flimsy shirts, bright-colored sashes suitable for a flamboyant showoff, weapons from the wrong century, and boots no self-respecting pirate would ever have worn. One or two women dressed as sailors left very little to the imagination, and I cringed at the thought of the rope burns they'd suffer if they actually wore such skimpy clothes while on a real ship.

Most of the women, much to my relief, dressed as ladies, although they'd picked gowns in fashion over a hundred years *after* the Golden Age of Piracy had come to an end.

"Please allow me to introduce myself, lady

pirate," Benny declared, returning his tricorne hat to his head without dislodging his wig. "I am Captain Benjamin Allen of the British Navy."

"You mean you're not in character? Pity, that. For a moment, I thought you were going to regale me with tales of your cunning at sea."

"There is no finer British captain than I, lady pirate." Grinning, he offered his arm. "Shall we, Captain Corona?"

He had no way of knowing how his words hurt or the past he exhumed from its watery grave, but he cut me to the quick and left my heart bleeding out on the sidewalk. A pirate captain didn't take the arm of a British captain, and I refused his offer with a huff and lifted chin, angling my head so I could stare down my nose at him. "Watch your step, Captain Allen."

Benny's bright smile warned me some game was afoot, one he'd enjoy playing, likely at my expense. He'd already gotten in his hits without knowing it, and I'd likely count the night as his victory just from how much of my past he'd managed to dredge up within a single day. Sometimes he surprised me, showing sparks of brilliance when he so often missed what was right in front of him.

Benny gestured to the museum. "Never fear, m'lady. I shall. This way, then."

Striding towards the museum's glass

doors, I took a moment to admire the blend of the old and the new. At ten stories, it towered over everything else in town. I'd seen it beside the aquarium on prior visits to Norwalk, but I'd never thought it housed a museum.

Within the lobby, paintings of famous galleons, frigates, and other ships from the Golden Age of Piracy decorated the walls. An anchor, pitted and worn from long exposure to the sea, rose from the marble floor, cordoned off with a red rope. A plaque proudly declared it had been found in the wreckage of *Queen Anne's Revenge*. My eyes widened, and I sucked in a breath, stepping forward to get a closer look.

I'd sailed the same waters with Edward Teach. I'd seen his proud ship on the horizon. Once, I'd had the misfortune of sharing the same air he breathed, and I lived to tell the tale only because he had never learned who I was or which captain I served.

He had thought of me as an amusing wench, one with enough fire and backbone to spit on even him, and he'd dumped me at the first lot of land when he'd been finished terrorizing his crew with the presence of a woman on board.

Where Blackbeard sailed, trouble surely followed in his wake. I'd heard his *Queen Anne's Revenge* had been found and pieces of her dredged up from the deeps, but I'd paid the news no mind.

The wise let the dead sleep and ignored a siren's call.

Like Blackbeard, we had fallen to the British, and the Crown had paid well for the sinking of our ship. At least in one way, we had risen above those aboard *Queen Anne's Revenge*.

The British hadn't taken our captain's head for all they had taken our lives. She had died with us, and our beautiful frigate had sunk before the British could lay their filthy hands on us and take captives—or heads. Only the curse of the sea had spared my life.

I had journeyed with them to the depths, watching their bodies sink through the currents and be swept away on the tides. One by one, I had brought them back to the *Calico* so they might sleep together beneath the waves, swearing one day to join them—to rejoin her.

Oh Captain, my Captain.

THREE

Over my dead body!

WHILE THE MUSEUM'S lobby contained treasures of gold and history, the antechambers guided visitors through a history of the high seas, portrayed the nations fighting to be the supreme rulers of the oceans, and showcased the pirate scourges menacing the tides. To those around me, the pistols, the cannons, the emptied kegs of gunpowder, the old jiggers for measuring rum, and the riggings of deceased ships represented the past, artifacts to be admired.

To me, they were memories.

Benny bounced from display case to display case with the enthusiasm of a child let outside to play after a long rain, taking in the exhibit with wide-eyed wonder. No matter how often I thought of him as dumb but sweet, he thirsted to experience the world, something I respected well enough.

I couldn't remember what had driven me

out to sea or how I'd become part of Captain Louisa's crew, but the wonder of discovering something new on the swelling waves or seeking distant shores never faded. I remembered many of the people represented among the pirates and their hunters. Most knew of Blackbeard, and there were numerous displays dedicated to him and his crew, but lesser-known pirates made a good showing, including the women. While Anne Bonney took the spotlight, some of the more interesting pirate queens from around the world were featured. Of them, Grace O'Malley of Ireland intrigued me. Neither one of us had liked the British, so we may have found common ground in our mutual enemy had we shared the tides.

For her, piracy began as a way to rescue family, something I appreciated although I didn't understand it. For me, the crew had been my family, and I had no memory of anyone else.

It took us almost two hours to work our way through the maze of rooms dedicated to pirates and the sailors who fought against them. For a small town to hide such a wealth of knowledge astonished me.

I snagged hold of Benny's sleeve to catch his attention. "Why did they bring this collection *here*?"

"The main exhibit was located not far from here. That's part of the reason why.

They needed a building large enough for it to fit, close enough to New York City to lure school groups, and access to the ocean." Benny grinned at me and tipped his hat. "That, plus I own the majority of the artifacts on display in this museum. I wanted them close to home."

Benjamin Allen, investor and general annoyance with an interest in baking, sometimes managed to surprise me, and when he did, it reminded me of the time I hadn't watched a boom and got cold-cocked and tossed overboard. My mouth dropped open, and words failed me.

Benny owned the majority of the exhibits within the museum? While he had taken interest in my outfit from last year's Halloween party, I'd never even suspected he had more than a passing interest in pirates or their history.

"And since we're on the subject of my collection, wherever did you get that flintlock? May I?"

Saved by the curious man I had always thought was dumb but sweet. Still absorbing the fact I'd been suckered somehow, I mumbled, "Sure."

I unholstered my pistol and offered it to him. With a practiced hand, Benny inspected the weapon, one of his eyebrows arching as he flipped it over and examined the wood, the bronze, and the steel.

"Dragoon flintlock pistol. I'd date this from somewhere between 1650 to 1720." Angling the gun in the light, Benny inspected the bronze insets, which coiled around the pistol in the shape of a sea serpent. "Most use a dragon design, but this looks more like a serpent of some sort. *Armi Da Fuoco Italiane*?"

I weighed the advantages of lying to Benny against the consequences of being caught in a lie. Considering he had correctly identified my pistol's age *and* its manufacture, I decided caution would serve me better than my normal bluffing. Then again, unless he'd been there the day Captain Louisa had slammed the oak box on top of the ship's logs, her flawless face blanched from fury over my display of rebellion, which had resulted in her beloved ship requiring a lot of repairs, he'd never know the truth.

Instead of making me walk the plank, she'd given me a gun, a gift from her lover, a jewel of the sea, along with a warning if I ever did something so stupid again she'd spank me. Of course, she hadn't expected me to answer her challenge with deliberate infractions, but that was hardly *my* fault.

She should've known not to challenge me, especially not after taking Ricardo and returning him to his crew. It hadn't been my fault his captain happened to be my captain's lover. *She* had challenged the norms taking a rival captain to be her lover, and I had resented the loss of the one man who convinced me love could be real—and obtained.

I decided to stick with a very modified version of the truth. "It was a gift."

"Someone likes you a lot. I don't suppose you'd be willing to sell it?"

While tempted to say, 'Over my dead body!' I gave a single shake of my head before reclaiming my weapon. The sea's memory was long, and it didn't like giving up its dead—or ending its curses. I'd learned that lesson well enough.

The day I died would be the day the ocean willingly gave up what rightfully belonged to it. Until then, I'd remain a living relic.

~

THE ANCHOR from *Queen Anne's Revenge* served as the gathering place of the rich and famous waiting for the moment they would behold the museum's main exhibit, and Benny basked in the glow of their attention. I, on the other hand, wanted to hide.

Unfortunately for me, my friend enjoyed the dichotomy of a pirate captain alongside a British naval captain far too much. Whenever I tried to slip away, he found someone else to introduce me to.

On my fifth escape attempt, he flagged down Franklin Benson, holder of my bank's largest accounts. In his late eighties, half the office looked forward to the man's death, which would result in financial chaos of the worst—and best—sort. We'd be freed from the influence of a money shark at the price of helping his estate liquidate his investments.

The job would fall mostly to me, and if his heirs didn't annoy me too much, I'd even scrape their pennies together to find extra dollars for them, too—if my cut of the pie was right.

"Ah, Benny. Have I told you today your collection is simply marvelous?" Bensen swept forward with the force of a tide, parting the crowd and plowing into my friend, giving him a hearty beating on his back.

With my luck, I'd be waiting a very, very long time for the energetic old man to realize he was supposed to keel over and die. Sighing, I braced for the moment of recognition, when Bensen realized his investment manager was dressed like a pirate and had worn makeup to mimic the dirt and gunpowder of surviving a sea battle.

"Not today, Franklin, but I'll accept your groveling as always."

"Good lad. That'll take you far. I see you couldn't resist the urge to dress the part. Good choice. Who is your… friend?"

Benny grinned, reached over and grabbed my elbow, and pulled me forward. "You've met."

For a brief moment, a frown darkened Bensen's expression, and then he looked me over head to toe before narrowing his eyes and studying my face. When he realized who I was, he burst into laughter. "Catalina Corona, if my eyes do not deceive me!"

"Mr. Bensen," I greeted.

"Franklin, darling. It's after hours. I had no idea you made such a striking pirate lass."

At a complete loss for how to deal with the situation, I decided to punt the ball back into Benny's court. "Benny invited me to come and asked a favor to get me to dress up."

"He does like showing off, our Benny. I'm impressed." Bensen turned to Benny, his eyebrows arched high. "Wherever did you find such an authentic costume for her? You must have been planning this a long time."

"Asked her yesterday, actually. She wore it to the Halloween party last year at her bank, and I had happened to swing in for some business and saw her in it."

With admirable speed, Bensen whipped a cell out of his pocket, tapped the screen, and put it to his ear. "Ah, darling Harriet. How are you?"

My worst nightmare unfolded in front of me, one I couldn't escape without murdering one of my boss's favorite—and wealthiest—clients. I knew exactly one Harriet, and she'd already dressed me down for daring to go to a museum exhibit rather than waiting on Bensen's whims.

When she found out I stood within five feet of the man, dressed like a pirate, she'd find a reason to fire me. Then again, it was high time I moved somewhere far away and picked up a new occupation, so no one realized I didn't age like everyone else.

"Yes, yes. I received it. If I have any questions, I'll make sure I ask her. She's, very helpfully, made herself quite available, thank you. I had a question for *you*. You are hosting another Halloween party this year, correct?" The pause made me think my boss had no such plans and was scrambling to come up with something on the fly. "I'd like to put in a special request."

I turned to Benny, put aside my dislike for his attire, and used his shoulder as a convenient forehead rest, closing my eyes so I could pretend the world did not exist. My hat tipped backwards but stayed on my head. Like he would with a child, my friend patted my shoulder. "There, there. I know. He's insufferable when he gets like this, but we have to indulge the old man. It's only polite."

I peeked through my lashes, canting my head to watch my client continue to insert an unhealthy amount of chaos into my life.

Bensen flicked his hand in our direction. "Quiet, you scurvy curs. Ah, I apologize, Harriet. I'd like to request that the ever-so-charming Miss Catalina wear her delightful pirate costume to the Halloween party this year. It would be doing me quite the favor. Oh, I'm sure she already knows. She's standing right next to me. Oh, dear. It seems that a haughty young British captain is trying to take her into custody. I better put an end to that nonsense right now. I will see you at the party, darling Harriet."

Hanging up, Bensen pointed at Benny. "Unhand the fair maiden, Captain."

A headache brewed behind my eyes. I straightened, swallowing back my urge to sigh. Lifting my hand, I gave my brow a brisk rub. "I think you're confused. Fair? Maiden?"

"Your outfit is a most clever disguise."

"Why am I here, Benny?"

"I believe I bribed you with beer and cookies, plus a nip of something to eat afterwards."

Damned those cookies, anyway. Why did I always fall for the cookies? Ah, right. Hundreds of years flitting around the world hadn't graced me with the ability to bake anything other than charred discs. I could cook, but my curse seemed to extend to baked treats.

Then again, my inability to bake likely saved me from becoming a beached whale, bloated on sugary confections.

Shaking my head, I heaved a sigh. "I may have undercharged you."

"I'm afraid it's too late to back out now. You had your chance to negotiate."

Since when had my dumb but sweet Benny become so ruthless and clever? I would really need to reevaluate my original opinion of him. With a grunt, I adjusted my hat. "Better be the best damned cookies you've ever made, and that nip better be good, or I'll be paying you a visit and plundering your house, me hearty."

I meant it, too. It'd beat having to face my boss tomorrow morning, especially when she had a little over a month to prepare for an office party she didn't want to host. Then again, she'd probably dump the whole thing on my lap in addition to my regular work without offering any help whatsoever.

Maybe I'd pay Bensen a visit, too. When the going got tough, sometimes it paid off to return to my roots and make like a pirate before busting out of the joint. That'd serve both men right.

Maybe in Benny's case I'd consider a different sort of plundering. Good—and bad—deeds deserved their proper reward, after all, and the man had somehow managed to outsmart me at my own game.

That'd teach me to lower my defenses and underestimate someone.

Then again, I'd have to go through the headache of finding out if Benny was married. If he was, that would end that. I didn't encroach on another woman's territory. I also had no desire to follow in my captain's path.

I missed her, but I also hated her, for thinking of her reminded me of Ricardo. Why couldn't I bury the dead and leave them to their eternal slumber? Why did I torture myself with what I could no longer have?

In my quest for forgetting about the past, I'd tried just about everything. Society and its many people still confused me. Women were scorned and abused for loving each other, but if those same two women were to find company with a man, they would become his conquest, and society would look the other way.

I hated people.

Benny turned to Bensen, and for a long moment, the two stared at each other with the largest grins I'd ever seen on either man's face. "The best part about this? I bet she would steal everything you own, and for some reason, I think she'd get away with it."

"Indulge an old man and give me a call if you get yourself arrested stealing from his home, Miss Corona. It'd be a crime if I missed all the excitement."

Unlike most corsets, which clung to my body and showed off my breasts without providing any additional value, mine had one special feature. Dipping my finger into my cleavage and into the hidden pocket, I pulled out my watch, lifted it up, and popped it open. "When does the main exhibit open, Benny?"

Both men stared at the old, dented pocket watch as though they'd seen a ghost. Its gold chain twinkled in the museum lights. I arched a brow at the two gentlemen. Like everything else, my watch was my original, a memento of my captain, ship, and crew.

It worked well enough for something so old. According to the device, it was almost ten o'clock. Snapping it closed, I returned it to its pocket. "Benny?"

My friend jumped, reached into his coat, and pulled out a pocket watch of his own. "Five minutes."

While neither man spoke about why my watch had startled them, I caught them staring at my breasts—and the hidden pocket—when they thought I wouldn't notice.

FOUR

We'd both resented our need to return to our crews and the sea.

I SHOULD HAVE KNOWN Benny would give a speech. Pirate captains liked speeches. Hell, everyone who wanted power of any form liked speeches. I'd given a few speeches in my day, too. Mine mostly consisted of threats to eat annoyances if they didn't buck up and get their damned jobs done.

Most pirate ships were hardline democracies, but some captains ruled with an iron fist, and mine had been one of them. It helped that they believed her when she claimed she would make any and all participating in a mutiny walk the planks to be fed to a shark.

That I was the shark that would eat them went a long way to ensuring obedience.

If I'd been as smart as I liked to think I was, I would have run for the hills before he dragged me in front of the crowd. His knowledge of pirates and sailing the seas came second only to his enthusiasm, and he had far too much fun giving the crowd a lesson on appropriate pirate apparel, starting with my hat and ending with my boots.

He even had the audacity to make off with my cutlass, teaching the curious landlubbers about the violence of swordplay through the collection of nicks and dents in the old, battered metal. Over the years, I'd developed an unhealthy ethics condition, which meant instead of beating my friend within an inch of his life and stealing his wallet, I smiled and pretended I wanted to be on display.

After all, a job was a job, and Benny was paying me. Maybe my payment came in the form of beer, cookies, and dinner, but I honored my agreements. Most pirates had a twisted sense of honor at best, but Captain Louisa had beaten one lesson into all of us: when we gave our word, we kept it, even when inconvenient.

Thirty minutes after he started talking, Benny finally turned to the double doors leading deeper into the museum and took off his hat with a flourish. The pair of guards stepped aside, and after Benny tucked his tricorne under his arm, he shoved through the doors, opening the final exhibit in the museum to those gathered in the lobby.

The sea-worn, rotten remains of a frigate loomed before me, her mast broken, her sails shredded to molded scrap, and her keel so encrusted with barnacles I suspected they had held her together long after she should have fallen apart. White capped waves rose from the floor and splashed against her hull, and the dim overhead lights gleamed on the resins forming the sculptures holding the ship upright.

I knew her well.

I'd always known the love of Captain Louisa's life had found her way to the bottom of the sea, too, although it'd taken her and her crew, including my beloved Ricardo, a lot longer to get there. I had heard of her disappearance, and I both cursed and blessed the day the ocean had gotten revenge on my behalf.

I'd mostly cursed the day I'd learned Ricardo had drowned along with the pirate queen who'd ruined us all.

The two frigates made by the same hand and carved from the same trees had set sail on the same tide for different waters. They differed in but one way, the proud figurehead gracing their bows.

Captain Louisa had chosen a mermaid, an enchantress of the seas and potential doom or savior of sailors.

Captain Maritza had chosen a sea serpent, so similar to the one decorating my flintlock it hurt, and unlike the rest of the ship, it had endured, its every golden curve shining in the light.

The sea serpent mocked me, an eternal

reminder Captain Maritza knew exactly what she had that I cherished. The figurehead hadn't protected my Ricardo from death. Time would have come for him eventually, but my cursed heart insisted on dreaming about what might had been if only things had been a little different.

"Behold," Benny announced, spinning on a heel and sweeping his hat out to take in the entire room, large enough to showcase the frigate and its bounty, scavenged from the ocean's depths. "The *Terrier* sank off the coast of New York in 1714 during a storm; witnesses declared her a ghost ship, devoid of crew, adrift and left to sink. One such accounting, discovered in the journal of a British sailor, claims the *Terrier* and her crew, captained by the Black Scourge, one Maritza Ludovici of Venice, had been spotted in deeper waters, alive and well. No one knows what became of those on board. When the shipwreck was discovered five years ago, there were no signs of combat, nor were there any skeletons discovered on the ship, which was, as you can see, remarkably intact. The crew's possessions remained on board, making it one of the best preserved pirate shipwrecks of our time."

The crowd gaped at the ship and hung to Benny's every word as he launched into a speech about the ship's recovery, the work involved raising her from the deeps, and the restorations done to preserve her for future generations. I stared, too, my gaze fixed on the serpent figurehead, a warning of the Black Scourge's treachery and her love of gold.

I wondered what would have happened if Captain Maritza's love for my captain had surpassed her fondness for wealth. When had the scales tipped out of my captain's favor?

More than three hundred years separated me from my first meeting with the Black Scourge and the day she had, out of love for my captain, cursed me with the ocean's blessing.

With her dark eyes harder than any stone and more turbulent than any sea I'd ever sailed, she had stared at me. I could have sworn she saw into the depths of my soul, and in her voice, I had heard the pounding of the surf on the shore.

With her words, she had cursed me to serve my captain well, to the ends of the Earth and all eternity if I must.

There was no one left for me to serve, but still I lived. When I succumbed to the ocean's call, I hunted the waters for what I would never find.

I LEFT Benny to regale the crowd with tales of the Black Scourge and her crew, abandoning his side to circle the frigate. Old cannonball scars marred the ship's right side, deep enough to leave their mark without compromising her ability to float.

I'd witnessed the ship's acquisition of those scars for myself during one of the rare times the pirate queens had shared the waters against a common foe, the British fleets—the same fleets who had later hunted the *Calico* down and riddled her with holes, boarded her, and ultimately sank her.

Every last item from the *Terrier* filled display cases around the room. The floors were modeled to represent coral reefs and the deep sea, covered in layers upon layers of epoxy, tricking my eyes into believing the entire museum would heave under me like swelling waves. The items closest to the door proved to be mundane, everyday tools a sailor needed to keep his ship afloat.

Step by step, I circled the room, taking in the Black Scourge's many treasures with an almost morbid fascination. Everything had a name and a purpose, and most of them the historians had even gotten right. I understood Benny's shock at my pocket watch; those a match for mine filled a case, although the sea had eaten away at them after so many years underwater. I'd forgotten that; like their ships, our captains had insisted their permanent crew share the same watch, a symbol of the promises made between the two pirate queens.

I couldn't even remember the promise, only that the Black Scourge had betrayed us a mere year before we—both captains and both crews—would have retired from piracy altogether. My beloved Captain Louisa had looked forward to taking us to the house perched high on a cliff overlooking the sea, hidden in deep waters off the beaten path, an island so small and unremarkable I doubted anyone paid it any mind. It didn't have a name, and the last time I'd looked over a chart of the oceans in its area, no one had bothered marking its presence.

Sometimes, when I had nothing else to do and the sea's call was too strong to resist, I left my home, walked to the shore, and slipped into the surf. Over the years, I'd learned if I stayed within a hundred feet from shore, I wouldn't succumb to the curse. Beyond, I struggled to avoid exchanging frail, human flesh for the sandpaper-rough hide of a shark.

The coincidence of a woman cursed to transform into a man-eating tiger shark serving on board a frigate christened the *Calico* had not been lost to me even then. It had been over a hundred years since I'd bitten someone, and almost two hundred since I'd killed someone.

Captain Louisa had promised she'd find a

way to undo what the Black Scourge had done, but that hadn't stopped the pirate queens from enjoying each other's company. In those early days, I'd spent a lot of time as a shark, taking out my fury over being discarded on the keel of Captain Louisa's beloved *Calico*.

In the same breath she'd promised to find a way to break my curse, she'd told me I'd deserved it for taking Ricardo, making him mine for a few months, and refusing to give him back without a fight. That had been the first time I'd lacked faith in my captain.

She viewed my cursed state as a suitable punishment for what she considered to be a betrayal. Ricardo hadn't even been part of our crew. But no, because Captain Maritza had dallied with Captain Louisa, *I'd* betrayed them both by taking one of the men. No, worse. To them, I'd weakened the bond between the rival pirate queen and her navigator.

It wasn't like I'd stolen Ricardo because of his skills with a map and reading the stars. He'd caught my eye, dared to be intelligent, and had flirted with me.

I'd viewed that as all the invitation I needed to make off with him and make him mine. I'd even made him like it.

We'd both resented our need to return to our crews and the sea.

The resulting fight had cost my captain

two weeks in port repairing bite holes in the *Calico's* hull, so the bilge wouldn't flood more than it was supposed to. In retrospect, I should have swam for deeper waters to freedom instead of circling the pirate ship, waiting to see if anyone was stupid enough to come within my reach.

I'd left marks on the *Terrier*, too, though not enough to delay the Black Scourge's return to the sea.

I found Captain Maritza's possessions at the very back of the room. Fashioned from pure gold, her pocket watch had endured exposure to the sea with little damage on the exterior, and I wondered if its gears could be resurrected from the dead. Unlike mine, which was fashioned of silver with golden inlays, hers was as perfect as the day it'd been crafted, and my captain's mermaid decorated its cap.

Her sea serpent decorated mine. Somewhere in the deep sea, it decorated my captain's watch, too. In the case, beside Captain Maritza's watch, the decrepit ruins of her flintlock rested on a bed of velvet, its gold inlays the only survivor of time and exposure to saltwater. The rest of it vaguely resembled the shape of a pistol. The state of her cutlass pained me; once a piece worthy of pride, it too had fallen into a state of ruin, its blade pitted and its hilt reduced to scrap, leaving the onyx pommel stone and the gold wires forming its guard as mementos of its glory.

Her personal keepsakes littered the display surrounding the watch, the pistol, and cutlass, including a necklace plundered from a British merchant and a promise ring gifted to her by my captain. Among the string of pearls, the rusted keys from the ship's treasure chests, and the coins from her stash, a flash of gold caught my eye.

I sucked in a breath, peering closer for another look. I recognized the key and its chain; the other half rested at the bottom of the ocean, clutched in my captain's hand even as the life fled her body. Combined, they would have opened every door in the house they'd built far off the coast of South Africa, trapped somewhere between the Old and New World. The island and its neighbors weren't a part of any storied history, thus were lost to time.

My captain had meant to call it home, but I had given it another name, a title as frivolous and idiotic as many of the ones foisted upon us: The House Lost at Sea.

It ranked as one of the dumber names I'd given to something. The house was hardly lost, for starters. I knew exactly where it was, and no matter how far I roamed, I could find my way back to it. If I entered the ocean in New York, I'd be able to find my way south and east through the deeps without error. In the years between leading false lives, before the government's surveillance had made disappearing far more difficult, I'd made the journey from Britain, arriving months later without losing my way once.

I'd thought the key lost, and I'd only visited the island long enough to leave the treasures of my long life hidden in the caves of a neighboring isle.

"It's quite remarkable, isn't it?" Benny murmured, leaning over to peer at the evidence of Captain Maritza the Black Scourge's existence. "In the next few weeks, I'll be adding her signet ring to the collection. There's still a great deal being inventoried, restored, and prepared for the museum. What do you think?"

What did I think? I turned and stared at the stern of the *Terrier* rising high overhead, the rotten boards gleaming with some clear substance preserving it from further decay. The ship alone surpassed my ability to comprehend its presence in the museum.

To know the location of Captain Maritza's half of the key, which led to the pair's greatest treasure of all, astounded me so much I couldn't find a single word to express myself. I settled with a shrug, turning to look over the wealth of an age long past.

The pirate queens had never made names for themselves in the way Edward Teach and so many others had, but they had left their mark on the world all the same.

"Nothing impresses you, does it?" my friend asked, his tone wry.

"Oh, I'm impressed," I corrected, taking off my hat and spinning around my finger to take in the room with a single gesture. "This is a marvel unlike any I've ever seen. You have outdone yourself, Benjamin Allen."

What I wanted to know was why, and how, someone who had presented himself as dumb but sweet for so many years could hide something as magnificent as raising a sunken ship from the depths of the sea and preserving it for the world to see.

For a few minutes, pirates once again ruled the seas, and the urge to set sail sang in my blood. But first, I needed both halves of one little golden key. One I would have to lift right out from under my friend's nose.

The other I would have to delve into the deeps and retrieve from my captain's cold, dead hand, long since turned to bone.

FIVE

Living with the curse would be easier if I didn't have to carry quite as many burdens around with me.

BEERS, cookies, and dinner stood between me and my plans to return to the House Lost at Sea, so I could close the book on my age of piracy once and for all. Without the final mystery of the house lurking in my memories, there would be nothing left binding me to either pirate queen. I could toss them aside and live with only my regrets of losing Ricardo. Maybe one day, I could move beyond him, too.

Resolving the house's mystery wouldn't break the curse, but I doubted anything would.

And so, I was punished for daring to love someone other than my captain.

If I made all of the right moves, I might gain a different sort of freedom, one I hadn't realized I lacked until I saw the reminders of the pirate queens' alliance hiding within the display case, scattered among other treasures classifying as knick-knacks in the grand scheme of the Black Scourge's plunders and wealth.

I didn't have to live with the pirate queens and their long story of love, loss, and betrayal. If I acquired the key, if I returned to the home that should have belonged to all of us, I could be free of them.

Living with the curse would be easier if I didn't have to carry quite as many burdens around with me.

The room held many treasures, but the key should have been the star, the showcased treasure of the exhibit alongside the *Terrier*.

Somewhere in the museum, a clock tolled the midnight hour. I stifled a yawn, watched the sleepy-eyed crowd still admiring the ship and mingling, and contemplated ways to torture Benny for having pulled so much wool over my eyes. Gone was the lighthearted, sweet man I'd met through work, who had been more than happy to let me rub his pennies together and turn them into serious money, even for a multi-millionaire. He'd played to perfection the role of a man smart enough to understand his fortunes were better off in the hands of someone like me.

I wouldn't underestimate him again.

I wouldn't underestimate Bensen, either, who verbally sparred with Benny at every opportunity. They made an unusual pair, their easy-going affection at odds with the challenge in their posture and sharp words.

In a way, they reminded me of the *Calico's* crew. As First Mate, second only to Captain Louisa, it had been my job to keep the general riffraff in line. Even when I'd spent weeks as a shark, circling the ship in harbor and at the early stages of the voyage, I'd served my role.

It'd taken one foray against a British ship to prove my worth and reinforce our captain's place as the leader. After the skirmish, during which she'd captured a handful of enemies while plundering and scuttling their vessel, she had made them walk the plank. I didn't remember much of it, except she'd cut them so their blood seeped into the sea, and I'd torn them apart within moments of them hitting the water.

I had a lot more reasons to hate my captain than love her, but I'd loved her all the same.

After her demonstration, Captain Louisa had put the crew to work fishing, tossing me the bounty of their catch, probably to keep me from wandering too far. The crew of the *Calico* learned a very valuable lesson: obey the rules or walk the plank. For those she wanted to survive to tell the tale, she offered hooks, line, and bait. Feeding the hungry First Mate Catalina de la Corona did a lot to prevent those who went overboard from being unnecessarily eaten.

I toyed with those who fed me when they fell overboard, nosed them through the rolling waves, and otherwise scared the piss out of them before returning them to the *Calico* alive and in possession of all their limbs.

In time, the crew had learned to trust me with their lives if they fell into the water, especially after the captain convinced me to haul my ass back on board where I belonged. We'd argued over that, with her screeching like some fisher's wife on the wharf while I slapped water at the *Calico* in open defiance.

On any other ship, I would've been the one walking the plank.

I wondered if the *Terrier's* crew had someone cursed like me, and if they did, what had happened to him. Unlike my captain, the Black Scourge allowed no women on board, marooning those who attempted to sneak into the ranks. I suspected Captain Maritza couldn't tolerate the thought of anyone competing for Captain Louisa's affections. After my months with Ricardo, I'd only seen him again as a distant figure aboard the rival ship, and I'd never been invited on to the *Terrier* when he might be around.

Yet another punishment for my actions.

Some days, I regretted I hadn't sunk the ship of my captain's lover, plucking Ricardo from the waves, and making off with him. I'd been branded a traitor for wanting him, but I'd stayed loyal until the bitter end.

I regretted that choice, as it had cost me everything.

Damn it all. Making off with a man on shore leave wasn't even a real betrayal anyway, and if Captain Maritza hadn't wanted him out of sight, she shouldn't have left him where I could take him at my leisure.

"I owe you a few beers," Benny announced, whipping off his hat and dipping into a bow. By some miracle, his wig stayed in place. "Why don't we take your car? There's a pub the next town over you'll appreciate more than the dive here."

Bensen crept up behind Benny and, with a wicked grin, cleared his throat. My friend's startled yelp caught the attention of the straggling social elite, who joined Bensen in laughing.

Even I cracked a grin at Benny's undignified reaction.

"Allow me to take you both for dinner. I asked my personal chef for a favor, and he is willing to whip up something for us at his home. He's a delightful young chap with a lovely cottage on the sea not far from here."

I'd never understand the wealthy. While I had a fortune in treasure hidden away on an island in the middle of the ocean, I only took what I needed to get by, using my hard-earned paychecks rather than the wealth I had plucked from the sea. In some ways, I benefited from the curse.

No human diver could beat me at looting shipwrecks.

"Sounds good to me. Cathy?"

"My boss is going to crucify me in the morning anyway, so what do I have to lose? I'm not driving you home, Benny, so you better bring your car."

"Nonsense. I'll have Edwardo pick me up when needed."

"Fine." I turned to Bensen and canted my head, arching a brow. "How about you?"

"I would not object to seeing your car. I was under the impression you only had a motorcycle, darling. How intriguing."

"Her car makes ours look uncouth. We've been outclassed, Franklin. Next, she'll tell me it's all original, and that we're heathens for even asking to touch it."

Laughing because it was expected of me, I shook my head and headed for the doors. "I've had to do some repairs to it over the years, but it's as original as it gets."

"What is it, anyway? It's a Rolls-Royce of some sort, but what model?"

"It's a 1955 Silver Cloud."

"Where have you been all my life?" Bensen demanded.

"I saw her first."

The pair started bickering, waging war

with their accounts to prove to the other who held the majority of my attention. At the rate they challenged each other, maybe I wouldn't have to worry about my boss's wrath in the morning. If they didn't try to one up each other by expanding their investments under my control by the end of the day tomorrow, I'd eat my hat and squawk like a parrot.

ONE DAY, maybe the absurdities of the modern-day nobility wouldn't startle me. When I got technical about it, I had the wealth to be one of them, although I hoarded mine in a cave like some long-lost, ancient dragon ready to breathe fire at anyone who got too close to my treasures.

I couldn't help but wonder if Bensen's chef had a chef, a butler, and whoever else the excessively rich hired to make their lives as pleasant and easy as possible. I expected a house—maybe not one as rundown as mine, but still a house. Instead, I visited a mansion, one so large my entire home could fit in the garage.

At least my Silver Cloud felt right at home beside the newer Rolls-Royce on display at the end of the chef's driveway. I liked mine better. Something about the modern version lacked the quiet elegance of my car. Then again, if I had my way, I'd blitz my way right back to 1690 where I belonged.

For almost three hours, I left my comfortable, sparse reality, stepped into a dream world where men with more money than any god served me, and crossed the chasm separating the elite and those who labored beneath them. The chef was a British import named Tyler, and I got the feeling late-night dinners happened more frequently than I initially would have believed thanks to one old man's enthusiasm.

Maybe Tyler held the rank of Bensen's personal chef, but he ate with us, laughed with us, and had no problems with making fun at their expense. Had I even dreamed of indulging in such easy-going and relaxed behavior with my boss, I would've been packing my desk within an hour due to my new status as unemployed.

Well aware I'd have to drive home, I indulged in only one beer before dinner, but in exchange, Benny gave me a second batch of cookies. By the time I got home, the first hints of dawn brightened the distant sky, and I wanted nothing more than to sleep for a week.

Instead, I returned my Silver Cloud to its rightful place in the garage, trudged my way inside my home, and got ready for work, taking a shower so cold my teeth chattered. It woke me up, and I pulled out my daily planner to check over my schedule. Once the Bensen account was settled, my work could be distributed between other members of the team for a few weeks.

I could take a two-week vacation, fly to South Africa and the Cape of Good Hope, and go for a swim. It wouldn't take too long to reach the *Calico's* final resting place, eight days if I took my time and lingered with the wreckage, leaving me with enough time for the edge to wear off from hunting the oceans as a shark. If I chartered a ship, I could make the journey in a day.

If I secured the Bensen account expansion, the acquisition bonus would more than cover my expenses without me having to loot my hoard until I had acquired both halves of the key. Excitement shivered through me, the one I associated with finally returning to sea after too long on shore.

Anticipation of reclaiming what was rightfully mine kept me awake through my dawn preparations. I applied my makeup with far more care than usual, erasing the fading ink stains from Maximus's escape back to the ocean. The patter of rain outside convinced me to drive the Rolls-Royce, and I chanced parking it beneath the bank.

The garage guards gawked, and I waved my pass to gain access to the employee level. Enough people worked in the building they didn't know me by name, although I expected rumors would spread of an antique car visiting the lot.

Armed with coffee enough for three, I made it to my desk with three minutes to spare. My boss stormed in, her fury a match for the time she'd caught one of the other investors rubbing pennies together, making extra dollars, and making off with more than his fair cut of the bounty.

"Do you care to explain?"

While I ranked high enough in the fold to have an office, my spot wasn't far from the open concept cubicle farm, and everyone stopped what they were doing to stare. At least modern society frowned upon taking pistols or swords to work; the temptation to run the woman through might have otherwise caused an incident, a very bloody and lethal one.

Of all the tricks I'd learned over the years, I selected a sweet, pleasant smile as my weapon of choice. "I wasn't aware Mr. Bensen was attending the exhibit until after my arrival, ma'am. He seemed quite upbeat last night. Hopefully, he'll—"

My phone rang, and as though my words had summoned the devil himself, I recognized Bensen's number. I held up a finger to indicate I needed to take the call, swept the phone off its cradle, and held it to my ear. "Good morning, Mr. Bensen. How can I help you?"

"Cathy, darling. It's been far too long since we've spoken."

I glanced at my cheap little desk clock. "Sir, you saw me several hours ago."

"Far too long, my dear. I've been looking over the proposal you sent over yesterday. I have a question about the African investment account."

Files upon files littered my desk, each one labeled with the client and the portfolios the bank pursued on their behalf. I grabbed Bensen's foreign investments summary folder and pulled out the appropriate page. "Yes, sir?"

"Can you expand the sea-trade investments account by two-hundred thousand? I have particular interest in the tourism industry surrounding the Cape of Good Hope."

Normally, when a wealthy client called asking to spend more money, it was going to be a good day. His desire to expand close to where the *Calico* rested beneath the waves, however, worried me. "I can look into it, sir. What sort of tourism were you considering?"

"Deep water dives for shipwrecks between South Africa and India. Submarine exploration, shipwreck analysis, documentation, and recovery. Expect a call from Benjamin later today, dear. We're following some interesting leads."

"Should I classify this as luxury adventure tourism, sir?"

"That will do, Cathy darling."

The first thing I needed to do was buy myself a little time. If Bensen's discovery of the *Terrier* spurred the men into a wild goose chase through the ocean depths, the *Calico* was at risk, and while she hadn't been officially found, too many had known we'd sailed those waters. "You're going to need a larger budget if you want to break into that market as anything other than a spectator, sir. If you want to do more than just grow your options, you're going to need at least one direct business partner in the industry."

"Make it happen," he ordered before hanging up on me.

I set the phone in its cradle.

"Explain," my boss ordered.

"Mr. Bensen wishes to expand into tourism around the Cape of Good Hope, and I think he has mistaken our investments office as a business acquisitions firm. While I could make arrangements to buy out stocks of existing companies, so he could become a majority stockholder, that's not necessarily our specialty."

"What's the problem?"

When opportunity knocked, I refused to turn a blind eye. "I'll have to do some research, ma'am. I will need a first-hand look at the products he's wishing to invest in. This is far beyond our usual scope."

Our usual scope involved sitting behind a

desk crunching numbers and obeying investor demands for the movement of stocks, bonds, and other financials rather than proposing expansions into specific industries with an expectation of hands-on participation.

If looks could kill, my boss was moments away from murdering me in my own office. "And what's the problem with that?"

"The research required would send me to South Africa to the Cape of Good Hope to see if what he wants actually exists, ma'am. It's very specialized."

"Will it secure the account expansion?"

I picked up my phone, dialed Bensen's number, and connected the call. He answered after the second ring. "News for me already, Cathy darling?"

"Will a full proposal on potential expansion options, including the proposals for potential stock acquisition of promising companies, secure your other investments? It will require a great deal of research to put together an action plan, so if I can push the rest of the investment portfolio out the door to the other managers on the team, I will be freed to pursue these interests for you."

"I will write in a modification to your original proposal to separate out the South African tourism project and have signed copies to you later today."

Why did people always hang up on me? At

least he gave me the answer I wanted, although I hoped he wouldn't regret his reckless decision later. Then again, with the amount of money the man had to burn, I doubted he cared if he lost half a billion dollars on a whim.

"He's going to remove the South African portion of the proposal from the account and send over the signed copies later today, ma'am."

"Book your flight. I'm expecting good things from you. How long will you need to handle your research?"

"Call it three weeks, and I'll take a week vacation out of my personal days."

"Approved. Don't disappoint me, Corona."

I fully intended to disappoint a lot of people with the South African expansion gambit, but with a little luck, no one would discover I worked hard to ensure no one looked too closely at the specific stretch of ocean hiding the *Calico*. And, if I could find something of use for Bensen somewhere away from my ship's sunken ruins, I would work miracles for him.

But my crew would not be found. Not by them. Not by anyone.

SIX

What sort of pirate wore lace panties?

It took two days to get my affairs in order so I could abandon ship and fly to South Africa, one day of which I spent transferring every piece of coral from my living room aquarium to a rental truck for transport to a store willing to take everything for their display tank. The store's manager even provided the containers, heaters, and pumps required so nothing would die during the two-hour drive.

The fish went, too, and it pained me to catch the seahorses, my favorite of my new acquisitions. Some pirate I had turned out to be. I'd gone from man-eating shark and scoundrel of the sea to a woman incapable of allowing twenty-dollar fish to die unnecessarily. Pirates with any sense of compassion didn't last long.

They became pirate hunters or privateers on a mission.

With several hundred million reasons to be happy with me, my boss had tacked on the two days for preparations to the three weeks I had requested, fully paid. The all-expenses-paid trip came with a new company phone and laptop, too, although I recognized those as the double-edged swords they were. My transition from investment manager to scout left a lot to be desired, but it worked for my plans—at least for the moment.

The first week I would spend scoping out potential businesses, indulging in every luxury tourism event I could find so I could build a potential portfolio. The next week I'd claim as my vacation, returning to the *Calico* to retrieve my captain's half of the key. The third week I'd use to find everything South Africa had to offer for me to use to lead Bensen away from the location of the shipwreck.

I would've preferred to go straight to the *Calico,* but patience would better serve me. Benny's interest in my watch and pistol worried me almost as much as Bensen's choice of locations for his diving project. I wouldn't make the mistake of underestimating either one of them again. Both had the funds to hire someone to watch me.

If someone was monitoring my activities, I'd spot them.

As a precaution, I stopped at a bank and left my cutlass, pocket watch, and pistol in a safe-deposit box. To make things even harder for anyone wanting to access it, I locked the key in a different box at another bank. I had seven more such boxes, and I made a point of visiting them all and hiding their keys around my home.

My satisfaction over my efforts to frustrate any would-be thieves lasted all the way from JFK to Cape Town, a nineteen-hour flight with a single layover. I planned to work myself into a state of exhaustion so severe by nightfall it'd take a crane or an explosion to get me out of bed.

Ships were so much better; they allowed a gradual adaptation to time zones rather than flying's swift punch to the gut. Returning to the United States would hurt just as much, although it'd be worth the price. I would have the first half of the key in hand with my eye on the rest of my prize.

I made my way through the airport, stifling yawns and dragging my ridiculous wheeled bag behind me, one the luggage salesperson claimed paired elegance and sophistication with function. It, like the leather bag from hell my boss insisted I pack my laptop in, fit the requirements of a proper businesswoman, as did every last piece of clothing I'd brought at her recommendation, right down to my lace panties.

What sort of pirate wore lace panties?

The only person who might appreciate the

lace panties had died hundreds of years ago, and he would've been more baffled by them than anything. It wouldn't have taken him long to remove them from my person, and I suspected their fragile nature would have encouraged him to use his teeth rather than other methods of removing troublesome pieces of clothing preventing us from indulging in each other.

The thought both disgusted and amused me all the way through the airport to the line for cabs, where I joined at least thirty other people looking to escape hell in a hurry. No matter how much effort my boss invested in dressing me up for business travel, she'd need a miracle for me to rise above plain at best. Brawn and brain I could do in plenty, but I let others worry about being pretty. It worked well enough in my favor; they enjoyed making themselves beautiful. I didn't begrudge anyone from enjoying the fruits of their labor.

Beautiful things deserved to be admired. While I wasn't beautiful, Ricardo had liked me plain.

I couldn't go a single damned day without thinking about the damned man. Obsessing over him was even worse of a curse than my actual curse, and there was jack shit I could do about it. All trying to drink him away did was leave me with a splitting headache and a bad temper. Forgetting didn't work.

Time refused to work its magic on me.

I had enough trouble considering my uncontrollable shapeshifting into a shark.

To try to distract myself from the realities of my life, I admired the men and women who captured their beauty and showed it off. A woman sauntered by, headed in the direction of the limousines parked farther down the line, and the sway of her hips warned me of a woman who knew exactly how good she looked and didn't mind gracing the rest of us with a good, long look. My boss had the wrong idea completely; lingerie better suited the leggy, gold-highlighted brunette in her black pencil skirt. The silk blouse caressing every last one of her curves didn't hurt, either.

Damn. I needed to find someone worth taking a tumble in a hammock with. Who knew finding someone smart, beautiful, challenging, and mutually interested could be so difficult? Even if I tried to open the playing field a little, the mutual interest part always shot me in the foot.

Maybe three hundred years ago taking what I had wanted worked, but times had changed, and so had men and women. Three hundred years ago, it had taken very little effort to find someone willing enough. Challenging and smart had taken work, but even a brawny wench like me had been able to hunt someone interesting down with little effort or protest.

I'd ruined myself with snatching Ricardo and taking my time convincing him I was worth spending time with. In the years after his death, I had indulged in a kidnapping or two to try to find a new flame. It hadn't worked, but pirates had a reputation to maintain, and I always returned my partners in good health, even the ones smart and challenging enough to put up a good fight. None of them had worked out. Half the time, none of them had been interested in a dalliance with me, and I'd sent them on their way without having scratched any itches at all.

Beauty was usually the first of my criteria to be sacrificed in pursuit of a relationship, whether I wanted it for a night or a little longer, something I needed a heady dose of soon. As usual, I got ahead of myself. Forget putting the cart before the horse, I needed a cart or a horse before I worried about either of them.

A blur of motion drew me out of my thoughts, and a chauffeur opened the limo door for the woman, who turned to slide into the vehicle. With her skin tanned from long exposure to the sun and her eyes darker than even mine, she reminded me of those who had set sail long ago.

I appreciated the honesty in her frown,

and while I waited for a cab, I wondered about her.

~

MAYBE ONE DAY I would understand the banker mentality. While I classified as an investment manager and moved money in high quantity, in the grand scheme of things, I ranked pretty low. I never met most of the clients I served; my boss usually took the glory of my preparations and left me in the shadows. In a way, it reminded me of my job as a first mate.

The captain took the glory, and I made certain everyone fell in line. I did my work best when I stood in the shadows, watching and waiting for the moment I needed to step in and bash heads together. I had taken command often enough, but when I did my job right, I didn't need to be hovering for my influence to be known.

The captain demanded respect and held authority, and I, as the first mate, enforced it. Most days, I had enjoyed the work well enough.

My boss had, in her infinite wisdom, reserved me a room at a tourist dive. While the place wasn't quite ready to give up the ghost and come crashing down, I worried the next storm might tear the roof off.

At least my room had a good view of the

ocean, and I spent a long time looking out over the sea. Soon enough, I'd be able to venture out. First, I needed to find out what Cape Town and the Cape of Good Hope had to offer. Since Bensen wanted adventure tourism, I abandoned everything but my keys, wallet, and new phone in my room. If something got stolen, it would serve as a consideration for his review. In a way, I hoped someone robbed the room. It would serve my boss right, as she'd have to replace everything stolen.

I wouldn't find anything in a hotel meant for those visiting South Africa on a budget.

Cape Town had a thriving tourist district, and with a little help from my phone and a travel agency, I learned a few important things: impulse planning trips in South Africa sucked, and there were very few options for those who wanted to spend more money than they had sense.

Instead of indulging in something interesting, such as a dive off the coast or a trip out on the ocean, I ended up exploring the Cape of Good Hope on foot while my travel agent, Lizzy, went on a hunt for something interesting—and expensive. She'd already booked me for a trip to go diving with the sharks the next day, which I viewed as a disaster in the making.

The last time I'd gotten into a scuffle with a great white, it'd ended badly for both of us. I had lived to tell the tale. The other shark hadn't.

An hour later, my phone rang. Something about the salt in the air, the hiss of the wind, and the crash of the surf brought out the pirate in me, and expecting Lizzy's call back, I answered, "Catalina de la Corona."

"Cathy?" Benny blurted.

Crap. I grimaced, reminded myself I needed to check caller id *before* answering the phone, and sighed. "It's me." I hesitated, scrambling for some excuse for using the Spanish variant of my name. "I'm overseas, and the locals like the Spanish flair. What do you need?"

"Where are you? I've been trying to reach you since yesterday, and you haven't been home. Your boss gave me this number."

"I'm on a business trip."

"A business trip? Overseas? Since when did you start going on business trips overseas? When will you be back?"

"Three weeks or so. I'm scouting some business opportunities for Mr. Bensen."

"Franklin has you out scouting business opportunities?"

"Not exactly. My boss has me scouting out business opportunities. I'm doing my job. I'm just doing it a little way from home, and it happens to be for some of Mr. Bensen's accounts."

I expected him to start asking questions,

but instead, he sighed. "Damn. I wanted to ask you a favor."

"What sort of favor?"

"I wanted to find out if you'd do a photoshoot with the *Terrier*. Your costume is one of the most authentic I've seen, and it'd be good publicity for the museum."

When opportunity knocked, I answered, and a photoshoot with the *Terrier* would get me close to Captain Maritza's half of the key. "If it can wait for three weeks until I'm back in town, I'd be happy to help you out. You still owe me a few beers. You can pick me up, drop me off, and pour rum down my throat to make it even more authentic."

"With a lime in it?" he asked, his tone wry.

"Can't risk getting scurvy, now can I?"

"Obviously not. You'll be back for Halloween?"

"Easily. There's the issue of the office party, though."

"It'll be an after-hours shoot. We can do it after the party. I'll make it worth your while, promise."

I sighed. If I withheld information on the joint venture, Benny would know I was up to something, especially if he verified any information at all with Bensen. "I'm in South Africa looking into adventure tourism. He said you were going into a joint venture with him?"

"You're in South Africa?" he blurted.

"I'm in South Africa. It's almost impossible to get good information on this area for what he wanted. Someone had to go in person, and I was owed some vacation anyway. So, I'm doing two weeks of work and slipping in a personal vacation on top of it. Good deal for me. So, here I am, scoping out South Africa on Mr. Bensen's behalf. Apparently, I'm going to be served up as bait for some sharks, as that is a popular activity here. If you don't hear from me by late afternoon tomorrow, I was eaten."

"How reassuring. What other things do you have planned?"

"Good question." My phone buzzed as someone tried to call me. "Got a call on the other line. If you're that worried, call me tomorrow."

"Will do." Benny hung up.

I swiped to answer the incoming call, and since I'd already blown my cover once, I went two-for-two and answered, "Catalina de la Corona."

Maybe having a fancy name would make me sound like a spoiled rich girl looking for adventure.

"Hi, Miss Corona. It's Lizzy. I have an opportunity that might interest you."

"Shoot," I ordered.

"How does a tour of the shipwrecks of the Cape of Good Hope sound to you? Since you're interested in diving, the captain of the yacht is willing to do a night dive to some of the more interesting wrecks off the coast. The tour would take you to some of the more prominent coastline wrecks and includes a five-course dinner served at sunset along with a late-evening dive."

"Book it." I thought about the planned shark dive, which provided all the needed equipment. I doubted a yacht operator—who likely wasn't captaining a real yacht, but rather a smaller pleasure boat—would have a full complement of equipment. "I'll need to buy gear for the dive. Mine is at home. Where would you recommend?"

Lizzy gave me the name of a shop, the location of the marina, and instructions to be there in two hours. I agreed, hanging up on her without finding out the cost to set sail. There'd be plenty of time for me to worry about expenditures later.

For now, I would return to the sea where I belonged and test my control of the curse before exposing myself to sharks—real sharks, and not cheap imitations like me.

SEVEN

Her captain had plenty of reasons to be proud of her.

WHILE I WOULD HAVE PREFERRED a proper sailboat, the sleek yacht Captain Naidoo led me to melded the past and present, its hull carved to resemble a sloop while fashioned with more modern materials and lacking masts. The blue trim on the white vessel came across as plain yet elegant, and I approved of the subtle signs of use and the discoloration promising the ship spent a great deal of time at sea.

At a solid thirty-five to forty feet long, it took pleasure ship to a whole new level, and I decided I couldn't call it anything other than a yacht, and her captain had plenty of reasons to be proud of her. The captain amused me almost as much as his ship. When I had been at sea, men as dark as Naidoo would've been stolen by the paler Europeans, chained, and taken as slaves, a practice I found revolting at best.

I valued the freedom to make my own choices, and while I hadn't been above the occasional kidnapping for nefarious purposes or hunting of other pirates, I had always disliked slavery and slavers, especially when the *Calico* was involved.

My Captain Louisa refused to discriminate between white and black, taking whomever she wanted as a slave on board her ship when necessary. She had kept a few over the years, a practice that opened more ports than it closed. People could tolerate a friendly pirate. Slavers, on the other hand, crossed a line with many. Captain Louisa had found it a suiting punishment to sell white slavers to black men as often as she'd return black slaves who had attempted to stowaway on the *Calico*.

On that, we had never quite seen eye to eye, and in the end, I suspected our differing opinions had been the reason why she had sided with Captain Maritza and taken Ricardo from me.

Bitch. I still loved her, but on days like today, I hated her.

"You would call her, perhaps, *Lady of the Lake*." Captain Naidoo gestured to the blue and gold script decorating his ship, the words in a language I didn't know. "Her lake is a little larger than most."

"Thank you for agreeing to take me out on such short notice, Captain. Unexpected business brought me here, and I won't have much time for enjoying myself."

"The pleasure is mine, ma'am. I have taken the liberty of having my chef begin preparing his specialties for your enjoyment for dinner this evening. Is this your first time in South Africa?"

It wasn't, but I doubted he'd believe me if I told him the truth. I hadn't been to the specific port we set sail from, so I smiled for his benefit. "This is new to me. My travel agent informed me we would be seeing shipwrecks today?"

"The Cape of Good Hope is an interesting place. Its name hides a dark history. Thousands of ships have ended their journey on the shores of the cape. On a clear day like today, when the waters are calm, you can see many of them on the bottom, an eternal reminder of ages lost, a history predating when pirates sailed the seas in earnest. The cape has many an interesting tale, including the fate of the *Flying Dutchman,* a rather famous ghost ship. You have heard of it, yes?"

"I know a little about the *Flying Dutchman,* but I didn't know it had history here?" It wasn't quite the truth, but it wasn't a lie either.

The old ship, believed doomed to sail the seas for all eternity, could appear on any of the oceans. Curses I understood far too well, and I was in no position to claim a ghost ship couldn't exist. The *Flying Dutchman* had, if stories were to be believed, set sail long after the *Calico* had sunk to her final resting place.

"Ah, then I would be delighted to tell you its story, Madam de la Corona. Please, be welcome on board the *Lady of the Lake*."

Whether Captain Naidoo simply enjoyed integrating the past and present, or he just wanted to lord over the seas no man truly ruled, his yacht sported the style of wheel I expected from the Golden Age of Piracy. A lounge chair near the bow offered me an unobstructed view of the sea, and I made myself comfortable while the captain and another man stowed my diving gear and prepared the ship.

During the bustle, the captain found time to bring me a frosted brown and white cocktail, setting it beside my chair with a flourish. "Amalyser, for your pleasure, made with Amarula, a coffee liquor, and a splash of vodka. It will be several hours until our dive, so until then, please enjoy."

"Thank you," I murmured, taking a cautious sip. Its sweetness surprised me, prompting me to take care with it. Drunken diving approached the bottom of my list of things I intended to do, although alcohol often hindered the curse, giving me better control over my transformations. Not even three hundred years had given me enough time to figure out the full consequences of the curse and the intricacies of its nature.

The *Lady of the Lake's* engine rumbled to life, and within ten minutes of boarding, Captain Naidoo coaxed his yacht away from the pier, guided the vessel beyond the safety of the harbor, and took her out to sea. I breathed in the salty air, and the steady rock of the gentle waves relaxed me as nothing had in longer than I cared to think about.

"It is said when the fog rolls off the coast and envelopes the sea, the *Flying Dutchman* might appear in the mists, its crew desperate to return to shore. At the dawn and twilight hours, there are those who claim they have heard the ship's captain, Hendrick van der Decken, calling out to parley with those who might spare the ship and its crew from their doom. All around the world, men weave a different tale of the man-o-war, but one simple fact remains."

Captain Naidoo's accent, thick yet rich, added a sort of mystique to his speech, and I tilted my head to catch his words over the wind and waves. "Oh? What fact?"

"It is here, off the Cape of Good Hope, the *Flying Dutchman* sank during a storm. She sailed with another vessel, who found safety in the port. As though angered a ship dared to escape, the sea protested, later catching its lost prey in a tempest near where the *Flying*

Dutchman disappeared. It is there the ghost ship's legend was born."

Along the coast, where a sandbar rose from the surf, the decrepit ruins of a ship listed in the water, its wood long rotten and rusted metal cracking where the waves washed around it. I pegged the vessel as a modern craft, built after proper masts and sails made way for engines but before metal and fiberglass took over as the material of choice.

Captain Naidoo told me the names and stories of the ships lost along the Cape of Good Hope, but the mysterious ships lost to time interested me the most. For every three ships whose history he knew, he presented one burdened with tales of drowned sailors seeking the souls of the living to warm them in their cold, watery graves.

I sipped at my Amalyser and tried not to smile at his efforts to frighten and entertain me.

As the sun slipped towards the horizon, Captain Naidoo brought me another African cocktail, something with a meaner bite and a harsh edge I appreciated more than the Amalyser. He also brought a salad of dark, leafy greens topped with seared fish and garnished with lemons and limes, something I approved of from my long time at sea.

To the average sailor, limes, lemons, and tamarind kept the bleeding, slow healing, and other malaises associated with scurvy at bay. After a good raid, Captain Louisa rewarded us all with stolen wine, an extra jigger of rum, and as much fresh fruit and vegetables from the enemy vessel as we wanted.

The time distancing me from my ventures out to sea hadn't diminished my appreciation for something as simple as a fresh salad while on the water. The novelty filled me with so much pleasure even Captain Naidoo noticed, and he seemed to take pride in my enjoyment of the first course.

In modern times, few approved of my tendency to eat citrus fruits rind and all, so I left most of the skins on my plate although the waste annoyed me.

After the salad, Captain Naidoo led me on a merry adventure through South African cuisine, ranging from boerewors sausage, piri piri chicken, and pap to bobotie, a ground meat dish in red sauce topped with egg. Long after I'd eaten enough for lethargy to take hold, he plied me with the South African version of a pumpkin fritter, a dish he called pampoenkoekies, and melktert, a pastry filled with a mild but pleasantly sweet cream filling.

To cap it all off, he brought me another Amalyser.

"We will reach a suitable spot for a night dive in approximately one hour. This is a bit behind our schedule, but I thought you might enjoy some of the more unusual sights the Cape of Good Hope has to offer. Is this good for you?"

Stifling a yawn, I saluted him with my drink and murmured, "Aye, Captain."

He left me alone to focus on his work. I recognized the dangers of sailing at night, especially in a region littered with perils lurking beneath the waves, but it didn't matter to me.

Even if the *Lady of the Lake* sank, I would survive. I always survived.

EIGHT

I'd bite a hole in his new ship, too.

KILLING ME WAS DIFFICULT, but apparently, drugging me was not. Instead of snapping awake as usual, I remained mired in molasses-thick exhaustion, and the sensation of a heavy weight pinning me down smothered me. Nothing hurt, which I viewed with cautious optimism.

The steady rolling ocean soothed me more than anything else, however. As long as I remained near the water, I would be fine. All I needed to do was slip into the sea and wait for the curse to take hold and tear away my humanity.

I could choose to let go. Maybe I'd only lose a few days to life as a shark, maybe I'd lose a few years, but it didn't matter.

I would survive.

The curse sometimes turned into a blessing, especially when I got snookered on what should have been an exploratory pleasure cruise with a dive. Revenge would be sweet, and I'd find Captain Naidoo's precious *Lady of the Lake*, drag her out from the safety of the harbor, and bite a hole in her hull. Once I sank her, I'd find him and bring him pieces of his lost ship, tormenting him until he replaced her.

Then I'd bite a hole in his new ship, too.

It took far longer than I liked to open my eyes, and when I did, the heat of the African sun beat down on my skin while the lapping of water and the distant call of gulls surrounded me. I turned my head, and the bright yellow of an inflatable raft assaulted my eyes. Stifling a groan, I lurched upright, aware of the give in the thick rubber beneath me.

Sun-kissed seas stretched out as far as I could see with only a few birds promising the presence of land somewhere nearby.

Had the *Lady of the Lake* sank, or had I been dumped and left for dead? If the ship had taken her final voyage to the bottom of the sea, where had Captain Naidoo and his cook gone?

The raft had plenty of room for three, which led me to believe I'd been dumped and left for dead.

Yep, I had a date with Captain Naidoo's ship, and I'd enjoy chewing through her hull.

I grimaced at the stiffness in my muscles and joints, and the tightness of my skin warned me I'd spent a long time exposed to the sun, which hung high in the sky. How long had I been unconscious? The faint memory of watching the sunset taunted me, followed by a big, black nothing. My clothes were as I remembered, although I needed deodorant, stat.

I didn't miss the old days when perfume failed to counter the stench of hard-working sailors and sweaty pirates. A dunk in the sea would get rid of most of the smell, replacing it with the tang of saltwater. Shaking my head to clear it, I took stock of the raft.

Me, myself, and I made for a pretty poor survival combination, which led me to two conclusions: either I'd been set adrift to die or wash up on some shoreline, or someone meant to fetch me when the time suited them.

Neither option appealed to me in the slightest.

Without a single clue on what I'd done to offend anyone enough to be set adrift, I patted myself down checking for anything useful and confirmed I'd been stripped of everything except my clothes. While an enterprising thief would get some money out of my credit cards and bank account, they were going to be very disappointed if they thought they were about to get rich quick.

What was the point of amassing treasures if I made it easy for someone to steal them from me?

I sighed, rolled towards the side of the

raft, and flopped my arm over the side, splashing my fingers into the cool water. After roasting for so long in the sun, submerging would shock the hell out of me and likely force my transformation, which served my purposes. A normal human wouldn't last long in the raft. Without fresh water, there was little hope of survival. Within a week, death was almost guaranteed.

If I wanted to be able to return to my human form, I'd have to enter the ocean and transform before exhaustion and dehydration took their toll. Waiting would make it harder to resist the curse. The last time I had succumbed to its power, I'd been too near death, and it'd taken me almost a decade to remember how to live outside of the sea.

Intentions mattered, and as long as I went into the water of my own free will, I'd be able to leave again. In a way, it worked well for me; I could return to the *Calico* and retrieve the second part of the key from my captain before making my way back to the drifting raft to watch for anyone hunting me.

I doubted anyone was. Only one person knew I had gone out on the *Lady of the Lake,* and I hadn't given Lizzy any reason to care what happened to me. It made certain things simple for me. Several phone calls and a reported theft later, I could resume my life without a ripple.

After all, it'd be my word against Captain

Naidoo's, and I'd give him no reason to counter my claims. My lies would serve him, and no one would learn of how I had ended up adrift somewhere off the Cape of Good Hope.

Then I could pay him a visit in a few months and obtain my revenge, using my next chunk of vacation time to swim across the ocean so there would be no evidence I'd returned to Africa.

Sometimes, the curse came in really handy.

~

AS OFTEN AS NOT, I lost many of my memories when I shifted from human to shark, retaining only enough of who I was to remember what I needed to do and to find my way back to shore. The sea welcomed me, and as though pleased I had entered its embrace willingly, it left my memory intact.

I circled the raft, contemplating how I might best taunt those who thought they could entrap *me*.

If I'd been left for someone to find, I knew one method to ensure their panic. I hungered, and a little bit of blood on the craft would go a long way to reminding the landlubber humans the ocean did not readily give up what it claimed. It wouldn't take much to trick them.

Diving deep beneath the waves, I hunted, and when I found a school of fish too slow to escape my hunger, I dined. I saved one of the larger ones so I could splatter its blood on the raft and carried my prize back to the surface.

As a shark, I often forgot how time slid by, and when I relocated the raft, someone had already come for it. Without a need to keep the fish, I swallowed it and lurked beneath the waves, careful to keep my dorsal fin from cutting to the surface and warning the interloping humans of my presence.

Unlike Captain Naidoo, the humans sailed in a proper, fully rigged frigate, one boasting three proud masts and sails, although they were furled so the wind wouldn't carry her away from the raft. In a nod to modern times, the vessel also possessed engines, and the vibrations of its idling passed through the water and annoyed me.

Why did such a beautiful frigate require something like an engine?

Several humans investigated the empty raft, and I slid through the waters for a closer look. Two stood in it, likely looking for any signs of my presence. Without fail, I would have left a few strands of my dark hair for them to find; it caught on everything, a reality I faced each and every day I maintained their two-legged shape.

I recognized the third figure leaning over the rail as a woman only by her slim shape and long hair, a rich brown gleaming with hints of red and gold. Something about her seemed familiar, but I couldn't isolate where I'd seen her before.

"Any blood?" she demanded, and her voice had a sharp, displeased edge about it.

"Nothing, just some hair."

"I will hang that fool by his entrails from the crow's nest."

Her words supported my theory I'd been left for someone to find, and I decided to give them a taste of what lurked beneath the waters they refused to take seriously. It'd take one solid strike and a bite to destroy the raft. I'd only give them a nip or two as a reminder to respect the ocean and its denizens.

Swimming deep, I circled around, angled upwards, and put every last bit of my strength into ramming the raft from beneath, using the force of my momentum to launch out of the water. I whipped my tail, catching one of the humans with my fin. I hit hard, lashing around to right myself, and turned, closing my teeth on the rubber and shaking my entire body like I would when I hunted seals or dolphins.

The two humans plunged into the sea, and their thrashing and flailing attempts to stay afloat amused me.

Releasing the raft, I turned my attention to one of the humans, and obeying my shark's basic nature, I toyed with my prey, stealing his shoe. His high-pitched squeals pleased me so much I nibbled his toes without claiming a single one of them as a snack.

The other one lost the seat of his pants to my teeth, and to ensure they both knew how close to death they came, I grabbed them both by their clothes and yanked them beneath the surface. I gave each a final bite, hard enough to make them bleed, though they wouldn't be long in healing.

With better things to do than torment the humans, I nudged them with my nose upwards before I sank into the depths. Somewhere far below, the *Calico* waited, and I no longer had any excuse to delay visiting my captain one last time.

~

THE *CALICO'S* final resting place remained engraved in my memories. The ship was so deep beneath the surface I couldn't tell if the day had made way for the night. It didn't matter. I assumed the curse gifted me with superior vision, as I had no problem spotting the encrusted, decaying vessel lying in the thick silt blanketing the ocean floor.

I glided through the wreckage, pausing at each and every skeletal form on the way into the heart of the ship. Faces and names partnered with the worn bones in my memories, and as though finally accepting their fate, the lightest nudge crumbled my crew, my chosen family, away to nothing more than fragments strewn across the rotten planks.

Even knowing the day would come when time would finally take its final toll on their bodies, it still hurt to watch them disintegrate, leaving me with nothing. I regretted my human soul.

Sharks of my kind limited their interactions to day-to-day encounters, remaining near other sharks only long enough to procreate, raise their young, and move on to better waters and plentiful hunting grounds. On rare occasion, I'd hunted with other sharks for large prey or to harass massive schools of fish, but those moments never lasted long.

Mourning went beyond the immediate needs of my kind.

Even knowing what to expect when I reached my captain, my presence disturbed the waters around her enough to destroy her mortal remains, leaving behind a pile of decayed bone and cloth. In it, I spotted her key, which remained attached to its golden chain. Her pocket watch likewise lingered, the saltwater unable to destroy its gold and glass. Even if time and the sea encrusted its insides, it'd work again.

I'd make it work again, no matter what.

In that, Captain Maritza had done well by my captain, giving her only the best. Not a single screw or gear would fall to time, every piece precious, a reminder of the eternity they had sworn to spend together. Mine, locked away in my armoire at home, came close. Everything always came close, but never quite close enough, a constant reminder of what I had longed for but couldn't have.

I lingered by her broken remains, and while the *Calico's* hull protected my captain from the stronger currents, the sea still wore away at her, taking her from me piece by piece while I watched, helpless to stop the inevitable.

Until nothing remained of her, I stayed and grieved for what I had lost and could never reclaim.

~

I TOOK her watch and the key, tangling their chains around my teeth. Until I changed back to human, I wouldn't be able to eat, else I'd risk losing them both. With my captain and crew truly lost, all that remained for me was a final return to the House Lost at Sea, where I might put their spirits to rest once and for all.

I only needed to return to the land and my mortal life long enough to take the second half of the key. Then it no longer mattered if the curse took me in its entirety.

Someone would find the *Calico* and put

her on display, just like the *Terrier*. They wouldn't find much on the ship; I'd already taken the rest, hiding it in the caves not far from the manor perched high on its island cliff. Maybe I would find answers or peace behind the locked doors I'd never been able to force myself to break down.

Enough had already been destroyed, and I couldn't bring myself to ruin what they, together, had built.

I slunk away from the old ship, gliding through the currents. If I swam long and hard, I would reach the island chain hiding the House Lost at Sea within several days. I could leave the watch and key in the caves hiding the rest of my hoard before once again crossing the ocean to South Africa, where I could wash up and play ignorant over my time at sea.

There were other places I could go, too, all of which would allow me to reintegrate into society, feign trauma, and escape without anyone realizing I was something other than just an unlucky human betrayed by a greedy captain.

I'd pay Captain Naidoo back for his daring, but I'd take my time with his ruin. I'd leave him with his *Lady of the Lake*, at least for a short while, but he'd find shark-infested waters more dangerous than ever before.

In that, my curse came in useful, and while my kin held no love for each other or humans, they took matters of revenge seriously. Maybe one day I'd understand the nature of magic.

Then again, I probably wouldn't, but I could live with that.

Or, I could return straight to South Africa, keeping the watch and key with me. I'd save time—and lower the risks of being caught in a lie—if I were to wash up along a barren coast. I could protect myself with the truth; I'd gone with Captain Naidoo on a cruise and a late-night dive, but remembered nothing until the moment I washed up on shore.

It wasn't far from the truth, and no one would believe I could transform into a shark. No one would believe I'd lingered for hundreds of years beyond my normal lifespan. Someone might locate the *Calico*, someone might even be able to identify her, but no one would ever believe the truth behind her sinking and the fate of her captain and crew.

No one would ever know.

The House Lost at Sea could wait until I recovered the second half of the key from its glass prison within a museum. I headed for the Cape of Good Hope, and I couldn't help but wonder if Benjamin Allen would reunite the twin vessels and put them both on display for the world to admire, or if my captain and crew would forever remain a mystery lost at sea.

NINE

I loved the South African coast and its broken shores.

I LOVED the South African coast and its broken shores. Miles upon miles of barren sands and hidden coves offered me plenty of places to wash up without prying eyes witnessing my transformation from shark to human. The curse released me with ease, and I even managed to transform without needing to dislodge the key and watch first. Their chains dangled from my human mouth, and I carried them that way through the pounding surf until I reached the safety of the rocks, panting to catch my breath.

More than ever, I appreciated how the curse transformed everything I wore, which allowed me to dodge a lot of uncomfortable questions. To play the role of the dazed castaway and kidnap victim, I'd have to ruin my clothes, tearing the fabric with stones and seashells. Baking under the sun on the raft would give my skin the cast of someone inflicted with exposure at sea, and my inability to hunt after leaving the *Calico* would serve me well when the doctors insisted on verifying my health.

While the curse preserved my life, my body could—and did—wither when abused, and I still bruised and bled like anyone else. Unlike proper humans, I suspected very little could actually kill me. Drowning didn't work; in the case of saltwater, I shifted into a shark. The few times I'd gone belly up in freshwater, I had resumed breathing as soon as I washed up on shore.

I'd been in several serious car accidents over the years, and what would have killed anyone else left me in a comatose state until my body healed enough for normal function to resume. It had happened once in the past decade, and the doctors had determined their miraculous workings had been the primary factor in my survival.

Lucky me.

The spot I had picked, within a mile from what looked like a popular beach, would work well for my needs. The waterline didn't quite reach the cliffs, and given a little time, someone would come around and find me. If someone didn't, I'd change tactics and stagger along the coast. After a few minutes climbing around on the rocks, I'd be able to convince just about anyone I'd been either lost overboard or had been involved in some sort of accident.

I tucked the key and watch into my pocket; unless someone searched me for them, they'd remain safe and hidden.

To keep the illusion of having washed up on shore, I flopped near the high tide line and settled in to wait. Patience born of endless hours hunting the ocean as a shark partnered with my more human tendency to enjoy the crash of the surf and the cries of gulls on the whispering winds. Both sides of my life melded into one, the closest thing I found to peace in my hundreds of years searching for the freedom I'd likely never find.

What the sea claimed it never returned, and I enjoyed deluding myself into believing it liked me. At least that way, I found it easier to tolerate the burden of my curse. It didn't matter, not really. Shark or human, human or shark, my nature didn't change all that much when I shifted.

Sharks hunted to survive, hunted for mates, and thrived within the seas. As a pirate, I had preyed upon men and women alike, taking those of interest and luring them to me, ultimately leaving them behind when the seas—and my captain—called me again.

The watch and key didn't weigh much, but they smothered me all the same. Why had

Captain Louisa chosen Captain Maritza over me? What had I done so wrong? Why hadn't I been good enough? Had I merely lacked the flare she desired? Had my loyalty faltered without my knowing?

Some questions couldn't be answered, some doubts could never be eased, and time couldn't erase my most painful memories. In my twisted little world, those three rules haunted me. Death wasn't a guarantee, and I was pretty sure if I really wanted to, I could find enough loopholes in the United States tax code to dodge giving the government any of my hard-earned money.

After several hours of waiting, I determined my choice of location had been a little too good, and I staggered to my feet to implement my second plan. Without my wallet, I'd have to sweet talk a police officer, assuming he didn't think I was an insane tourist and throw me in prison for breaking some law. At least I'd be honest when I claimed I had no idea what happened, as I didn't, not really.

Captain Naidoo selling me out stung, but I'd figure out a way to stack the odds in my favor, and when I finished with him, I'd make sure he regretted crossing me.

That's what good pirates did, and it'd been far too long since I'd indulged in any treacherous activities. I needed to practice, or I'd lose my edge.

I'D SPENT LONGER than I thought as a shark, and I didn't even have to make up a cover story. Captain Naidoo had laid out the foundation for me, and with wide eyes and trembling voice, I played my part as an adventure diver on an expedition gone terribly wrong.

The police took me to their station, so rustic in nature I found the place charming in a reminiscent sort of way. I worried it'd come crashing down around my ears, and I suspected it'd been built before I'd been born.

The police officer in charge of me, a big black man with a voice so deep I felt his words as much as heard them, kept staring as though he expected me to vanish if he looked away for even a moment. I found him amusing, although I questioned his superstitions.

"The Captain of the ship..." he mumbled, giving an expectant pause, waiting for me to fill in the blanks.

"Captain Naidoo of the *Lady of the Lake*." I hated myself for forcing a pleasant, almost ditzy chirp rather than my more direct snap, but if the backstabbing man wanted to paint me as a dimwitted landlubber who bit off more than she could chew playing with sharks or looking for sunken treasures, I'd cooperate—for now. "It must have been those sweet little cocktails he gave me for the first part of the cruise. I didn't have many, but your liquors sure seem to be strong here, sir."

"It happens to the best of us," he reassured me again after making me tell the same damned story for the tenth time. "And you don't remember going on the dive?"

I held my hands up in surrender. "Nary a thing. Next thing I knew, I was alone in the water. I must have ditched the gear. I wasn't wearing a wetsuit, which baffles me. Guess the water must have been warm last night, so it shouldn't have been needed, right? Must have been why. Lesson learned. Those little cocktails and the ocean do not mix. I guess Captain Naidoo must have my wallet; it would have been left on the *Lady of the Lake* when I dived, right?"

"Yes, your personal belongings were turned in by the captain when he reported you were missing yesterday. It seems he stayed out on the water searching for you before he gave up and brought his ship back to the harbor. We'll have your things ready for you as soon as we're done with your questioning."

I wanted to stab the man and leave him on the floor to bleed out for wasting my time, but I forced a smile instead. "I understand. I'm just so very tired. Could I bother you for another glass of water?"

At the rate I was guzzling water, I'd float away long before he finished questioning me, but since they didn't seem to think being missing at sea qualified as a medical concern, I'd at least do my part to keep from collapsing.

The first thing I'd do once I got my hands on my wallet was find something to eat.

"Of course, Miss Corona." He got up, went to the door of the interrogation room, and said something to someone outside. If they had any modern technology at all in the place, they had surveillance equipment installed in the room, watching and listening for any signs of deceit. If the cop knew his stuff, his getting up and going to the door was to reinforce the illusion I wasn't being watched.

He returned with a small paper cup of water, which would give me a few swallows at best. I sipped at it to make it last through however many other questions he intended to ask until he finally got around to accepting I wasn't going to change my story.

"I'm so sorry to be a bother." I used my best fake smile, the one I reserved for when I needed to work with an insufferably rich client who believed the sun, moon, and stars all revolved around him without having the wit or intellect to intrigue me.

"Are you certain you don't remember anything else?"

"I wish I did, sir. The last thing I recall before waking up in the water was watching the sunset after dinner. Captain Naidoo told me it would be another hour before we reached the dive spot. I don't remember anything after that."

"This is not the first time one of his passengers has ended up lost or stranded at sea. One gentleman was left adrift on a life raft, where he was picked up later by another sailor who happened to be in the area. Another had a small rowboat and had been set adrift near shore, close enough to find his way. He has reported several women lost during dives, but you're the first to be found. Are you certain you don't remember anything? Do you recall the dive at all?"

I shook my head. "I don't, sir. It's possible I went diving in my clothes, but I normally wear a wetsuit or swimwear. I've dived before. Waterlogged attire can be lethal. I was close to shore when I woke up, and I suppose I must have had something to hold onto until then—or had swam without being conscious of it. I'm sorry, sir. I just don't know what happened."

"Yes, Captain Naidoo claimed you had your own gear, but he didn't have it. He had your wallet, keys, and a phone. Would you please confirm he returned everything you had with you when you boarded his ship?"

"Except my diving equipment," I muttered.

He acknowledged my complaint with a

nod, got up, and once again spoke to someone outside the door. Within two minutes, he presented my wallet, keys, and cell phone in a plastic bag. I opened it, dumped everything out, and began a systematic check.

"Everything's here," I reported after a second check. "Including my cash."

"Then theft was unlikely the motive, if he had one." The cop scowled. "Captain Naidoo is a wily one."

"How strange. He seemed so polite, too. My travel agent arranged for his ship."

"Which travel agent?"

I gave the police Lizzy's information, the agency I found her through, and the circumstances surrounding my booking the *Lady of the Lake*. "I suppose I got exactly what I paid for, although it would've been preferable if I could remember the adventure. Preposterous."

"I'd like to apologize again for how you've been inconvenienced, Miss Corona."

I waved my hand in a dismissive gesture before shoving my wallet, phone, and keys into my pocket. "It's hardly your fault. Are we finished here? I'm starving, and it's not often I get to mean it quite so literally. I could really use a shower."

"I'll have someone take you to a good place for something to eat and drive you to your hotel, Miss Corona. Once again, I apologize for the inconvenience."

I nodded in acceptance of his apology and stood, grimacing as every muscle in my body protested moving. "Thank you, sir. I'm so sorry I couldn't be more help."

He led me out of the police station to a waiting white, yellow, and blue cruiser.

TEN

Ricardo would've been proud of me for contemplating a conquest.

WORD HAD SPREAD ALL the way to my boss about my disappearance, so instead of sleeping and eating like I wanted, I spent several hours convincing her I wasn't actually dead. She asked more—and better—questions than the South African police had. By the time I managed to get off the phone, I had a plane ticket for home and a promise I could take a real, proper vacation a little later in the year.

She hung up after making a stern promise Bensen could do his own research and risk his own personnel.

I read between the lines; she needed me for something, probably one of the more active accounts requiring a little more attention than most of my co-workers were willing to put in. On a good day, she tolerated me because I worked magic with numbers that she couldn't. On a bad day, she probably wanted to maroon me on an island so remote no one would ever find me.

Instead of complaining about the vacation that wasn't, I packed my bags and headed home. I cleaned my captain's watch, so it looked like something an eccentric businesswoman might use and wore the key as a necklace tucked under my blouse, adding to my eccentricity when I passed through security to catch my flight back to the United States.

My plan had changed, and I didn't need to return to the House Lost at Sea until I had the second half of the key in my possession. Getting the second key would prove problematic, but I'd dust off my rusty skills and partake in a little plundering. I'd feel a twinge of guilt for swiping a friend's property, but it wouldn't last long. I'd call us even after the adventure cruise that came too damned close to ending with me as the booty.

I had no idea who the sea witch on the modernized frigate was, but if I met her again, I'd turn the tables on her. She could be my booty instead, and I'd enjoy every minute of turning the tables on her.

If she put up a good fight, maybe I'd talk her into becoming part of *my* crew. Wenches were so much more fun when they were willing participants, and smart wenches so often made witty conversationalists on top of having delightfully nasty mouths.

I realized how ridiculous my thoughts were, but I couldn't help it. I didn't find many women with nice looks, an active interest in piracy, and great taste in ships—even though she had polluted her frigate with an engine. I yearned to know what she wanted to do with *me,* who appeared to be nothing more than a banker in South Africa doing research for a wealthy client.

The best covers were the real ones, and I'd shown no signs of ever having been a pirate myself.

I spent most of the flight contemplating the odds of taking the woman and her frigate and making them mine. If her crew seemed clever enough, maybe I'd take them, too. Once I had them, I'd find out what they wanted with me before deciding what I'd do with them.

Ricardo would've been proud of me for contemplating a conquest, and it cost more than I wanted to spend for something like a frigate. Hers would be an acceptable alternative to a proper one, although I wouldn't be pleased with its engine.

First, I needed to pull off a modern-day raid, plunder the most important of treasures from the *Terrier,* and close the book on my past. It wouldn't break the curse on me, but it'd be one last chance to take a stab at the woman who'd taken everything from me with her treachery.

There was no finer way to get revenge against a pirate queen than taking her treasures and legacy away from her. If her ghost lingered, I hoped Captain Maritza recognized me for who I was and regretted her broken vows. More importantly, I hoped she would realize my thirst for revenge stemmed from Ricardo's loss.

Had we been given a chance, I would've been truly loyal, but no.

When I finished my work, the only ghost left to haunt me would be Ricardo's.

I would take her half of the key, and I would uncover the secrets of the House Lost at Sea. Closure would be mine, and the lost pirate queen's wealth would complement my cavern hoard. Maybe I would take up the life of a treasure seeker, exchanging gold for cash and living the life of the wealthy, the dream of many a pirate.

Between my boss's insistence I get on the earliest flight back to the United States and my idiocy for doing what she wanted, by the time the plane landed, I trembled, felt—and probably looked—like death warmed over, and if I wasn't careful, I'd be a candidate for hospitalization.

My boss waited in the terminal, and she looked me over with narrowed eyes and a frown. "You look like hell. What'd the doctors there say?"

"They didn't. The police didn't feel I was in any need of one."

"You're fucking kidding me."

I couldn't help it; I raised my eyebrows at her snapped words. "I called you as soon as my phone charged after they released me from the police station. They questioned me for a few hours before deciding I didn't know anything of use."

"Lovely. Should I be driving you to the hospital, then?"

I thought about it. Having not had a chance to eat anything of substance, I'd probably match doctor expectations. I could claim prior good physical health and exercise to explain my condition if I had recovered better than I thought. "Might be wise," I mumbled.

Existing without anyone discovering my second nature involved a lot of lies, and after an experience like mine, no one would question my surrender to the inevitable.

"All right. I'll take you to the ER. If it looks like you'll be there a while, I'll arrange for someone to pick you up when they're ready to release you. Do you have your insurance information with you?"

I nodded; I paid through the nose for insurance I didn't really need, but if something did go wrong, at least I wouldn't have to go digging into my treasure hoard to pay for it.

"Good. Can't be too careful. I'll take care of informing Mr. Bensen he may not wish to invest too much into such a dangerous part of the world."

I forced a laugh. "Well, if it's an adventure he wants, South Africa definitely delivered—in an unpleasant sort of way, unless you're into that sort of thing. I'm not."

After I played the part of a banker dealing with a traumatic experience and retrieved Captain Maritza's key, I would hunt down the brunette pirate and her fancy little frigate. When I did, I'd show her what it meant to be a true pirate of the seven seas.

~

I DID a fifteen hour stint in the ER, most of which I spent with an IV stuck in my arm, replenishing lost fluids. All in all, the doctor fell in line with my plans, crediting my good health and tendency to exercise as the reason I had survived exposure to the sea and sun in such good condition. I thanked my Spanish heritage for my lack of a severe sunburn, although he annoyed me by asking which part of Mexico my relatives came from. It took several minutes to explain I was literally a Spaniard—from Spain.

I confused the doctor, and I wondered how someone smart enough to be a doctor could be so ignorant about global geography. With a little help from my phone, I showed him pictures of the Spanish coast, not far from where I'd been born.

Time had changed the place, humans had moved in en masse, and life went on, but I imagined the untouched shores of my youth and pretended they hadn't been overrun by modern times like everything else.

My boss arranged for someone to pick me up from the hospital, but the last person I expected to see waiting in the lobby was Bensen. The instant he caught sight of me, he hurried over, grabbed my shoulders, and dropped kisses on my cheeks. "When I got the call you had gone missing in South Africa, I was worried. What happened?"

One day, my boss wouldn't leave me to make the uncomfortable explanations—maybe. "I was scouting for additional opportunities for your portfolio and found that you may not wish to expand *too* much in the region, at least not without hiring your own captains—or importing them. I don't think they quite understand the difference between a good adventure and a bad one."

"You're all right?"

"Nothing food, sleep, and a few hours with an IV jabbed in my arm won't cure."

"What on Earth happened?"

At least my stint in the ER had done me some good; the doctor had done a blood test, and they'd found trace amounts of some sedative in my system, one I'd been informed could cause limited memory loss. "I don't remember much, but it seems the captain of the ship drugged me before a dive. When I woke up, I was washed up on shore."

The lingering residue of drugs in my system made sense; while transforming into a shark cured a lot of ailments, poisons and drugs tended to stick around in my human shape; they wouldn't kill me, but they didn't metabolize out of my system when the curse influenced me.

It occurred to me the South African police might have somehow been involved with Captain Naidoo's treachery. Why else would they avoid having me see a doctor, unless they knew I'd been drugged?

Later, I would think long and hard on the issue.

"I simply must insist on you coming home with me then, dear. It can't be safe or healthy to be home alone after such a traumatic experience. I'll have my chef make you something for dinner, then you can rest however much you need. I insist. It's my fault you were put in such a position." He took hold of my elbow and pulled me towards the doors. "You could have been killed."

If I refused, he would argue with me until I agreed to do what he wanted, and while I bristled at his meddling, fighting with him wouldn't do me any good. "I'll be fine. I think my boss expects me to come to work…"

"I have already discussed the situation with her. You'll stay at my house tonight and tomorrow night, and I'll have someone drive you to work. Arrangements have already been made for you to be taken home, too."

Wonderful. The last thing I needed was an overly wealthy man micromanaging my life, but instead of complaining, I smiled and thanked him for his generosity.

A few days wouldn't change anything, nor would the lost time make any difference in my plans. Captain Maritza's key waited for me, broken and useless to the casual observer, a curious trinket and nothing more.

Of all the wealth discovered on the *Terrier,* the second half of my key was worthless to everyone save me, who knew of the House Lost at Sea and longed for the treasures hidden within.

ELEVEN

They even broke into your walls.

In the two nights I spent at Bensen's home, I suspected someone had somehow cast a second curse on me.

Theft happened, but I wrinkled my nose at the thorough plundering of my home. The shredded ruins of my couch had ended up in three different rooms, and they'd gone as far as to break apart the wooden frame during their search. At least I hadn't kept the aquarium and its precious corals and sea life; I suspect the thieves would have killed everything.

As a proper law-abiding citizen with nothing to hide, I called the cops from my front step, took pictures of everything, and took care where I walked so I wouldn't ruin any evidence—if any had been left behind. It didn't take long to confirm my fears: the thieves had taken every last one of my safe deposit keys. While waiting for the police to arrive, I called the banks, expecting the worst.

It didn't take long to confirm someone had accessed the most important of my safe-deposit boxes and taken my three prized possessions. They'd gone as far as finding someone who looked a little like me to make the grab. Both banks promised to get in touch with my insurance company and the police, giving them all the information on who had accessed the boxes.

Within twenty minutes, a curious pair of police officers entered my home, both men whistling at the extensive damage.

"They even broke into your walls," one observed, a man easily in his sixties but built like a linebacker on a mission, and he gestured at the gaping holes in my drywall. "Did you have anything of value to justify this?"

I stuffed my hands into my pockets, and my fingers closed over Captain Louisa's pocket watch. "I had a few antiques which were quite valuable, but little else."

"What sort of antiques?"

"An original flintlock pistol from the Golden Age of Piracy, a cutlass from the same era, and some golden doubloons and similar trinkets I'd bought at auctions over the years. I'm a collector." I braced for the worst, guiding the two officers to my bedroom.

My armoire lay broken and scattered across my bedroom floor. "The keys for the safe-deposit boxes where I stored many of them used to be in there. That used to be my armoire, which I kept locked."

"What would you estimate the value of these items to be?"

I drew in a deep breath, closed my eyes, and grimaced at the hike my insurance bill would take when I reported the thefts. "North of half a million dollars, sir. The insurance policy for all the items sits at six hundred and twenty-five thousand, appraised three years ago."

Both cops stared at me with wide eyes.

"It's the gold. The flintlock and the other trinkets barely reach twenty thousand combined. I've been on some scavenge dives, which is where I got some of it, and I bought the rest at estate auctions."

It made for a pretty story, one composed almost entirely of lies. In a way, I *had* acquired the booty on scavenge dives, three hundred years ago while the ships were in the process of sinking. While I did sometimes do modern-day dives as a shark to add to my hoard, the bulk came from the *Calico* and other ships we'd preyed upon before our final voyage.

"We're going to need a full list of everything disturbed, broken, and stolen," the cops informed me, and they spent the next forty minutes poking through the wreckage, taking photographs, and otherwise documenting the extensive damage done to my home.

I got the feeling they never expected to see any of my things again, nor did they intend to put much effort in locating anything. They didn't even attempt to dust for fingerprints, claiming there was no way they'd find anything thanks to the very thorough destruction of my home. They took photographs of some footprints they found in the mud, took pictures and measurements of my shoes to confirm they hadn't been made by me, and noted the fact my classic car and motorcycle remained undisturbed in my garage.

After they left, I confirmed the most painful truth: not a single scrap of evidence of my life with Captain Louisa remained. My watch, my gun, and my cutlass were gone, as was my outfit, right down to my hat.

I wanted to cry, but instead, I dialed Benny's number and scowled at what I'd have to tell my long-time friend.

"Cathy, welcome home," he answered. "You doing okay?"

"No."

"What's wrong?"

I drew in a slow, deep breath. "Someone decided to come into my house and trash the entire place while I was gone, and since taking my shit wasn't good enough for them, it looks like they did structural damage to the house, too." I shook from a mixture of rage and grief. "The police just left. I know you wanted me to dress up for Halloween, but it isn't happening. I'm sorry."

"They took your pirate outfit?"

I wandered into my bedroom, pushing through the debris with my toe. I nudged the scraps of torn fabric, which I identified as having been one of my shirts. "Took isn't the word I'd use. Shredded is closer to accurate. They probably took some of the stuff, but it's a mess. I just wanted to let you know I won't be able to dress up this year for you, sorry. I have to go. I need to call the insurance company."

Not in the mood to listen to his pity or deal with sympathy, I hung up, dug through my contacts, and began the process of filing an insurance claim, giving them the police report number. I also filed for a home inspector to judge the amount of structural damage to my house at the same time. To support my claim I hadn't been home, I gave the insurers a full list of my whereabouts, including the police report from the South African police, my plane itinerary, and visit to the ER, all of which supported my claim and my inability to be the one behind the destruction of my home.

It took three hours on the phone for me to force them to send a claims adjuster to my home, and I waited two hours on the front porch for their arrival.

At least the man had been wise enough to bring a flashlight, as the thieves had managed to knock the power out. It didn't take long for him to go through my home, whistling at the damage done. "I was told you had made a claim of extensive damage, but it seems their definition of extensive doesn't match yours. This is far worse than I was led to believe."

I snorted. "You can always trust an insurance company to downplay the severity of an incident."

"I'm Henry Hughhaven, and this won't take long to get situated, filed, and processed. I'll have to photograph everything. Have you taken anything?"

I shook my head. "I moved some things after the cops left to confirm what was missing, but everything is almost exactly as I found it."

"Your antique collection was the primary target?"

"I think so. They left my Rolls-Royce and my Knucklehead in the shed, but tore up everything in the house. I found pieces of my couch all over the place. Looks like they were looking for small valuables."

"According to your file, you have small valuables in plenty. You can verify your location since you were last home prior to the theft?"

"Easily. I already gave the insurance company the information, including a police report from South Africa, my flight itinerary coming home, and the reference numbers for my visit to the ER upon my return. I was staying with a business associate following my stay at the hospital—a stay your insurance company has on file, too. My co-workers can verify Mr. Bensen drove me to work this morning, and one of his associates dropped me off here. From the outside, nothing looked disturbed, so the driver left before I made it inside."

"Can you give me a list of names and numbers?"

I gave him the requested information. "I'll be staying at a hotel in the interim, as I suspect they've done enough damage to my house to make staying here rather unsafe."

"I don't need an inspection license to make that call. If the building isn't condemned due to the damage they caused searching inside the walls, I'll be very surprised. The inspector will be by in the morning to make a full list of damages and estimate the cost for repair. I think it'll be a complete write-off, which would be beneficial for you. Your policy easily allows for a complete rebuild, and the property would be better off as a result. The rest of the claim will be dependent on the police investigation."

"They said the place was such a mess they couldn't even get prints."

Hughhaven shook his head and sighed.

"Typical. Hopefully, we'll be able to recover the pieces, but I doubt you'll see any of the gold again. The more distinctive items, however, might be recovered; they are rather unique."

"That's one way to put it. Please let me know if there's anything I can do to help."

"Of course, Miss Corona. It's a rare time I'm able to say this, but I don't think it will take long to process this claim at all, and I'll make certain the head office is aware you were being upfront and honest regarding your situation. Please keep all of your expense receipts in the interim, as this is not a habitable space."

I thanked him and waited until he left to snarl enough curses to guarantee the spirit of my captain rolled in her grave over the foulness of the words spilling out of my mouth.

I PICKED a hotel with an indoor garage near work as my base of operations. Using the tarps and canvas piled in my garage to protect my car, I barely managed to squeeze the Knucklehead into my Rolls-Royce for the trip, unwilling to leave it easy pickings for someone to take.

When I found out who was responsible, I'd turn the sea red with their blood. I'd enjoy dangling them overboard and playing tug-of-war with the local shark population. If I had my way, I'd use my new frigate for the expedition.

I showed up to work two hours late in clothes so new their tags burned a hole in my pocket.

My boss took one look at my face and decided against yelling at me for my tardiness. "Cathy?"

"Since a near death experience wasn't enough, someone decided I'd just love to come back to my home thoroughly vandalized with everything of worth inside either trashed or stolen. At least they weren't interested in my garage." I somehow kept my tone even, just on the right side of professionally acceptable. "I'm at the hotel down the street while the insurance company deals with the inspection."

"For a robbery?"

"It seems the thieves believed I had things hidden in the walls. When they didn't find anything, they continued searching and destroyed the studs, but I had nothing hidden in my walls." I sighed. "I'm sorry I'm late. They shredded my clothes, so I had to go shopping this morning."

"They shredded your clothes?"

"I found pieces of my couch all over my house. Compared to my clothes, the couch got off lightly."

"Do you need to take a personal day?"

"No. There's nothing I can do, so it's better if I at least get something productive done here. You're off the hook for the Halloween party, I suspect. What wasn't destroyed of my costume was stolen, and there's no way I can replace it in time, so I'm out. I already told Mr. Allen."

"I heard. He seemed quite unhappy someone would ruin your apparel. I told him I'd still host the party. Maybe you can find something else to wear?"

I sighed and shrugged. "We'll see."

Maybe buying a sewing machine and all the right fabrics would keep me busy. If I got too bored, I could sew the whole damned thing by hand. It wouldn't replace what I'd lost, but it'd be a start, and maybe I'd figure out a plan while working my needles and threads.

If all else failed, I'd at least be dressed to kill, so if I crossed paths with the thief, I'd be ready to show them a pirate's version of revenge.

TWELVE

Turnabout was always fair play.

INSTEAD OF RESTORING my pirate attire, I fixated on the past. Unwilling to trust anyone with Captain Louisa's pocket watch, I systematically dismantled it, photographed every last screw and gear, cleaned the gold inner workings, and put it back together again, muttering prayers while I worked, hoping I wasn't doing irreparable damage to it. The task kept me from other thoughts, including the others I'd lost in my long life.

Working on the watch almost kept Ricardo's memory at bay.

And so I worked, and I muttered prayers. I didn't even know who I prayed to, but it didn't really matter to me. Religion was for those with a chance of seeing the heavens, something I'd discarded as a possibility centuries ago.

After a week and a half of spending four or five hours a night meticulously cleaning the inner workings of my captain's watch, I put it back together again, using tiny tweezers to work each delicate piece back into place. I wound it up, bit my lip, and muttered one final prayer.

The second hand began its slow, steady journey around the clock's face, and its gentle ticking, a sound I hadn't heard in so, so long, cut me to the bone. I cupped it in my hands and held it close to my chest, swallowing several times so the heat in my eyes wouldn't turn to tears.

Some god out there must have pitied me, and for once, I didn't even mind. Maybe my captain's bones had decayed away to nothing, but her two most prized possessions lived on. I would focus my attention on claiming Captain Maritza's key and returning to the House Lost at Sea.

If my gun, my watch, and my cutlass surfaced, I would track down those who had stolen them from me, and they would regret their theft. If they showed up before I had Captain Maritza's half of the key in my possession, I would bide my time.

If someone suspected who I had once been, I wouldn't make it easy on them. I would turn it into a game, one where I would feign disappointment over the loss of antique treasures with little other value. I'd take my time and savor my revenge.

I'd also plunder from them, because turnabout was always fair play.

A week and a half after informing Benny I wouldn't be dressing up, he called me on my cell, and I glowered at the device before answering, "Cathy."

"Any luck recovering your pirate costume?"

I snorted. I expected the insurance check in the mail soon, since replacing my belongings wasn't possible. "No."

"A pity. Is there no way you'll be able to make a costume in time for Halloween?"

"I'm thinking I'll wear a black sheet, cut some eye holes in it, and buy a scythe from the farm equipment store. I'll go as the grim reaper."

"You are far too beautiful to cover up with a sheet."

"You're full of shit, and it's leaking out, Benny."

"You have such a way with words. How about two beers and a batch of cookies, and they'll involve coconut and limes, just for you. No one else will get a single one of your cookies. I'll even pay for whatever supplies you need for it. You made that all yourself, didn't you?"

"Damn it, Benny. I don't have the time. I have work."

"I'll get you a few days off. I'll tell that witch if I don't have you for my museum gala, everything'll be ruined. Where else am I going to find someone who looks the part of a pirate so damned well?"

"I thought this was for a Halloween party."

"Gala. At my museum. The office party was just a good excuse to get you dressed up for my gala. We can do the photoshoot at the same time."

"Look, they stole my cutlass, they stole my flintlock, and they took my watch, too. My hat's gone. The rest of the costume was cut into tiny pieces. I really don't feel like rebuilding it, okay? That was years of effort. I'm done with it."

"Two batches of cookies, and the second one will be chocolate chip with hazelnut?"

"If you feed me that, I'll be too fat to fit into the costume."

"I'll beg, Cathy. I made arrangements for the photoshoot weeks ago. You'll be the star. There's just no one else who can fit the role like you."

I frowned, thinking it over. A slow smile spread over my lips as I considered my options. "All right. I have a price, and it isn't in cookies or beer."

"Name it."

"You want me to pose for your museum gala? My whole collection was taken, stolen." I paused so I could rub it in a bit. "Lost. Irreplaceable. I want a piece from one of your cases. A token piece no one will probably care about. My choice. Nothing interesting or too distinctive, of course, but pretty. Obviously not something excessively valuable, but if I'm going to have to do this, it better be worth my while. Nothing stupid. If you're going to talk me into this, then you can let me restart a collection with something *you* cherish."

Silence.

"Well?"

"You drive a hard bargain. Dare I ask if that's all you need?"

"I don't have the time to find a cutlass or flintlock, so I'll have to go without. You're responsible for any accessories you want me to wear. I'll see if I can put together a hat, but I make no promises. Period accurate, authentic hats aren't exactly easy to make *or* find."

"All right. What do you want from the collection? I'm sure you already have something in mind."

"That necklace from the captain's case—it had a gold chain and the broken key pendant on it. I want that. It was a bit unusual, but no one will miss it. It's pretty, and at least I can wear it. That way it'll be difficult for someone to steal."

"Interesting choice. I would have thought you'd want the pocket watch or something more distinctive from the collection." Benny sighed. "I have a condition. I would like a replica of it made, but whenever I need it for study or for the exhibit, you would need to loan it to me."

"Bring it to me by tomorrow, and we have a deal. I'll start the work on making the costume. Do you have a pen and paper handy? I will need a lot of supplies to make this."

"I do. Tell me what you need, and I'll make sure I can get everything for you."

I began rattling off materials, yardage, and the supplies I would need to recreate my pirate attire. Because I was annoyed he had asked me to posture for him, I demanded only the best, right down to gold buttons and exotic feathers for my hat.

~

I TURNED my hotel room into a sewing station, and true to his word, Benny arrived ten minutes after I got off work. It took him three trips to bring all the material I had ordered, and he even brought two machines, one of which could handle working with leather. When he had everything situated to his liking, he held out a blue and gold jewelry box to me. "This is the piece you wanted."

I sat on the edge of the bed, took the box out of his hands, and set it on my lap. I opened it, and my breath caught in my throat.

Captain Maritza's half of the key waited on black velvet, and Benny had taken care to clean every last link of the gold chain so it gleamed in the room's light. "It's lovely. So mysterious. Why would a pirate captain bother to keep something like this? It's not useful for anything. What's the point in having a necklace like this?"

I asked the question to maintain the illusion of ignorance layered on top of the natural curiosity of a collector of eccentric items.

"You like collecting things that make you ask questions, don't you?" Benny chuckled before he turned to the massive pile of bags taking over my hotel room. "I find it incredibly hard to believe this will become a pirate costume."

"If I were being truly authentic, I would be doing everything by hand, but I don't think I have the time. So, I'll make an unauthentic outfit first—something made with the sewing machine so I have an outfit. If I have time, I'll make something a bit more authentic."

"How many days off work would you need to make the costume fully authentic?"

I frowned, grabbed my cell phone, and checked the calendar. With a little over two weeks until Halloween, I could sew the entire outfit if I took a few days off, but I needed to give the appearance of lacking the skills—it took longer for those without practice to craft anything, and there was no way I could reveal I had hundreds of years of experience making my own clothes. "A week, I guess. I doubt my boss would give me the time off, especially after the disaster trip to South Africa."

"Ask her, and I'll see what I can do to encourage her to give you the time off. I'll also ping Franklin and get him to give her a nudge in the right direction. He'll be attending the gala, too. He was quite upset to hear you'd lost your collection. Your pieces were exquisite."

I grimaced. "It is what it is. I doubt I'll be able to replace them. The insurance company sure doesn't think so; they cut the check for the policy on it already. It should arrive this week."

"If you don't mind me asking, how much was your collection worth?"

"Over six hundred thousand."

Benny stared at me, and his mouth dropped open. "Excuse me? Did you just say six hundred thousand?"

"Yes. I had a valuable collection. The cutlass, watch, and flintlock were only twenty or so thousand of it. The insurance adjusters expect the rest of my collection will be melted down, but I have a no-liability policy should the pieces be recovered. They're currently looking at antique markets to see if they turn up."

"So if they turn up, you don't have to pay them back?"

"Oh, I'll pay them back if they show, but I

wouldn't be accused of insurance fraud. That's important. There's a market for those who have their own items stolen so they can get the insurance money. I laid out my agreement with the insurer so if my items turn back up, I pay them back the insured amount. They have a set period of five years to recover my pieces. If they're found after that, I owe them nothing, and they can't file any claims against me."

"That's smart of you. How on Earth did you negotiate that?"

"I'm liable for other items in the collection, just not those pieces. They were priceless to me, and there is such a limited market for them. They can't be replaced, and the insurer knows it. For them, it's only twenty-three thousand dollars, and when they look at my policy as a whole, it wasn't worth fighting me over it for those three pieces."

"So you're liable for paying them back if found, but they can't press any charges against you?"

"Correct."

"I'll keep an eye out for them and spread word you had those pieces stolen; I have photographs from the museum opening I can spread around. Maybe I'll get a hit for you. I'll do what I can. Can you put me in touch with your insurance company should I locate the items?"

I went to my wallet, pulled out my insurance manager's card, and handed it to Benny. "I don't think you'll have any luck, but stranger things have happened, I suppose."

"I'm really sorry this happened. It must be hard losing so much at one time."

I shrugged. "It's not all bad. I get a new house out of it, and the insurance company is paying for the rebuild and everything inside. And since I was in the ER, have records of being abroad, and the police estimate the theft happened sometime while I was on the flight and within the hospital, the insurance company can't even accuse me of insurance fraud. There was no way for me to plan the destruction of my home while in South Africa lost on a dive expedition, and Mr. Bensen confirmed my trip was an unexpected one. It'll work out."

"I'm still sorry."

I waved him off. "Go home, Benny. You owe me cookies, and they better be good ones."

He chuckled, reached into his pocket, and pulled out a plastic bag with a single chocolate chip cookie inside. "With hazelnuts, your favorite."

I grabbed it before he could change his mind about giving me the cookie. "I knew there was a reason I liked you. Emergency cookies."

He laughed, offered me a flippant salute,

and headed for the door. "I'll see you on Halloween, then? In costume?"

I looked over the plethora of material taking over my hotel room, sighed, and nodded. "Stop asking me for miracles, Benny."

"Maybe if you'd stop making them happen, I wouldn't keep asking for them."

THIRTEEN

I thought you'd never ask.

My boss was more than happy to give me a week off before Halloween, and I suspected she felt guilty over my less-than-ideal trip to South Africa.

Humans. Why were they so ready to accept the blame for things outside of their control? I found the custom of apologizing for everything absurd, although I was guilty of it in order to better meld with modern society. I tried to save my apologies for when I actually meant them, which didn't happen very often at all.

At least they accepted a weaker sorry in lieu of one carrying more weight and sincerity.

I appreciated the days away from the daily grind of scraping pennies together in search of an extra dollar. It gave me the time to convince the insurance company to just demolish the old wreckage and put something appropriate up in its place. I issued a few snappy warnings over how I better get my money's worth out of my new home, and if they had the extra thousand in the budget, my counters better be granite and my tiles better be real ceramic instead of flimsy linoleum.

The rest of the time I spent sewing, and I wore Captain Maritza's key around my neck while I wrapped the golden chain of my captain's key around my ankle, safely hidden from prying eyes. I kept her pocket watch tucked beneath my clothes, its chain clasped to my bra in case it slipped from its spot nestled between my breasts.

I took care with my shirts to ensure no one noticed its presence.

It didn't take long to slap together the unauthentic costume, cut in the same style I'd worn at sea. Only those familiar with old sewing techniques would recognize it'd been made by a machine. I could probably get away with wearing it to Benny's gala, although I'd used the cheaper materials for it.

The rest of the time I spent recreating a proper outfit, stitch by painful stitch. The hat took the most work, and I cursed the leather and myself for choosing durability and prestige over ease. I cheated on the boots; I couldn't afford to spend the time cobbling my own pair, and I doubted I'd remember how to do it quite right, so I bought a pair made by an artisan who swore they were as close as they got to the real thing.

When they arrived in the mail, I had to give the man credit; they were close—close enough I couldn't tell they weren't the real thing.

I sent him a tip for doing such a nice job on them.

When Halloween finally rolled around, I looked the part of a pirate, and I walked to work, aware I lacked a flintlock and cutlass to round out my outfit. I'd gone over the top, adding in a few braids to my hair and decorating them with scraps of colored fabric and beads to add a little flair, as I had sometimes done when my captain wanted a more imposing image.

The workday went by in a blur, and Bensen and Benny showed up together at the office Halloween party to fetch me for the gala.

"This better be good enough for you," I warned, narrowing my eyes at the two men. "Don't even ask how much time it took to put this together. I will bludgeon you both to death with my chair."

"Your other costume was fantastic, but this one is exquisite." Benny circled me like a shark, a behavior I knew far better than most. I stiffened under his scrutiny, and he crouched beside me, giving the folded top of my black leather boots a tug. "Did you make these, too? They're absolutely gorgeous."

"No. I bought these, and don't ask how much they cost. You might faint."

"I'll reimburse you for their cost. How much?"

"A thousand, plus I tipped him for doing such a good job on them on such short notice."

"I'll cut you a check. I didn't even think about the boots, and I should have—I bought everything else! Is this the one you sewed on the machine?"

I shook my head. "Hand sewn, every last detail. It's not authentic if it isn't done by hand—pirates didn't have sewing machines." I made a thoughtful noise. "Of course, I suspect few pirates could actually sew at all and likely stole their clothes or bought it with their booty. Clothing production among pirates isn't exactly studied. Ah, the joy of educated guesses when making a period-accurate costume."

"Well, you look stunning, Cathy. You have far surpassed my expectations. Did you order the hat, too?"

"Made it. Squeezed out just enough time around everything else."

"If I wanted a costume like yours, how much would you charge me for the work?"

I huffed, turned my nose up, and planted my hands on my hips. "What sort of self-respecting pirate makes clothes for navy bilge scum?"

"Ouch. That hurts me, Cathy," my friend complained, clutching his chest. "But I'm not even dressed as a navy captain—yet. I might be dressing up as a pirate, too, for all you know! I'll be changing at the museum. Are you ready to go?"

I grabbed my coin purse, which was lined with chainmail and contained all of my important cards and my cell phone, and tied it to my belt. "All ready."

"No purse?"

I patted my pouch. "You wanted accurate, so you're getting accurate. I definitely didn't have time to make a satchel of any sort."

"Dare I ask how much time you would have needed for the other accessories? I'm really impressed, Cathy. I never knew you were so into reenactment and had such a good eye for period-accurate details. Had I known, I would have hired you to help with my museum. Did you bring the necklace with you?"

"Of course I did." I lifted it from beneath my white silk blouse, careful to avoid tangling it in the frills. "Safe and sound. It stays with me at all times. I learn from my mistakes."

"You can hardly be faulted for someone robbing your home while you were away on business."

I shrugged. "If we're going to reach this

gala on time, we better hit the road. It's a long drive, and if Bensen's driving, the average turtle will beat us there."

"Think you can do better?" the old man groused, pulling out his keys and dangling them in front of me.

I snatched them out of his hand. "I thought you'd never ask."

~

I PROBABLY SHOULD HAVE CARED a little more about what sort of sports car had four doors and a backseat, but the instant I got behind the wheel, the urge to put it through its paces took hold. Benny kept making funny noises behind me, which only served to goad me into taking the corners a little tighter to test the vehicle's grip and handling in addition to its speed.

"There's something to be said about modern cars, isn't there, Cathy?" Bensen teased.

"You're just jealous you can't have my Rolls-Royce."

"Who taught you to be so mean?"

"Born that way." Glancing in the rearview mirror, I smirked. "You know, Benny, I'm disappointed in you. I thought you'd be the type to like a wild ride in a sporty car."

"I have an intact sense of self-preservation, unlike the old man in the front."

I chuckled. "I just wouldn't want you to be late for your own gala. While it rarely occurs, I can be a generous and considerate soul."

Twin snorts answered me, and Bensen shot a glare in my direction. "I feel like I should call for an inspection of hell. It's surely frozen over."

"I got dressed up today, didn't I? If that's not generous and considerate, I don't know what is. I didn't even complain very much, either."

Benny kneed my seat. "You conned me out of one of my museum pieces."

"I didn't con you. I asked nicely in exchange for a favor. It's really pretty, and I enjoy wearing it. I could have been mean and asked for that captain's sword to replace mine—or that flintlock. Or the watch, or some of those jewels, or…"

"I'll concede. Since you mention those items, you were very considerate of my wallet."

"The pendant is unusual, but it's not a showcase item, not like one of those. You really did put together a fantastic exhibit, Benny. I'm really impressed you managed to get such a large collection. To think you brought an entire pirate ship up from the bottom of the sea. How long did it take you?"

"The better part of five years of continual work, restoring and preserving each piece as it was salvaged. A lot of pieces were at risk of deteriorating, but we found a way to encase them in resin to preserve and protect the wood. We got lucky—the first few ships we attempted to bring up fell apart before we could preserve them. The *Terrier* was our only success. I'm hoping we'll be able to find the location of her sister ship."

I thought back on the museum's opening, and I couldn't remember if he had mentioned the *Calico* or not. "There's a sister ship?"

"An old sea tale claims the *Terrier* was built at the same time as another ship. The limited records I've recovered claim the ship's name was the *Calico*, and it was owned by a rival pirate captain, although very little is known about the captain and the rivalry they had with the Black Scourge."

I frowned, slowing the car enough I could glance at Bensen before regarding Benny in the rearview mirror. "They? The *Terrier's* captain was unusual because she was a woman, was she not?"

"The records seem to imply the Shark Tamer was actually a woman, too. There hasn't been any substantial proof of this."

"The Shark Tamer?" I blurted, astonished the nickname had survived the centuries. To cover my thoughtless mistake, I added, "You're making these names up to make this museum seem more interesting, aren't you?"

"Not at all. The records we found listed the *Calico's* captain as one Louise or Louisa, the Shark Tamer. Unfortunately, the writing is smudged, and the difference between an e and an a is a gender. It could be Louis, too, with flourish on the s. The records we found indicated that the two captains were once allies, possibly lovers, which supports the Shark Tamer being a man. But, I find the story of two rival pirate queens far more interesting. Don't you?"

"I find it unlikely at best. The wise women hid their genders, and when there were pirate queens, as you call them, they were the only woman in the crew. Everything I've read indicated that sailors were highly superstitious."

"You're likely correct. The *Calico's* first mate was confirmed to be a woman."

A chill swept through me, and in order to hide my apprehension, I played along. "Oh?"

"There were two records of her. The first called her the Tamer's princess, the Cat Princess, likely referencing the ship's name."

"No name?" I prayed to the uncaring gods my name had been lost to time, because there was no way I could explain away such a strong coincidence.

Benny grumbled something, which I suspected was a curse or a string of them. "Unfortunately not. She was listed as C-C in the records both times. The other documents with her name were too ruined to make out. We're not even certain of the *Calico's* port of origin, although we suspect she came from either Italy or Spain."

"And you know nothing of the ship and its crew beyond that?"

"I've isolated her final resting place to one of two possible locations. One is off the Cape of Good Hope, and the other is deep in the heart of the Indian Ocean. It seems she ran afoul of the British navy. We found limited records from the British supporting the sinking of the *Calico,* but they didn't list the captain's name, origin port, or anything other than the fact she was a frigate matching the general description of the *Terrier*. The records implied the *Terrier* was the original target of the fleet, but they had found the *Calico* instead."

I couldn't—didn't want to—believe what Benny told me, and the possibility I'd had it wrong all along stabbed through me, a dagger to the heart, and each of his words twisted the blade a little deeper. "What sort of records?"

"Navy captain logs. I don't have the originals; those are in a history museum in the United Kingdom, but I was given an opportunity to go through the records and found the listing. Until I can verify the existence of the *Calico* beyond the two references I currently have—or get the captain's full name—I am not making any announcements regarding the ship. I'll be organizing some dive teams to check shipwrecks off the Cape of Good Hope to begin my search. I've already charted out the locations of the identified shipwrecks, so it's a matter of confirming the identities of other ships. Fortunately, the *Calico* likely has a distinctive figurehead like the *Terrier*, if the rumor of them being twin ships is true."

"What will you do if you find her?"

"There's room for a second frigate in the museum. I'll stage them together in conflict, representing the downfall of the *Calico* and the eventual perishing of the *Terrier* and her crew. Alas, until I find proof of the second ship's existence, it's just a story and nothing more."

"That's quite the story," I muttered, shaking my head and forcing my attention on my driving. "Implausible at best."

"Never say never, Cathy. This is part of why the Golden Age of Piracy intrigues me so much. Sometimes the strangest stories prove to be the truth."

FOURTEEN

I'm going to have to keep you on a short leash.

THANKS to my decision to view speed limits as a general guideline and recommendation rather than a rule, we reached the museum an hour before the start of the gala. I handed the keys to Bensen's car to the valet. A security guard checked Benny's identification before letting us into the museum early.

The general lack of Halloween decorations intrigued me. Since my last visit, Benny had added some new pieces to the entry room, including several anchors belonging to famous pirate ships and five new figureheads, one of which was fashioned of gold. The mermaid coiled around a pointed battering ram, something I found curious. "That's odd."

"I wish I knew its story. It was salvaged from an unnamed ship in the Arabian Sea, and I haven't been able to find any ships on record with a figurehead matching its description. The ship was in really bad shape, but the figurehead and ram were intact."

The *Calico* also had a golden mermaid figurehead, a beautiful woman with outstretched arms waiting to embrace any sailors fortunate—or unfortunate—enough to cross her path.

"Type of ship?"

Benny shrugged. "Your guess is as good as mine. It had been reduced to a few timbers scattered across the ocean floor. From the best I can figure, it came from a smaller ship, something riding low to the water, so it could ram larger ships and punch through their hulls. She probably broke apart during a ramming attempt."

Circling the mermaid, I inspected her. If she'd ever hit anything, I saw no evidence of it in the smooth gold polished to a high shine. The ram, like the *Terrier,* was encased in resin to preserve it. "Did you have to repair the mermaid?"

"Minor repairs. Part of her tail was damaged, but all it needed was hammered and smoothed back into position. The ram was broken, but we fitted it back together and secured it before preserving it. Those are all original pieces."

"Wouldn't she have been a lot more damaged if she had rammed a ship? Gold's a softer metal. It would be ruined if it hit another ship at ramming speed, wouldn't it?" I reached out, but before I could touch the figurehead, Benny caught hold of my wrist.

"No fingerprints on my mermaid, you heathen pirate!"

I laughed but relented and didn't touch his precious figurehead. "I'll smear my prints all over her shiny scales before this night is over, just you wait and see."

"I'm going to have to keep you on a short leash, I see."

"I thought you wanted me to play pirate today." I gave him my best innocent look and struggled to hold back my mirth. "I'm pretty sure pirates don't see golden statues and walk away without pawing them—or trying to steal them."

"They also don't sew or negotiate for plunder, either. You're a terrible pirate, Cathy. You have the look down to an art, but you really need to work on your act."

"Do you have a plank? I think I need to make you walk it."

Bensen came between us, took hold of Benny's shoulders, and steered him across the room. "All right, you two. At least wait until we're all in costume before you start fighting, that way it looks like part of a show."

While I wrinkled my nose at the thought of putting on a show for anyone, I followed the pair. "How many people are supposed to be here tonight?"

"No more than fifty. It'll be a fairly quiet

social event, then we'll do the photoshoot afterwards. I'll be surprised if people stay more than an hour or two. Most attended the opening, so they've already seen the majority of the collection. It won't be too strenuous, I promise."

For some reason I couldn't quite put my finger on, I didn't believe him, not for a single moment.

~

THE BROWN-HAIRED WOMAN with golden glints in her hair, the one with the modernized frigate, prowled through the museum, and she wore an outfit similar to mine while carrying a cutlass and flintlock resembling the ones stolen from my home. No, they didn't just resemble them, I was certain they were them—I knew every etching of them better than the back of my own hand.

To add insult to injury, a man with heartbreaking resemblance to Ricardo shadowed her steps, just as he had shadowed the steps of Captain Maritza.

Life was truly cruel and uncaring.

If I could have staked my life on a bet she held my prized possessions, I would have. I stood stiff and tense, aware I lacked any form of weapon at all, and it took every bit of my will to keep from balling my hands into fists.

I couldn't afford to let anyone know I recognized her, and with each passing moment, my temper frayed. I'd been whipped enough times by a frayed rigging line to understand the pain it caused when it lashed out. A stray line could cut through skin and break bones, especially during a tempest.

Benny sidled up to me, dressed in his British navy coat with golden buttons. While tempted to whip my leg around and knock him off his feet, I kept still, although I allowed myself a frown. "You didn't find me accessories. I look out of place."

Until I got a closer look at the flintlock and cutlass, I couldn't confirm they were mine despite my gut feeling they were. Pretending I hadn't noticed them would serve me better—and give me a chance to get near the woman.

I wanted to rip my blade out of her hold and slice through her clothing, leaving her with nothing but a few scraps to wear. The men in the room would thank me, and I'd blow off some steam at the same time. Maybe she had the looks to warrant the stares of so many attending the party, but I wasn't going to fall for her pretty face, not if she had my prized possessions.

I knew she did. They were unique, so unique I'd never seen any others quite like them.

"I know. I'm sorry." Benny glanced in the direction of my would-be kidnapper—or whatever she would have been if I'd stayed on the raft—and averted his gaze.

Fury heated my blood. Benny knew she had the flintlock and the cutlass; he either knew or suspected they were mine, and he didn't mean to do a single thing about it. If I pressed, I could guess what he'd say.

He'd claim he didn't recognize the pieces. After all, why would anyone so boldly wear stolen property?

"I'm going back to my hotel. If you need a proper model, use the wench over there. She's fully accessorized." I spun on a heel and headed for the doors.

"Cathy? Hey, wait, Cathy. I'm sure this is just some misunderstanding."

Bingo. He confirmed my suspicions without me having to ask a single question. I halted, lifted my chin, and slowly turned, angling my head to mimic my captain at her haughtiest. "Catalina de la Corona. There is nothing to misunderstand, Benjamin. My sword, my flintlock. They are unique. You know this, and you knew the instant you saw them, you who collects things of the era, too. You want your pictures? Take them with her."

He grabbed my arm, and I regarded his hold on me with clenched teeth and narrowed eyes. "Cathy, I'm sure it's a misunderstanding. Don't be melodramatic, please. This isn't like you."

Of course it wasn't like me. For so long, I

had tolerated everything so I wouldn't do more than cause a few ripples. I'd learned to do that after losing Ricardo, to survive after losing everything of value to me. When my anger had shown, I smothered it far more often than not, using words and my glare as weapons rather than staging a retreat or dramatic exit.

"This is the one thing I can't forgive."

Benny frowned.

The woman approached, her every step even and calculated, looking me over before shifting her gaze to Benny. "Benny, darling. What's the meaning of this?"

I recognized the lilt in her speech and her accent as Italian, and I flexed my hands. "I'm finished here, Benjamin. Let me go, or I'll show you how the ship's doctor actually dealt with injuries during a voyage. It'll get bloody, and you'll be putting in an order for a hook, assuming the ER can stitch the rest of you back together before you bleed out. I wouldn't bet your life on it."

Either my words or my lifeless tone got the point across, but he let me go. Shaking with anger, I stormed towards the doors. Without a weapon, there wasn't anything I could do, unless I added theft to attempted murder charges.

Escaping from prison took far too much work and closed too many doors for too long.

With only my name left, I wouldn't smear it, not over some worthless traitor.

My frustration peaked. With both halves of the key in my possession, I no longer needed to continue living the mockery of my past life. I'd lost the place I had called my home, and the too fresh betrayal of someone I had foolishly considered a friend still stung. Benny called my name, but I ignored him and headed into the night.

I would follow the coast home, and when certain there were no prying eyes to watch me, I'd slip into the sea. If someone asked in a few days when I finally showed up, if I bothered to, I'd add to the piles of lies littering my long and bitter life.

I MADE it all the way to the pier before Benny caught up with me, and he panted from exertion. "Come off it, Cathy. I'm sure there's an explanation."

"My home was leveled to rubble, and some wench shows up with items you know are mine, and all you do is look away from her without a word? Did you beg me to dress like this just so you could humiliate me? We're finished. You'll have to find some other banker to handle your accounts, and Bensen's, too."

"Or you could give me a chance to ask Lucretta where she got them."

"And if I hadn't gotten angry? Would you have just ignored it because the wench, your Italian *ramera,* is one of your darlings?"

Benjamin had the decency to flinch at my accusation, and his silence confirmed my suspicions. "I would have talked to her after the photoshoot. I need you for this, Cathy."

I stopped and turned, once again canting my head so I could regard him in Captain Louisa's cold fashion.

The woman strode up behind Benny, halting a half-step to the front and side of him, and she arched one of her perfect brows as she once again looked me over. "Problem, Benny?"

"You're only the symptom of the problem. I should be thanking you for the reminder of where his loyalties lie. If you want him, you're more than welcome to have him. Start watching your back, because he isn't going to watch it for you." I lifted my hand and flipped my fingers in a farewell once favored by many in the *Calico's* crew. "I'll just give you a free piece of advice, *ramera*. Avoid the water."

"Are you threatening me?" The woman straightened, and the disbelief coloring her tone forced a laugh out of me.

"When you take what belongs to others, expect curses." I smiled at her before turning my stare to my cutlass and flintlock. "You have what is mine, so I'll have to take what is yours. That seems fair enough to me."

If they wanted the *Calico* so badly, I'd guide them to it, sinking the Italian *ramera's* frigate to the bottom of the ocean to mark its final resting place.

That seemed fair to me.

"Cathy!"

I took a single step back and laughed. I hated the modern world, its easily broken friendships, and the shallow depths of its waters. I loathed the masks I had worn for so long. Discarding them would make things so much easier.

The House Lost at Sea waited for me, and my curse would become my blessing. If I lost a hundred more years to life beneath the waves, I would do as I'd always done. I would adapt.

A smothering weight fell off my shoulders and dissolved around me, breaking apart like foam tossed on a churned sea. "I'm tired. Go enjoy the rest of your party, Benny."

"I really need you for the photoshoot, Cathy."

I regarded him. Weariness took hold of me in a smothering grip. "Why? Your *ramera* is certainly prettier than I'll ever be, and she's a proper pirate. I will not lower my head to some worthless thief, if that's what you are hoping for, nor will I pretend to like anyone involved with the ruin of my home."

"Your home, ruined?" the woman asked, and she once again arched her eyebrow at me.

"Everything in it destroyed, the walls broken, until it was no longer fit to stand. Demolished, all for my flintlock, my cutlass, my watch, and my gold. Because it wouldn't do to leave me with anything, right? That's just not the pirate's way, is it? The round is yours. The next round is mine. Remember that."

Her eyes narrowed. "You exaggerate."

Benny sighed. "She isn't exaggerating, Lucretta. Just give her her gun and sword. I'll pay you whatever you spent on them."

"They are truly yours?"

Without anywhere to focus my anger, it burned out, leaving me an empty, hollow shell. "On the butt, the flintlock is engraved. You will find the marking near the dragon's heart. Four letters."

Lucretta pulled my weapon out of her holster, flipped it over, and examined the engravings decorating the handle's butt. "The letters. Tell me, what are they?"

Sometimes, the truth served me best. "CDLC. Catalina de la Corona, handed down to me as was my name."

Benny sucked in a breath. "They're heirlooms?"

I shrugged.

"And the sword? What proof do you have that it is yours?" Lucretta slid my flintlock back into the holster, and her hand dropped to my cutlass's hilt.

"You'll find the same initials on the pommel. If you'd like to discuss it with the police and the insurance company, I'm sure they can provide all of the photographs you could ever want of them and my pocket watch. If the photoshoot is so important to you, reschedule it for another day. I've had enough of this bullshit for one night."

I left. Instead of walking—and swimming—home, I hunted down a cab, refusing to speak another word to either one of them. I abandoned them on the curb, where they watched me.

Lucretta kept my weapons, and I wondered how I would find the woman's frigate when I only knew her first name.

FIFTEEN

Get used to the idea.

I GAVE my boss two choices: she could assign Bensen and Benny's accounts to someone else, or I would quit.

I suspected she thought I'd at least hesitate before living up to my ultimatum. I left her with my resignation, effective in two weeks, while she gaped at me. To add fuel to the flames, I used the bank's policy against them.

Since they wouldn't cash out my unused vacation time, I packed up my desk in a small box, informed her I was using the time the bank owed me, and left. She could have fired me over it, but she didn't, at least not while I was still in the office. It took me less than ten minutes to leave, and on my way out, I turned in my security passes.

I had been betrayed before. I remembered the sting, the bone-deep pain, and the lingering regrets. I had put too much trust in modern humans, and they had done exactly what I should have expected.

Benny and Bensen had chosen a beautiful Italian, just like my captain. That part wasn't their fault.

They had no way of knowing their choice would hurt me beyond the loss of a few possessions. I pressed my hand to my chest to feel the shape of my captain's pocket watch, reassuring myself of its presence. In a way, I wanted to thank them.

The years had softened me too much, and I had adapted too well to the complacency of so many comforts and an easy life. Anger had served me on the seas long ago. It would serve me again. I would become something more—and less—than Cathy, the account manager with a knack for finding treasure.

I headed to my hotel to find Lucretta waiting in the lobby. She frowned when she saw my box. "Cathy," she greeted.

She wore a business suit and a blazer. I headed for the elevators. "Lucretta."

"About last night…"

"Since you're such close friends with your Benny darling, you can tell him he'll have a new account manager in the morning." I shuffled the box in my hold long enough to jab the elevator button. "Have a good day."

I could be polite sometimes, when it served me best.

Instead of going off and having herself a

good day, she stepped into the elevator with me. I ignored her, pressing the button to take me to my floor.

"We got off on the wrong foot."

I waited, shaking my head at her audacity. "Let me give you a clue, since you seem incapable of figuring this out for yourself. If I had a match and stood next to your house, I'd light it on fire so I could roast marshmallows. If you had a car, I'd slash its tires. Do yourself a favor. Don't show your face anywhere near me. I might forget if you stay out of my hair long enough. Or not. If I were you, I'd go with the 'or not' option. I'm the kind to hold a grudge."

I went to my room, and she followed me. I dumped my box on the floor, dug my key out, and unlocked the door, wrinkling my nose at the disaster of fabric scraps and sewing supplies still taking over most of the room.

Lucretta made a surprised sound. "Benny told me you had made your costume yourself, but I hadn't believed him. It seems I was mistaken."

"Worry less about your looks and a little more about the dead space between your ears. That'd help." I shoved my box into my room and slammed the door in her face.

Infuriated Benny had told the woman where I was staying, I stormed through the room, packing away the scraps and returning the supplies to their proper place. The costume, which I'd spent so long slaving over, went into the trash.

I kept the boots but shipped them to myself so I wouldn't have to deal with what they represented; destroying a piece of art in my anger wouldn't do me any good, and Benny hadn't polluted them with his influence. I'd get a modern pair on my way to the airport, cheap in comparison but nice by most's standards. With everything in the room organized, I went to work packing a suitcase.

My cell rang halfway through the task, and I glared at the display, which informed me Benny wasn't done with me yet. While ignoring him would have been satisfying, I answered, "Haven't you done enough?"

"I'm sorry, Cathy."

"What do you want, Benny?"

"Lucretta told me you had mentioned I would be getting a new account manager? Can't we talk about this?"

"I quit. You're getting a new account manager, so get used to the idea."

He sucked in a breath. "You quit?"

"Get your ears checked. You seem to have difficulty hearing me." I hung up and tossed my phone on the bed. "Sorry isn't going to cut it, you landlubbing bilge rat!"

My phone rang, and I glared at the device. Ignoring my ex-boss's call would have made sense, but I grabbed my phone, reined in my temper, and answered, "Hello?"

"Can we discuss your resignation?"

Thinking on my feet, I considered the estimated amount of time for my home to be rebuilt, the time I would need to explore the House Lost at Sea, and how long it'd take me to hunt Lucretta down, steal her precious frigate, and blast a hole in its hull near the *Calico's* sunken remains. "Until my home is rebuilt and I have a chance for a proper vacation, I'm not even considering it. Maybe in two to three months. I'm burned out."

The excuse would work; people burned out in banking all the time.

My boss sighed. "I understand you're under a lot of stress, but you're one of my best managers, and you're the best person for the Bensen and Allen accounts. Both of them are concerned."

A snort burst out of me. "For some reason, I find that difficult to believe. They just don't like change, especially when it is beyond their control. It's not like I am the only good account manager in the office. Call me in a week or two. Maybe I'll change my mind after I get some fresh air."

"I'll be ready with a proposal, hopefully one you won't be able to refuse."

"I'll hear you out, but I make no promises."

If she wanted anything else from me, she'd be waiting for a long time.

A DUMPSTER behind the hotel served as the perfect place to be rid of my unwanted clothes, and I took fiendish delight in chucking the bag and its burden up and over the side, where it landed in the bin with a satisfying thump. While it would've been appropriate attire for what I planned to do, I'd take the more modern approach with jeans, a comfortable shirt, and a leather coat.

I confirmed two months with the hotel, giving me all the time I needed to pursue my more nefarious affairs. It'd been far too long since I'd indulged in my true nature, and I almost wasn't sure where to start.

Almost.

One convenience of modern times included the internet, and there were few women named Lucretta in the United States. It didn't take me long to find out the Italian woman had a bit of an Irish heritage. Like me, she had an interest in the past, one that fell in line with Benny's fascination with the *Terrier* and the *Calico*. Unlike him, her interest ran a bit deeper.

I didn't care much about the legacy of other pirates, but among enthusiasts, Lucretta held an interesting rank as the direct descendant of a pirate queen. I found it intriguing how many children Grace O'Malley had had before her death, especially with her reputation of being, like my captain, far more interested in the fairer sex than in men.

Then again, the woman had been married, so I assumed Lucretta was descended from a child born prior to O'Malley's time as a pirate queen.

I wondered if my Captain Louisa would have partnered with O'Malley instead of the Black Scourge had we sailed the same seas. O'Malley's final tide had washed out long before our first voyage. I sighed and gave the dumpster a glare before I turned and headed for the hotel's basement garage.

Some time with my Knucklehead would give me a chance to think and come up with a plan. I'd also find a bookstore and indulge in a leather journal, one I could use to log the important details on my hunt for revenge. Lucretta O'Malley would learn pirates of the old ways were cut from a different cloth, and my defeat would only serve as kindling for the fires of my triumph.

~

IT TOOK me several hours to find a store with a leather-covered journal with a fold-over flap and strap ties. It wasn't quite the same as what I had once used, but it came close—as close as a book with modern binding could. I hoped the pages wouldn't fall out from heavy use. When I returned to my hotel, Benny was loitering in the lobby, and he straightened when he saw me.

"You're not going to leave me alone, are you?"

"I'm really sorry about what happened on Halloween. I really have no idea how Lucretta got a hold of your pieces. I really don't."

"Considering she hasn't seen fit to give them back, I'm not really all that interested in hearing any of your excuses."

"She is having them molded so she can have a replica set made of them. They'll be returned to you, I promise—and if there's any restoration work that needs done on them, it'll be done. She claims she bought them fair and square. Didn't even want to believe they were stolen goods until I showed her the insurance documentation and police report of the theft. I… I took her to your property to show her what had been done to your home. They're tearing it down tomorrow, did you know?"

I hadn't known the specifics. I shrugged. "They told me they'd have something new built in its place in the next month or two. Seems logical they'd have to tear down the old one."

"She seemed really bothered by how much damage had been done."

"That's her problem, isn't it? You're wasting my time, Mr. Allen. I'm going out of town for a much needed vacation."

He blanched. "Is there anything I can do? I'd really like to do the photoshoot."

"I tossed the outfit, so no. Forget it. Lucretta has friends in the community. I'm sure she can find someone who can fit the role."

"You threw it out?" Paling several shades, he stared at me as though seeing me for the first time. "But why? You worked so hard on it."

"I worked so hard on it because you had asked me to. You threw that work in my face with this stunt. Letting her do what she wants with things you know are rightfully mine? Then you expect me to just happily accept this, because in her pretty, empty head, she thinks it's all okay because she wants a replica? I'm not sure you could get more insulting even if you tried. Leave me alone. You assume your *ramera* bothers to do as she claims."

"You've used that term several times. What does it mean?"

"It's Spanish. You like to believe you're so smart. I'm sure you can figure out what it means on your own. Didn't you know, Mr. Allen? I am a Spaniard."

That couldn't be taken from me, nor could my heritage and legacy.

"Can't you at least try to be reasonable about this?"

I clenched my teeth. "I was. Instead of calling the police and my insurance company, notifying them I have located the possessor of my stolen property, I waited. I see no reason to continue extending either one of you that courtesy."

I left Benny in the lobby, aware of his attention on my back. Times had changed, and I would use the law against them.

I smiled, pulled out my phone, and gave the insurance company a call to report I had seen one Lucretta O'Malley at a museum dedicated to pirates with my possessions in her custody, attending a gala hosted by one Benjamin Allen. If they were busy dealing with the police and my insurance company, they wouldn't have time to bother me.

SIXTEEN

At least one of you has a single grain of common sense. It's a miracle.

IT TOOK a little over an hour to deal with the insurance company, and by the time I finished, I almost felt bad for Benny and what he'd have to do to talk his way out of a theft charge. If he didn't understand my need to protect myself, he'd learn a valuable lesson. I also made a point of informing the insurance company of the pirate-related groups Lucretta O'Malley belonged to, which gave her motive to steal from me—or hire someone to steal from me.

To add to the shit storm the pair would have to endure, I made a point of mentioning the uncanny resemblance my weapon and pocket watch had to the one in the captain's case at Benny's museum, which gave him motive to steal the pieces.

My next step would be to take the keys to the House Lost at Sea and discover its secrets before the pair realized it wasn't just a pendant. If Benny realized its worth, he'd want it back so he could have a mold made to replicate it. Without the second half of the key, it wouldn't do him any good.

Then again, considering the lengths the thieves had gone to to take my cutlass, flintlock, and pocket watch, I suspected they'd have no scruples about breaking into the manor. The building likely meant nothing to them.

I grabbed my suitcase, called for a taxi, and headed for the airport. I'd have to take steps to reach the House Lost at Sea, and after what had happened in South Africa, I couldn't afford to use the Cape of Good Hope as my base of operations. Instead, I'd head to South America, find a sea-worthy ship I could sail solo, and take it to the island. I'd visit my hoard first, hidden away on a neighboring isle, and I'd pick suitable replacements for what I'd lost, anticipating they wouldn't be returned.

If Lucretta adhered to pirate ways, what was in her possession counted as hers, and its history wouldn't matter one bit to her. I could respect that, but I wouldn't allow it to deter me from sinking her precious frigate in retaliation. Maybe I wouldn't bother leading them to the *Calico*—I'd do them one better. I'd buy an underwater camera, record a video of my captain's ship in the deeps, and send it to

Benny anonymously, leaving him to wonder where she was and how to get to her.

At the airport, I booked a flight to Brazil, where I would head to Suape to hunt down a ship suitable for my needs. It wasn't the closet port to the islands, but it would serve me well enough.

Unfortunately, the next flight to the airport I wanted left in two days. If I wanted to reach Brazil earlier, I'd have to head to a busier, larger airport and drive almost two hundred miles to Suape or leave from a different port.

I considered my options and bought a ticket for a flight departing in three hours.

Bensen called me twenty minutes before my flight was scheduled to board, its gate only a few feet away from where I waited in a cafe. I considered ignoring his call before answering, "Hello?"

"Are you all right?"

Any other day, I would have found his concern gratifying, although I suspected he only cared because he knew I wouldn't be the one handling his money anymore. "Do you want the pretty answer unlikely to offend your sensibilities, or would you rather have the truth?"

"If you could give me the truth with training wheels, that would be ideal."

I almost laughed. He wanted me to soften the blow a little, but he acknowledged I would likely offend him and was prepared to accept my answer even if he didn't like it. "Training wheels? How youthful of you, Bensen. Benny's girlfriend has my flintlock, she has my cutlass, and it wouldn't surprise me if she has my pocket watch, too. Because she wants to have them replicated, they weren't returned to me, and Benny's quite all right with this. So, I'm finished. I quit, I'm going to take some well-earned time off, and I really don't want to be bothered. That about sums it up."

Bensen remained silent long enough I wondered if he had hung up on me, but a quick check of my display showed the call remained connected. When he was ready, he'd answer. It didn't matter to me if he never spoke to me again.

Perhaps considering him guilty by association did our relationship no justice, but I wouldn't make the same mistake twice, not anytime soon. I sipped my coffee, wished I'd gotten a beer instead, and watched people hurry towards their gates so they wouldn't miss their flights.

"This must be what my mother meant when she warned me about scorned women."

"And since the three items were involved in a huge policy claim, he forced me to report I had seen the items at his gala. I even gave him a day to return the pieces. I'm not becoming the victim of an insurance fraud accusation because he prefers this woman's friendship over mine. He made the bed, so he can sleep in it."

"Have you told him that?"

"I'm sure he'll figure it out when he and his girlfriend are visited by the police investigating my report. Since he has matching pieces in his exhibit, he's going to have to do a lot of talking to convince the police he wasn't involved. So, while I didn't mention your name, you were involved in the alibi, so perhaps you should be prepared for questioning, too."

Bensen sighed. "I understand you're angry, but was that truly necessary?"

"The insurance claim was for over six hundred thousand, Bensen. First, I'm contractually obligated to report it if the items surface, where they were located, and the circumstances. So yes, it was truly necessary. You're a businessman. I shouldn't have to explain this to you. Second, my property could have been returned, and they could have asked if I would consent to a molding of the original being made. Had I been treated with even a hint of respect, I might have even agreed to it, especially knowing Benny had similar pieces in his exhibits. I wasn't asked. I was told I might get my items back after the fact. I'm supposed to be happy with this?"

"No, you're right. You have no reason to be happy with that arrangement. If those were the terms of your policy, then it was unavoidable."

"At least one of you has a single grain of common sense. It's a miracle."

"Why don't you let me talk to Benny and see about making sure you have your things back. He really wanted you for that photoshoot for his museum."

I sighed. What the hell was so important about his photoshoot? Was it an eccentricity of the overly rich? Was there something I was missing? "No can do, Bensen. I tossed the outfit. It's probably in a landfill by now, and if it isn't, it'll be there soon enough. I'm not recreating it, and I'm not getting dressed up for his pleasure again. That Lucretta O'Malley has the pedigree he wants, and I'm sure she can call in some of her friends to fill any roles he may need. He can have his photoshoot, but it won't involve me."

"And knowing you, there's no force on Earth capable of convincing you to make the costume again, is there?"

I pinned my phone between my ear and shoulder and clapped loud enough for him to hear. "He made his decision. It seems only fair he pays the consequences for it. It's not my fault she's prettier than me, but it is his fault he chose to sacrifice his honor and my friendship for her. That's the problem with the wealthy. They think money can fix anything. No amount of money on this Earth can buy my trust or respect. Without that, there's no way I'm going out on a limb and inconveniencing myself for his benefit. I have nothing to gain out of this arrangement."

"I would suggest you'd have your property to gain, but that would imply that your material possessions are worth more than your principles, and I'm pretty certain that isn't the case."

"Correct."

"At least let me talk to Benny and see what I can do. I can smooth feathers with your insurance company, too. I'll make sure it works out for everyone."

I laughed loud enough to earn glares from the other travelers in the cafe. "What makes you think I want everything to work out? That implies I'm willing to forgive and forget. I have a long memory and a mean streak. I'll leave you to figure out the rest from there."

"Still, give me a chance to talk to him. Let's meet for lunch tomorrow?"

"No can do, Bensen. I'm leaving on a jet plane, don't know when I'll be back again." I hung up, laughed at my own joke, and finished my coffee before heading for my departure gate.

~

AIRPLANE MODE SPARED me from having to talk to anyone for several long, blissful hours.

Unfortunately, I ended up crammed between a teenager so frightened of flying he looked ready to cry and a businessman who looked ready to kill the poor kid if he cracked. Maybe I had a skewed moral compass, but kids always struck a nerve with me. I'd killed for far less than making a kid cry, and since gouging out someone's eyes with my nails on a plane would land me in a lot of trouble, I went with my second plan, which involved distracting the teenager from his fear.

"Hey, kid. First flight?"

The teenager jerked and stared at me, his brown eyes widening as he realized I was talking to him. At first he hesitated, but when I didn't jump down his throat and showed no sign of impatience, he nodded once, so subtly I wouldn't have noticed if I hadn't been watching him carefully.

"It's safer and faster than driving, although the security lines are not my idea of a good time. You know what the best part of flying is?"

The teen looked at me like I'd grown a second head, but his shoulders relaxed, and I got the feeling he'd grow into a handsome man given a few years and some confidence. "No. What?"

"It's when you land. You can end up anywhere in the world. One flight could take you to somewhere warm, somewhere cold, somewhere far from civilization, or right into the heart of a big city. Everything's different. Every flight could take you on an adventure."

"An adventure," he echoed, and his tone was so full of skepticism I laughed.

"I'm going to purchase a yacht and set sail for a few weeks. It should be an interesting trip this time of year."

Depending on how far north I went, I could run the risk of making the acquaintance of a hurricane, which would be a good way to ensure spending the rest of my trip as a shark.

"By yourself?" he blurted.

"Solo," I confirmed. "I wanted an adventure, so I'm making one."

"On a yacht. By yourself."

"Is it really so unbelievable?"

"You're a *lady*."

I shouldn't have laughed so hard, but I couldn't help it. Me? A lady? While I sometimes wore skirts for work, especially if I wanted to distract a businessman so the bank benefited from his carelessness, I couldn't imagine myself as a lady.

Hell would truly freeze over first.

SEVENTEEN

Sometimes, I even went to their funerals.

I DIDN'T LEARN the kid's name, but after the plane landed, an older man and woman met him at the airport. After watching them for a while, I wondered what it would be like to have a family. How would my life be different if I had someone who cried when they saw me, caught me in a hug, and acted like they never wanted to let me go?

Ricardo might have become that for me; I'd never know. When I'd held him as my most prized captive, I'd never let him out of my sight. He'd enjoyed my affections enough, and he'd sought out hugs after the first few weeks.

I'd refused to allow anyone else that sort of intimacy. I'd taken men to bed, but I'd never cuddled with them after we both took what we wanted from our shallow relationships.

Perhaps worse than Captain Maritza's curse was how relentlessly he haunted me.

That someone who resembled him, right down to his shorter stature, dark hair, sun-kissed skin, and Spanish flair, kept Lucretta O'Malley company served as a reminder of why I was better off vanishing and reappearing after a few decades.

What would it be like if I had someone who cared for *me*, not for what I could do for them or what I owned? What would it be like if I found someone I didn't want to live without?

I doubted I could ever have children even if I wanted them. Birth control and protection had been uncommon when I'd been cursed, but I had been promiscuous enough to have earned at least a few brats during my life as a pirate. After three hundred years of partners, if I could have children, I would have by now.

In a way, my infertility was far more of a blessing than just another facet of my curse. I wouldn't have to watch my children grow old and die around me, taken away from me one by one. I'd seen too many friends age, and my circumstances forced me to drift out of their lives so they wouldn't suspect there was something unusual about me.

Sometimes, I even went to their funerals, wearing a low-brimmed, veiled hat so I could wish them well on their journey to the next life.

Melancholy settled over me, and I made my way from Sao Paulo to Santos so I could find a seaworthy vessel. I hired a cabbie for the trip, and he treated the roads as challenges and ignored speed limits in favor of ditching me in the port as quickly as possible. I tipped him for breaking records and not getting me killed along the way before hunting for the first respectable marina I could find.

Life had taught me a few important lessons, and for every wealthy man, there were two or three who wanted to appear wealthy and bought things they couldn't afford. Yachts often fit the bill, and given a few hours and my credit card, I'd find one for sale.

The first marina proved a bust, its facilities so worn down I didn't even bother looking at the available ships before abandoning it for the next in line. With at least nine miles of marinas and docks, I'd find *something* eventually. Unfortunately, as I continued hunting for a seaworthy ship, I drew far more attention than I liked.

If a downtrodden dockworker or other bilge scum wanted a run at me, I'd show them I'd forgotten more about dirty fighting than they had ever known. I kept my chin up and stayed alert, waiting for one of them to decide he would try his luck.

To my amusement, it wasn't a Brazilian who decided he liked the look of me. I guessed he was a mix of some sort, white American and something darker, though I couldn't tell if his other half came from Africa, the Middle East, or even somewhere else in South America. Whatever he was, he wasn't easy on the eyes, which went against the predominant beauty-comes-first attitude favored by many of the Brazilians I'd met.

He approached at an angle, likely hoping to dislodge my purse and make a run for it. I pretended not to notice him, although I shifted my stride and took slow, light steps, ready to move when he decided to act.

I had made it halfway to the next marina when he grabbed for my purse. I stepped out of his path, plunked my elbow into my palm, and rammed my fist under his chin, using my left arm to add strength to my blow. On the follow through, I smacked my palm over my fist and smashed my elbow down on his face.

Little satisfied me more than breaking a would-be thief's teeth, and he crumpled to the ground at my feet. While I could have stepped over him, I put my boots to good use, and after I kicked him onto his back, I marched over him, making sure my heel hit his groin. "Not today. I'm not in the mood."

He groaned, and I left him writhing on the ground in my wake.

The others found something else to do in a hurry, and their cowardice disappointed me. My victim would live, although he'd need to have someone help rearrange his face thanks to my two strikes.

Back in the day, it would've taken me at least three good hits to flatten someone. Were modern men so weak, or had I honed my edge?

Unless someone else decided to try me, I'd have no way of knowing. I shook out my hand and wiped off the blood on my coat so it wouldn't damage the leather.

The next marina didn't look quite as disreputable as the first, and while wary of a con, I appreciated the selection of new boats available for sale. New worked as well as used, although I worried how long it'd take to get a new one seaworthy.

"American?" the store employee asked, looking me over.

"Alas," I replied with a shrug. "I'm looking for a ship. Something I can take out on the open ocean solo. I'd like to stock her for a week to a week and a half, call it two weeks to be safe. I prefer sailboats, but I'll take anything good. I'll be paying in credit because I don't want to bother waiting on a wire. I'd like something I can launch sooner than later. Impress me."

The man's brows rose towards his hairline. "That'll be expensive."

"My budget is two hundred grand, US dollars. I'll go over if you can handle the stocking. I'm looking for used, but if you have something new in my price range, I'll take it."

His eyes widened, and I could practically hear the coins chinking together as he realized a good profit waited if he managed to please me. "I think I have a few ships you might like. Please, come with me."

I followed him to the shipyard, where several yachts waited on dry docks for their chance to return to the sea. The ones he had in stock ranged between seventy-five to a hundred feet, and while he had used ones that fit my price range, they were far too battered for my liking and too large to easily manage on my own, so I directed him to his smaller offerings.

The smaller luxury ships he showed me ranged between twenty to thirty feet long, plenty spacious for my needs. If I did find Lucretta and her frigate at sea, size wouldn't matter much on my end; I had my ways of boarding and bringing havoc to her ship without even breaking a sweat.

He pitched me a hundred and fifty thousand for a nice thirty footer with a spacious cabin, which included a sitting room, three bunks, a kitchen, and a pantry. It even had an onboard shower, which filtered ocean water through a heater. Like Lucretta's frigate, it was a hybrid of a sail and motor boat, so if the winds didn't favor me, I wouldn't be stuck. If the motor failed while I was out on the open ocean, I wouldn't be stuck. On inspection, I found several problems, little things I could manage to repair—or ignore—on my own, but I managed to knock off twenty-five thousand from the price and secure enough supplies to last for two weeks on the open ocean, including fishing gear.

The only downside was it would take two days for the marina to make her seaworthy, a delay I accepted with a wrinkled nose. I bought the ship, dubbed her the *Wanderer*, and found out where the best hotel in the city was. The marina called a cabbie for me, sparing me from having to venture out into the docks again.

Part of me regretted the lost opportunity to engage in another fight.

A good fight might help dull the edge of betrayal.

~

THE HOTEL REMINDED me of the place in South Africa except it was even dingier, which awed and disgusted me. I regarded the place with a scowl. The cab, which could have taken me somewhere better, sped off as though frightened of the building's deteriorating veneer. I had two realistic choices: I could stay, or I could go.

I'd been in worse. I appreciated the health codes of the modern times. Then again, I held the opinion too many landlubbers couldn't fight off a basic cold without an intervention, all thanks to their unwillingness to go out and get dirty.

On the other hand, I liked how I could go to a doctor, have them poke me with a needle, and their medication would ensure I wouldn't come down with the worst plagues the Earth had to offer. I'd survived through several epidemics thanks to the curse, and I would rather avoid repeating the experience.

I stepped inside the building, bracing to enter a home for rats, fleas, and other unsavory beasts.

Instead, sunlight gleamed on polished wood floors, and simple elegance surrounded me. Bursts of color stood out on a backdrop of pale walls, and it took me a moment to recognize the feathers and sequins of Brazilian dancer attire on display for guests to appreciate. Rich red and gold rugs protected the floor from several couches and armchairs perfect for lounging.

Maybe the marina worker hadn't been out of his right mind after all.

I headed for the desk, and a man in a black, classic suit offered me a smile and said something in Portuguese, a language I knew all of three words of despite its similarities to Spanish, reminding me how much I'd neglected my native tongue and heritage. "Sorry, do you speak English?"

The man's smile widened to a grin. "Of course. How may I serve?"

"Any available rooms?"

"How long will you be staying?"

"Two nights." It didn't take long to get checked in, and I chuckled at the use of actual keys instead of cards. I got his recommendations for places to eat, headed up to my room, and ditched my suitcase. I took off my modern, cheap boots, a poor replacement for the ones I'd left in the United States, and wrapped the chain of Captain Maritza's key around my ankle. After a moment of thought, I found a spot to stash my captain's pocket watch as well.

If anyone wanted to hunt them down, they'd have to take off my boots, and if they managed that, I was in more trouble than I cared to think about.

I lingered in my room for an extra hour, giving my phone a chance to charge before heading out. Brazil intrigued me in some ways; violence seeped into so many elements of its culture, with a staggeringly high murder rate. Life—and death—were cheap, and so were the guns and knives used in so many crimes.

I considered hunting down some protection for myself, something with enough firepower I wouldn't want to risk smuggling it back to the United States.

My phone rang, and the display warned me Bensen wanted to continue our talk from earlier. Sighing, I grabbed the device and answered, "Cathy."

"I was starting to think you were ignoring me."

"I told you I was leaving on a jet plane, Bensen. It's traditional, when one boards a plane, to turn the phone off or use airplane mode. I just turned it back on, as I am no longer in the air. What do you need?"

"The police have confiscated your pistol, your cutlass, and your pocket watch. After investigation, it'll be returned to your insurance company. They'll give it back to you."

I chuckled. "That'll be at least a month or two. That works. I should be back in the United States by then—or I can have them courier them to me. Thanks for the tip. I'll make sure to give the insurance company a call. Is there anything else you need?"

"Benjamin was hoping you might urge the insurance company to move a little quicker and begged me to ask you if you'd reconsider the photoshoot."

"Hell might freeze over first, Bensen. Today, I have a plan. It involves the hardest liquor Brazil has to offer and as many bar fights as I can find before the police show up.

I might even hunt down a man, as long as he's capable of counting to ten without having to stop and think about it. I'm very busy."

"In Brazil. Are you trying to get yourself killed? What are you doing in Brazil?"

I laughed at the alarm in the old man's voice. "Getting good drinks, participating in rowdy fights. What else would I be doing in Brazil?"

"Please tell me you're joking."

"Would I ever joke about drinking and brawling?"

"I don't know, and that worries me a lot, Cathy. You're joking, right? You're not really in Brazil about to go looking for a fight, are you?" He hesitated. "While drunk, looking for a man who can count to ten."

"When you put it that way, you make it sound like I'm doing something completely reckless. Don't ruin my fun, Bensen."

"Actually, I think I make you sound like you're a real pirate, and I don't mean the nice kind kids dress up as for Halloween."

I smiled. "Then I best get on with the plundering and pillaging."

"I'm worried, Cathy."

My smile broadened to a grin, and I chuckled long and loud. "Plundering, pillaging, and fighting are all on the agenda. Fortunately, I prefer my partners to beg me for it, so I'll leave my conquests to that."

I hung up, and still laughing, I called my

insurance company to confirm the truth of Bensen's words, arrange for them to debit my account for the recovery of my three most prized possessions, and ensure they were kept under lock and key until my return to the United States.

EIGHTEEN

He didn't mind his temporary captivity

I FOUND a woman who could count to ten in six different languages, but she had eyes only for her husband, and while his attention wandered early and often, the battered remnants of my morals barred me from pursuing their company. Since I couldn't indulge in a two-for-one special, I hunted a man who wore his suit a little too well.

Alcohol, and copious quantities of it, made it a lot easier to accept I'd have to compromise on my requirement for clever wit and settle for handsome, capable of opening doors for others, and willing to pay my booze tab. Knowing how much it'd take to get me drunk enough to ignore his less than artistic turns of phrase, I decided the combination would work for a night.

Or two as the case was, since he was good enough in bed to warrant keeping him there. I considered him hangover therapy, and by the time I finished with him, I left him an exhausted wreck in his hotel room.

I got the feeling he didn't mind his temporary captivity. He hadn't been as good as Ricardo, but he'd been the best I'd had in the past hundred years or so. The curse would eradicate any potential diseases he might've been carrying, although he'd been as much of an advocate for condoms as me.

I added Brazil as one of my preferred countries to visit when in search of a good time and a fight.

I left him with the feeling of having scratched an itch rather than fulfilling a deeper need. I wanted to curse Ricardo for having ruined me, but I missed more than the sex. The little things, his affection that went beyond physical touch, continued to haunt me.

That Lucretta O'Malley had found herself a man who resembled my Ricardo hurt even more than the other betrayals. I'd find some way to even the scales between Benny, Bensen, and me—but I'd ruin Lucretta to help exorcise my long-lost lover's memory.

Maybe if I transformed Ricardo into a betrayer in my mind, time might begin doing its work on me.

Annoyed at myself for fixating on a past I could never revisit, I wandered back to my hotel, gathered my bags, and checked out.

Trouble found me before a cabbie did, and

with four-against-one odds, I'd need a little bit of luck and one of their knives to put up a good fight. I'd find out if I had the luck soon enough, which left the matter of disarming one of them. Like I had with the dockworker in the port, I pretended not to notice them stalking me. Instead of standing around and making it easy on them to surround me, I headed down the street with my suitcase in tow.

If a fight was what they wanted, I'd give it to them, and if they gave me a good enough run, maybe I'd consider taking one of them on my cruise with me, marooning him somewhere to be found if he wasn't sharp enough in wit to keep me amused.

I viewed it as the winner taking all, and I had no doubt they'd take everything they could from me if I let them get a hold of me. Some things didn't change, including the depravities of four men ganging up on one woman.

Unfortunately for them, I didn't fear death or anything else they could do to me.

I found a promising alley, one filled with garbage. Its stink was so strong it wouldn't have surprised me if there were corpses among the rubbish. As expected, they followed me, and I set my suitcase in one of the few cleaner spots, knelt as though adjusting my boot, and waited.

Their footsteps drew closer, and I dusted

my leather boots, flexing my hands in preparation for a fight. My boots would end up scuffed or torn, especially if they came with their switchblades out and ready. I expected pain and a lot of it; the curse didn't stop injury, it merely halted death.

If they cut me, I would bleed, and it would hurt. In a perfect world, I'd deal with them without doing more than damaging my boots and scraping my knuckles. If that happened, I suspected hell would be entering the ice-making business with a promising first quarter.

I waited until I glimpsed the first pair of worn, dirty sneakers before lunging forward, switching directions, and sweeping my foot out in a kick. Without a good fix on my first victim, I relied on luck alone for a good hit. My heel clipped his arm and startled him into jumping back. His knife, closed but still a threat, dropped into the trash. Using the wall to stop my momentum, I came in low, snatched the fallen weapon, and popped it open with a flick of my wrist.

The young men backpedaled, their eyes locked on the shining blade of my new toy. With a swish of my wrist, I held their attention, shifted my weight, and kicked, twisting to the side. I came in low, aiming for the knee of the youngest, who had, in his enthusiasm, attempted to flank me in the alley's confined space.

He yowled, and his pained cry woke his friends to their predicament. I gave credit where it was due; he staggered, but he didn't fall.

Had I been a better person, I would've felt a bit more guilt over teaching them a lesson, but I figured I was doing them a favor: they'd think twice about following a strange woman into an alley. A nicer person might've given them a chance to run, but I wanted one to talk to me, and I didn't care what happened to the others.

If they were wise enough to run, I'd let them go. Smiling, I kicked my young victim's knife out of his hand and launched it in the direction of the street. His friends dove out of the way of the spinning weapon, and they yelped and stammered something in Portuguese, which I decided was some form of disbelieving curse.

To make sure my chosen victim didn't go anywhere without me, I bit the handle of my knife to free my hands, smacked my right palm against my left fist and drove my elbow into his gut so hard he collapsed against me and slid to the ground, curled and writhing from pain.

I'd be nice to the kid later. I'd make sure he wouldn't die. It was the least I could do for picking him as my kidnapping victim. I smiled around the mouthful of rubber and metal and took a single step forward.

Only one of them had the intellect to realize they'd bitten off far more than they could chew. I rarely viewed someone who ran as a coward. In a pointless fight with life on the line, cowardice showed intelligence. There were a few types of people who stuck around in a fight, and I'd been—and met—them all, including the stupid, the brave, the stupidly brave, the desperate, and the competent.

I beat them until they ran and claimed their little knives as trophies of my conquest.

Shaking my head over the waste of time and disappointing lack of bloodshed, I turned to my victim and nudged him with the toe of my boot. "All right, kid. You're not going to die, so get up and stop whimpering. It's embarrassing." All I could see in his eyes was blank terror, and I sighed and hauled him to his feet. "Man up and walk it off."

My new acquisition was no Ricardo; while I'd stunned my lost lover and had earned more than a few incredulous stares, he'd never been afraid of me.

Keeping a firm grip on my victim's elbow with one hand, I closed the blade of his knife and pocketed it before retrieving my suitcase with the other. He didn't fight me when I dragged him along, and all it took was a hissed warning to keep him in line while I hunted down a cabbie so I could set sail for the House Lost at Sea.

THERE WAS BOLD, then there was 'taking a hostage in a cab to the port' crazy, but for some reason I couldn't fathom, my victim played along, not saying a word the entire drive to the water. I had the driver drop us off several blocks away from the marina.

"All right, kid. You speak English?"

He nodded, and his Adam's apple bobbed when he swallowed.

Ricardo would've had a field day beating the boy into shape and teaching him how to be a proper man. As far as pirates went, Ricardo had more of a soft side, making sure his chosen targets actually learned in his rough care. Back in those days, he'd been the equivalent of a pacifist while still being capable of killing.

Captain Maritza hadn't wanted Ricardo for his capacity of violence; she'd needed his skills with maps, charts, and the stars.

I regarded my new companion with a raised brow. He recoiled, as though my expression promised his death. Idiot kid. He'd learn soon enough he was useless to me dead. "Good. We're going to go on a little cruise, and you're going to talk. You tell me the truth, and I'll drop you off somewhere comfortable with enough cash to find your way home, and you won't even have many bruises to show for it. Since I'm nice, I'll even give you your little toy back in case you need it. I get the feeling Brazil's a rough place to wander around if you aren't armed. Got a name?"

"Abrahan."

"Abra*han*? Not Abraham?"

"Abrahan," he confirmed.

"Here's how this is going to work, Abrahan. I've got a little ship waiting for me in the marina up ahead. We're going on a cruise. I'm going to take you along the coast for the afternoon and drop you off. If they ask, I know your parents, and they thought you'd like a chance to see the water, since it's not something you normally get a chance to do. Got it?"

He mumbled something and nodded.

"Make yourself useful and bring my bag." I thrust my suitcase into his hands and marched him along the docks to the marina, keeping a close eye on the workers. Either they saw something in my expression warning them off, or word had spread to avoid messing with me, as all of them found something else to do whenever I looked their way.

I spotted the *Wanderer* on the water, and she had a fresh coat of paint and her name was written in elegant lettering on her bow. I nudged my victim, gesturing towards my ship. "That's your new home away from home until I decide I'm finished with you. Isn't she pretty?"

"If you say so."

I smirked and headed for the pier. "I do say so."

Within an hour, I'd be back on the water where I belonged, and as though sensing I meant to return to the sea, the winds favored me, ready to fill my sails and send me towards the House Lost at Sea.

The marina staff took me and Abrahan on a tour of my ship, showing me the supplies they'd acquired, and I nodded my approval of their choices, most of which were practical, and the items that weren't went into the refrigerator and freezer, both of which were powered by solar panels mounted on top of the ship's cabin.

They had stocked for three weeks, filling every inch of pantry space with fresh supplies. I took the time to check the expiration dates, nodding my satisfaction. Whether in an acknowledgement of the past or because limes were simply a part of the Brazilian way of life, there was an entire case of the citrus fruit in storage. Nothing would spoil within a month except for the perishables, and I'd use them up long before it became a problem.

To make sure I wouldn't be followed, I made the marina employees an offer: I'd give them ten thousand dollars each if they erased any mention of the *Wanderer* from their logs and swore they never saw me or Abrahan. I also gave them instructions that if they were asked about my credit card, it was used by a woman who did *not* match my description. I suggested they concoct some Brazilian woman, as my name sounded native enough.

The three men on staff didn't need to be asked twice.

I lowered myself to using the motor to leave the harbor, respecting the other ships coming in and out of the busy port.

I'd have plenty of time for indulgence once I was in deeper waters, and until I figured out what Abrahan and his friends had wanted, I wasn't going to take chances with my brand new sails and rigging.

The *Wanderer's* motors purred, and she cut through the waves as eager as I to voyage into the open sea beyond the breakwaters.

"Where are you taking me?"

I looked over my ship and gestured to one of the leather-covered seats where he wouldn't get in my way once I unfurled the sails and really went to work. "Wherever I feel like, kid. It's nice having a second set of hands on board during a voyage, and I've provisions enough for the both of us for a while. Don't worry. If I wanted to kill you, I would've left you to rot in the alley. This is how it'll work. You'll tell me why you and your friends followed me into an alley, and we'll go from there."

"We were hired to get something from you."

I laughed. "Oh, this is going to be good. Let me guess. Was it a necklace by any chance? One with what looks like a broken key?"

If the poor kid's eyes widened any more, they'd pop out of his head. He nodded. "That's what he said. Wanted the necklace. Said he'd wring our necks if you came out of it with more than a few bumps and bruises. Said you liked to talk big but were gentler than a mouse." Abrahan's expression soured. "You have him fooled."

"I do that. Act a certain way, and I just become big talk but gentle. Then I can do what I want without anyone thinking twice about me being the actual culprit. Paid you good for the work?"

"A thousand each if we got that jewelry he wanted. American dollars."

I snorted. I assumed it was either Benny or Bensen behind it—or both. They knew I had the necklace, and Bensen knew I was in Brazil. I wouldn't put it past him to figure out where I'd gone in some fashion or another. He had money and connections, especially within the banking sector and the FBI. Twisting rules wouldn't bother him if it meant he got what he wanted.

I had no trouble believing either one of them would use Brazil's reputation to get the necklace back. It also made me wonder if they knew the value of what I had coerced out of my ex-friend.

"What's got you and your friends so desperate you'll follow a woman into an alley?"

Abrahan shrugged and slumped onto the seat. "Need the money."

"Figured it'd be a quick and easy buck, and you liked that no one would really get hurt, huh?"

He grunted, which I interpreted as an agreement.

Some problems I couldn't fix, but if he needed money, I could buy his loyalties for a while and solve his immediate problems. "All right, kid. I got five thousand in cash for you, but you have to do one thing for me."

His eyes widened. "You want me to do one job for five thousand?"

When opportunity knocked, I answered, and with a bit of quick thinking on my feet, maybe I'd make the situation work out in my favor. "You'll come on this trip with me, run a few errands with me if needed, and do what I want. You'll earn every dollar of it, and if you do a good job, you'll earn extra. I'll feed you, and I won't even oppress you too terribly much during our little voyage. Your *base* pay'll be five thousand American dollars."

He sat straighter and stared at me, his expression eager. "What do you need me to do?"

I dug my cell from my purse. "You know the number of your contact?"

"I know it. I'm the one who did the talking. My English is the best."

I chuckled and decided the friendly approach would serve me better with the kid than threats or bullying. "Your English is very good. I used to speak Spanish, but I've forgotten most of it." Speaking my native tongue hurt too much, as I'd spoken with Ricardo in Spanish; our crews had used Italian, although both of our captains had spoken many languages. Anyway, the Spanish I knew wasn't even spoken anymore, not really. Modern Spanish, like every other language on Earth, had evolved over time. "It turns out you really do forget if you don't use it for a long time. You look pretty young. How old are you?"

"Sixteen."

I nodded, understanding all too well the hardships of being on the cusp of childhood and wanting to be treated as an adult. By the time I had turned sixteen, I'd already served on a pirate ship for years, pretending to be a boy until I couldn't anymore. My breasts had betrayed me, but my fists had served me well, and I'd beaten up half the crew before the captain declared I was neither man nor woman, and if they had a problem with it, they could take it up with him.

No one had dared until we reached port, which was when he kicked me off the ship. At least he hadn't marooned me on some deserted island.

"So, you up for it? A little time at sea helping me out, a phone call, and maybe a few odd errands. You'll walk away with plenty of cash. You'll have to lie a little, though."

"That's it?"

"That's it."

"I'm in. What do you want me to do?"

Ah, I loved when my victims became allies. It made my life so much easier. Smiling, I handed him my phone. "You went to do the job, you cornered me, started a fight just like you were told, and another group edged in on your turf. You took the phone off my body after the gunfight, and the last you saw of your friends, they had scattered—and make sure they scattered *before* I was gunned down. Tell them you don't know what happened to the necklace, but it wasn't on my body."

"You want me to tell them you're dead?"

"I do. You can also inform them that my credit cards were taken out of my wallet, but my identification was left inside. Simple enough, right?"

Abrahan nodded. "So, what should I call you?"

Digging out my wallet, I handed over my driver's license. "If he didn't give you my name, just go by what's on the card. That'll cover you. If he asks about the sea sounds, just say you're on a dingy off the shore lying low."

He looked over my license. "Not bad thinking, Corona."

I killed the *Wanderer's* engine and set the ship to drifting, taking a seat near the wheel. I'd use the satellite navigation system to get my bearings before digging out the sea charts to see if they were any good. If they weren't, I wouldn't have any problems finding my way.

Technology simplified so many elements of sailing.

"Make it real good, and I'll teach you how to actually use that knife of yours as part of your bonus, kid."

Abrahan flashed me a grin and tapped in the numbers of his contact, and when he sucked in a breath, I knew the number belonged to someone registered in my phone. He didn't connect the call, instead looking up from the device to stare at me. "Someone you know did this to you."

"Shit happens, kid. I have it pegged as either Benny or Bensen—or both."

"Says Benny."

Shaking my head over Benny's idiocy, I settled in and gestured for Abrahan to get to work. My friend should've known to hide his tracks better. It hurt, but the pain would fade in time.

Most pain did.

Abrahan frowned at my silence, but he

tapped to connect the call, holding my phone to his ear. "Boss, I'm on the broad's phone. Second gang came in and gunned the bitch down. What you wanted wasn't on her when they cleared out. They messed her up pretty bad. Doubt she lasted long. Nothin' we could do about it. We went in with those knives, just like you told us. They brought guns, and I ain't talkin' the little ones, sir."

I almost ruined the ruse with laugher, but I covered my mouth with my hand so no sound would betray my presence. The kid had enough nerve to shoot a glare in my direction, which earned him more of my approval than anything else he'd done so far.

"They left her wallet, but if she had plastic, they took it. Yeah, I saw her identification. Her last name was Corona. Yeah, that's her. Catalina. You want what? Fine. We waited outside that hotel you told us, just like you said. We followed her a few blocks away, and we got her into an alley. I don't know where you got your info about her, sir, but she wasn't no wilting flower, that's for sure. She knew her way around a knife, and she had us scattered before we knew which end was up. Not even sure we could've gotten the necklace off her if she had it without having to mess her up ourselves. My gang left me with her, and that's when the other group opened fire and took her down. I left. I had a knife. What'd you expect me to do? Suicide?"

Maybe the kid made a bad mugger, but his acting skills impressed me enough I contemplated keeping him. Given the right opportunities and a little bit of help, I bet he could run a con with the best of them. The scorn he injected into his tone also carried the sharp edge of disgust.

"Sir, with all due respect, who is gonna care about some American broad, even if she looks like some Spanish whore, and not even a pretty one at that? Just another day, just another mugging and murder. Nothin' new around these parts. I'm sure someone'll find her soon enough. She wasn't that far from the main road. In boots that nice? Someone'll stop, figure out she's a tourist and report her. You wanted us to keep quiet, we did that." Abrahan shook his head, rolled his eyes, and lifted his hand, making his fingers and thumb quack like a duck.

Benny had a lot to say, and the kid waited him out with so much patience I got the feeling he had endured a lot over the years and learned the hard way to keep his mouth shut when needed. When he sighed, the resigned sound made me wonder what Benny had said. "I ain't a doc, sir. I couldn't tell you if there was any chance the broad lived. Looked like they turned her chest to swiss cheese despite not offing her right away. I got no way of knowing. I doubt it. Who was gonna do anything about it? Where was anyone gonna take her? Who was gonna pay for it? She didn't have nobody to miss her. That's all I know. You didn't hire me to get shot, sir, and you didn't hire me to go rescue some broad who got shot. I don't know nothin' about who might've wanted the necklace, either. What you want me to do with the phone?"

Several moments later, Abrahan made a disbelieving noise. "No, I didn't keep anything else, just the phone. Can do that, but not this moment. Laying low, sir. Don't want whoever got her to get me, too."

The kid hung up, shook his head, and turned my phone off. "You got yourself some twisted friends, Corona."

"I don't have friends, kid."

Abrahan shot me a glare, got up, and handed me my cell and license back. "I think he missed the memo. He went ape-shit on me, and guys just don't do that without a good reason. From the sound of it, some other folks with him missed the memo, too."

"He hired you to rob me. I'm pretty sure that doesn't fall under the 'things friends do to friends' column."

The kid shrugged. "Point. I'm just saying is all."

I accepted his words with a nod. "Point. So, what *did* he want you to do with my phone?"

"Mail it to him. I'm gonna need some blood to make this look real, Corona."

"Blood's something I got plenty of," I replied, pulling out the kid's knife. "I'll swing near a port, and we'll mail it off. He gave you his address?"

"Said he'd send it to your phone. I don't know why he wanted it, but he did. Guess he thought it had value for some reason."

Sentimental idiots. What good would giving them my phone do other than confirm I'd gone to South Africa and Brazil? "Good enough. Now, I'm going to teach you a very important lesson about fingerprints, kid. Benny's smart sometimes, when he really wants to be. Gloves are your best friend, and after I wipe my phone for prints, I'll take care of getting it messy. You're to leave no prints or hair or anything when you ship him the device. Why give him someone to frame?"

"You're the boss, Corona."

NINETEEN

I had a mean streak at times.

I GAVE the kid enough cash to mail my phone to the United States, and I found a pair of gloves on the *Wanderer* that would keep him from leaving his fingerprints everywhere while avoiding unwanted attention. I located a quiet little dock near a town, dropped him off, and took my ship out into deeper waters to wait for his return.

After two hours, I suspected Abrahan wouldn't be coming back, but almost three and a half hours after I sent him on his errand, he ran onto the dock, and I brought the ship in to pick him up.

"That took longer than I thought it'd take." I waited for him to scramble on board before easing the *Wanderer* back out to sea, her engine purring as I guided her out of the harbor to the safety of the open ocean.

"Had to bribe someone to get the box sent without it getting checked through customs."

"You had enough for it?"

"You owe me fifty."

I pulled the cash out of my wallet and handed it over. "Good job, kid."

"So, what're you going to do with me now?"

I left him waiting for thirty minutes, which I spent guiding the ship out to waters deep enough to drift safely while I looked over the navigation charts inside the cabin. Abrahan followed me, his eyes widening as I spread the papers out over the cabin's single table, made to sit two comfortably, possibly three or four in a pinch.

Fool that I was, I hoped to find that third or fourth body to fill the space, cramp the cabin, and drive me crazy—or force me to buy a new, larger ship. Or steal Lucretta O'-Malley's.

Stealing her ship—and her Ricardo looka-like—would make up for a lot of my problems. Lighting it on fire would do the trick, too.

I had a mean streak at times.

While modern maps included most of Earth's islands, the charts lacked any notation for my cluster of tiny islands, most of which weren't fit for anything. The reefs surrounding them were flagged as a danger zone to be avoided, which likely justified their exclusion from the charts. Too small to be used for naval or aviation purposes, too barren for anyone to survive long without supplies, and lacking wildlife worth notice, they only existed on the most accurate maps, and even then, I doubted they had a name, and I doubted anyone cared enough about them to investigate their secrets.

I pointed to the reef. "We're going here."

"But there's nothing there."

Shaking my head, I tapped the part of the chart where the gap in the reef would allow the *Wanderer* to slip through without her hull being torn apart by the rocks and corals lurking beneath the waves. "There's a group of islands here. Hundreds of years ago, it was used as a pirate isle, a launching point for crews hunting the seas of South Africa and India. They would take supplies that kept well and store them on the island, replenishing their stock without having to return to the major ports."

"Pirates?" Abrahan gaped at me. "You're interested in hokey pirate nonsense?"

If seeing was believing, I'd be giving Abrahan plenty of reasons to change his tune. In the 1690s, his words likely would have resonated with the more skeptical, but no one then had reason to doubt the existence of pirates. We had made our presence known in every port around the world, and fear of our prowess and ruthlessness kept people wary of new ships in the harbor.

Wise pirates nurtured relationships with those on shore in favored ports, a tactic Captain Louisa favored, as had I.

"Benny is a collector, an enthusiast, and a bit obsessed with the Golden Age of Piracy. He made a bargain with me for the necklace he hired you to retrieve. I owned a cutlass, a pocket watch, and a flintlock pistol from that era, and I suspected he wanted them. My home was robbed and destroyed in the process, and they took my valuables, including those three pieces. Benny's girlfriend had them in her possession, and they didn't see fit to give them back to me. Ultimately, I involved my insurance company, and the items were recovered, although I doubt I'll get them back, as I've conveniently been removed from the equation."

I would miss those pieces, but perhaps I'd be able to recover them down the road. It would be a long time down the road.

When I was honest with myself, letting go of those damned items would, perhaps, allow me to let it all go.

"Why is he after you so much?"

"He's chasing history, and I had something he wanted. Rather like a pirate, really. I can respect that."

"You can? Are you loco?"

I laughed and shook my head, sliding my finger across the map to the *Calico's* final resting place. "No, I just know things he doesn't. He's after a shipwreck, and I know where she's at. I also know what he's after, and since I'm rather like a pirate myself, I'm going to enjoy taunting him with what he can't have."

"I'm very confused."

Unless I started at the very beginning, he'd never understand. I put the sea charts away and gestured for him to join me on deck. "Did Benny tell you anything about the necklace?"

"Only that you had it and he wanted it, and he'd give us each a thousand American dollars if we retrieved it without messing you up too much when we took it."

"Understand this is just my perspective on it. I'm sure Benny has his reasons. I probably won't like them, but that's not his problem. That's mine." I took a few minutes to check the *Wanderer's* engine and make sure it wouldn't get in the way of me properly sailing the ship. When I finished my preparations, I checked the wind, got my bearings with my compass, and went to work preparing the rigging and unfurling the sails.

Abrahan followed my every move, watching me with wide eyes. "You really know how to sail this thing? Benny said you were a poser playing a pirate."

I threw my head back and laughed. It took me several minutes to recover enough to focus on the tasks at hand. While I worked, I nodded in the direction of the boom. "If that hits you, you're going to regret it, so stay out of its way."

"Got it."

"Tell me, kid. You superstitious?"

"You mean like don't walk under ladders or break mirrors type superstitious?"

"That among others."

"A little, I guess."

"This story starts in the 1680s when a pair of pirate queens joined forces and had a pair of ships built, the *Terrier* and the *Calico*. These two queens ganged together, hunting the seas until the late 1690s." I considered what Benny had told me, and I decided to continue the story the way I had lived it versus the romantic tragedy he seemed to believe was the truth. "One betrayed the other, and as a result, the *Calico* and her crew were lost. Later, the *Terrier* likewise sank without a trace of her crew. Benny recovered the *Terrier* and her treasures. The necklace was on board the *Terrier*. The three items I possessed belonged to the *Calico's* first mate, gifted to her by the *Terrier's* captain."

Comprehension lit Abrahan's eyes. "He wanted them because of their history!"

"A missing piece of his puzzle."

"Who was the first mate of the *Calico*?"

"Catalina de la Corona."

"But that's your name."

I smiled. "So it is."

"Does he know that you have her name? Wait. Her. I thought pirates hated women on their ships."

"They did."

"So this first mate was one of your ancestors or something? That's why you had her stuff? But I thought you said the ship sank, her crew killed. How do you have her things?"

In my long life, I had never considered telling anyone the truth of my existence, but I considered the young man I'd kidnapped and, with an offer of five thousand dollars, had made part of my crew, although he didn't know what he had signed on for when he'd accepted my deal. "That's a tale for another day. For now, that's all you need to know. I have what he wants. Tell me, Abrahan. How much would it cost me to buy your loyalty?"

I'd asked that question of Ricardo, too. He'd laughed at me, and on the next breath, he'd promised I'd never have to buy his loyalty because I'd gotten something better.

It had taken his death to truly understand what he'd meant.

Abrahan. frowned. "What do you mean by that?"

"Your service. Your sworn oath to serve no other, to sail these waters with me should I decide the land bores me. That might happen often. I will pay you, I will pay you well, and I will be responsible for your education, your livelihood, your well-being, and everything you need, until the day you tell me you can no longer serve and wish to be released from your oath. If it is for weeks, so be it. If it's every day for the rest of your life, so be it."

"I hope you're aware that sounds absolutely loco."

"You seem smart enough to me." I meant it, too. He observed, he noticed the little details, and he had the courage to ask good questions. "I value that. Your English is good, which tells me you've had some education."

"My mother's American. She came to Brazil for my father."

Something in his tone warned me her choice hadn't worked out very well for her—or for him. "And are you American, too?"

Abrahan reached into his pocket and pulled out a US passport. "She returned to the United States to have me, stayed long enough to get my American birth certificate, then brought me to Brazil. Against my father's wishes, she didn't get me Brazilian citizenship. When she died, he tossed me out, because his son wasn't Brazilian enough for him, but he loved my mother enough not to shame her while she still lived."

"What a ray of sunshine. So your mother taught you English?"

"Right."

"And your father shoved Portuguese so far down your throat you'd do just about anything to forget it?"

"Close enough."

"I can work with that. I won't promise you a traditional schooling, not yet at least, but as long as you're on my ship, you're going to learn a lot. You'll learn how to sail. You'll learn how to fight with that knife of yours. You'll learn how to handle a gun, from a flintlock to something with a bit more punch. You'll learn how to read maps without the help of a phone. I'll teach you everything I know about banking. I'll make sure you'll be able to take placement tests as though you're homeschooled, and I'll get you set up to be good enough for any college smart enough to accept you. You won't be applying for student loans, as I'll pay for your education."

"So you're paying for my board, my schooling. What else?"

"A stipend, because every man needs a reason to work, something he can claim as his, that he built with his own hands." I finished unfurling the sails and setting the rigging, perching on the captain's chair with a hand on the wheel. I'd hold my course until nightfall, see where the winds took me, and decide where to go from there. "We'll negotiate each voyage. This one will earn you five thousand while you test the waters with me. If you don't like it, no harm, no foul, and I'll release you from your oath with no questions asked, plus I'll take you to any port you want in the world. What you do from there will be your problem."

"What if I said I wanted to go to China?"

I chuckled. "Then I would take you to China."

"Antarctica?"

"I would question your sanity for wanting to go, but I would take you there."

"You'd really sail anywhere? Why? What's in it for you?"

"I keep my word. That's what's in it for me. If you keep your word to me, I will keep my word to you."

"This Benny broke his word to you, didn't he?"

"His specific word? No. But he broke faith with me and betrayed me all the same. For me, there's little difference."

"All right. I have nothing to lose."

So few did when they signed on to join a pirate, but given time, I'd make certain he had everything to lose and gain by sticking with me. That was how Captain Louisa had built her crew, and it would be how I built mine, one worn and ragged landlubber at a time. I pulled one of my trophy knives out of my boot, flipped it open, and tapped a finger to the tip of the blade, not hard enough to slice through my skin—yet. "A blood oath, then, kid."

"You know you mean it when you bleed for it." He took out his knife. "How do we do this?"

I regarded my left hand with narrowed eyes. I held the blade's grip steady and curled my fingers around the weapon's back, pressing the edge into my palm deep enough to part the skin, waiting for a few drops of blood to well up. "Like that, carefully. You want a few drops, not to bleed yourself out on my nice clean deck."

Abrahan followed my lead, and I appreciated his caution, ending up with two blood drops on his bronzed skin. We shook, and I held his hand in a firm grip. "You have my sworn word and oath to provide for your care, pay you as promised, and safeguard you for as long as you're part of my crew, for as long as you choose to sail with me."

The words weren't the same as I'd sworn hundreds of years ago; mine were kinder, and I thought Captain Louisa wouldn't have approved of my gentle hand. Then again, maybe she would have.

She'd taken me in, after all, although she had sworn to kill me if I ever betrayed her.

Abrahan swallowed before replying, "You have my sworn word and oath to serve you loyally, until the day you release me from my service."

Releasing my grip on his hand, I got up, leaned forward, and clapped his shoulder. "Welcome aboard, kid."

All I could do was pray to the uncaring gods we wouldn't regret our decision.

TWENTY

Do you know how to fish, kid?

IF I STUCK to sails only, it would take a month to reach the cluster of islands. With the *Wanderer's* engine and a stop in the Cape of Good Hope to refill the ship's gas tanks, I'd be able to make the journey within fourteen days, especially if I taught the kid how to handle the ship and navigate.

Neither one of us would be navigating the old way, but it didn't matter much to me. I needed to reach the House Lost at Sea and learn its secrets, raid my stash for enough wealth for two lifetimes, and make a plan. Abrahan's ruse would buy me the ability to appear anywhere, feigning amnesia. A knife, some pain, and a week spent healing, and I'd have scars matching gunshot wounds, supporting the kid's story of how I'd met my supposed demise. As long as I kept him playing along with my scheme, I could show up anywhere in the world.

Or, with a good enough act and no identification, I could become a brand new person, resetting the clock on my age, giving me time before I'd need to disappear again to hide the fact I didn't age.

I almost wanted to show up where Benny and Bensen could find me to learn what they'd do.

It took four days for Abrahan to find his sea legs and adjust to the constant roll of the ship on the waves. I caught him staring at the fishing rods, and after checking our location on the sea charts and verifying it with the GPS system, I furled the sails, lashed them down, and decided to teach the kid the glories of life at sea.

"Do you know how to fish, kid?"

"No."

"Then it's time for you to learn. We've come far enough for the moment." In reality, the *Wanderer's* engine worked better than I had hoped, and when I opened her throttle, she plowed through the waves and proved eager to speed her way across the Atlantic towards the Indian Ocean. "We have a live well on board, so we can keep fish for a while before having to eat them. It's always good to have extra provisions."

"Live well?"

I hopped off my seat and headed for the empty well. It wouldn't take me long to get it running, and I'd be able to flush it with ocean water to keep the fish alive and healthy until we were ready to eat them. "I'll fill this with water. We'll keep the smaller fish in here. If we luck out and get a tuna, we'll have plenty for cold storage and leftover to chum the water. Of course, we might end up with sharks, but that's the way of it."

Within twenty minutes, the kid was perched on a chair with a fishing rod, trolling the seas for dinner while I pointed the ship towards the House Lost at Sea.

He lost the first tuna, but after an hour long battle, whimpers, and a great deal of panic on his part, he landed the second, the ship rocking side to side as the two to three hundred pound fish struggled to free itself from the kid's hook.

"What the hell is this thing?" he wailed, clutching the heavy rod, his entire body straining to keep from losing his catch.

I couldn't help but chuckle at his struggles. Taking pity on the kid, I lashed the rod into its holder. If the tuna wanted to take the rod, it'd have to take the entire ship with it. "You're all right, kid. You've done a fine job. That's a young bluefin tuna."

"That's a *young* one?"

"They get twice that size fully grown, maybe bigger. I need to get a hook to get it on the deck. Once it's out of the water, I want you to go into the cabin until I've killed it, all right? No need to get yourself hurt getting hit by a fish like this." I eyed the mast, my gaze locking on one of the pulleys. With a little work, I'd be able to rig it for cleaning the fish for cold storage. "I'll have you get the freezer and fridge ready. Go check the stores for packaging. We'll need the brown paper rolls. You can also sharpen the knives once it's on deck. All right?"

"How do I bring it in?"

"Just hold it, and don't let it get away, kid. I'll be back with a hook and rope in a minute."

It didn't take long for me to hunt down the foot long, barbed hook and rope thick enough to keep the tuna from staging an escape. It took me several tries to hook the kid's tuna securely enough for my liking.

I wrapped the line around my wrist and took hold of his rod with the other. "All right, kid. You get in the cabin and stay there until I tell you it's safe to come out."

For a long moment, he stared at me with wide eyes before he gulped and scrambled off deck. I waited until I heard the cabin door slam shut before I turned my attention to the tuna. "Here, fishy, fishy, fishy."

It took me five minutes to wrestle it onto the deck and give it a humane death. At least I wouldn't have to explain to the kid the source of my strength this time. I rigged the pulley, hung the fish, and took care of the grisly work so he wouldn't have to be exposed to one of the more brutal elements of life at sea quite yet.

With malicious glee, I made him swab the decks and earn every cent of his pay while introducing him to the misery of serving as a cabin boy on a pirate ship.

~

IT TOOK eight days for us to reach the Cape of Good Hope, and I picked a port so small everyone would remember the *Wanderer* and the kid who sailed her alone. I gave him enough cash to fill the ship's tank, a shopping list capable of feeding us for an extra two weeks, and set him loose.

"How much cash are you packing, Corona?" he muttered, flipping through the twenties I'd thrust into his hand.

"Enough until I hit a stash. I'll have you broker a few deals for us when necessary."

Abrahan nodded and took care of bringing the ship alongside the pier. I held my breath right up until the *Wanderer* gently bumped to a halt. He tossed down lines to the men waiting below. He pulled out his passport, bribed them with a twenty each, and to my amusement, recruited them to do half of his work. With his three minions in tow, it took him an hour to get the gas and the majority of the items on my list.

Staggering into the cabin, he slapped my

list on the table in front of me. “We’ll have to go to another port if we want the rest.”

I picked up the list and checked over the items he had circled. He had made substitutions for several things, most of which I liked. I had no idea what I’d do with the amount of potatoes he’d purchased, but I’d figure something out. “This’ll do. We’ll have to have a talk about the evils of potatoes, however.”

“You obviously haven’t had them made right.”

I glanced up from the sheet and arched a brow at him. “And are you going to be the one to ensure I’ve had them made right?”

“I can do things with food that’ll make you cry.”

“From terror?”

Abrahan leveled a glare worthy of a first mate in my direction. “No, terror is what you do to rice, Corona.”

Great. My cabin boy had developed a sharp tongue and unerring accuracy with its use. “You’re just angling for a pay raise, aren’t you?”

“No. I don’t want food poisoning or to lose my sense of taste. I’m at risk of both. I bought spices with the change.”

“All right, kid. I’ll give you one chance, and exactly one chance, to impress me. Don’t make me force you to walk the plank.”

“We have a plank?”

“I’ll improvise.”

"Can I get a parrot?"

I pinched the bridge of my nose and prayed for patience. "You want a parrot."

"Pirates had parrots, didn't they?"

"Cabin boys don't get parrots." I scowled when he pouted. "Pouty cabin boys in particular don't get parrots."

"What do you have against parrots?"

"They talk back."

Abrahan laughed, left the cabin, and prepared the *Wanderer* so we could set sail.

~

THE WINDS SHIFTED before dying to stagnant air, the bane of sailors around the world. I could have charted a course to take advantage of the currents to reach the islands, but I relied on the *Wanderer's* engines instead, cutting my way across the waves, dodging the *Calico's* final resting place in the slim chance someone followed us.

Abrahan watched, he learned, and he took over the cooking duties, a battle I conceded with a grunt, a shrug, and a few curses strong enough to peel paint from my ship's hull. Instead of being properly cowed, he laughed.

Four days later, running full throttle day and night on alternating shifts, we approached the islands I'd once called home, back in the day when my captain had found—and lost—the love of her life. In the gleam of the setting sun, the manor perched on its cliff glowed an eerie red while the blue-green of the sea skirted the rocks and crashed white on the shore.

"There's a house," Abrahan blurted, rubbing his eyes. "There's really a house up there."

"When she was built, I named her the House Lost at Sea, since only those who knew the way would be able to find her." I braced a hand on my hip and directed the ship through the channels between the reefs towards one of the smaller islands. With a great deal of care, I'd be able to coax the *Wanderer* into the cove near my stash, and I'd test my cabin boy's mettle.

If he had the courage to face the waters with me circling him as a shark, I'd keep him, groom him, and treasure him until I set him free, and unlike my captain and her lover, I wouldn't bind him to a long life of misery and regret.

I would give him power and unleash him on the world, and when he'd lived a full life, his legacy would pass down to the next generation.

"Why is there a house here?"

"I will show you, on a condition."

"What condition?"

"This secret dies with you."

Without any sign of hesitation, Abrahan pulled out his knife and flicked his wrist to reveal its blade. He'd gotten good at the move, and I nodded my approval when he gripped the blade and spilled a single drop of his blood to seal the oath. "Your secret dies with me, so do I swear," he said, gripping my hand when I'd matched him drop for drop in blood.

"All right. Sit while I head to the cove. This'll be touchy work, especially this close to dark. If I hit the reef, we'll sink, and trust me, it's a long swim to civilization from here."

"No shit."

I shot a glare at him, settled behind the wheel, and eased the speed down as slow as the *Wanderer* would go without stalling the engines. It took thirty minutes to reach the right island, and time hadn't done much to the cove since my last visit, although I'd been a shark rather than sailing a thirty footer and dodging the rocks and coral lurking beneath the waves. Abrahan held his breath, gasping when he couldn't anymore, only to try again and fail, and the pattern amused a low chuckle out of me. "Relax, kid. We'll be fine."

"You're loco, Corona! I can see rocks under the water."

"It's a good thing we can see them. Imagine trying this when you can't."

My cabin boy whimpered, but he leaned over the rail to stare into the shallows in rapt fascination. Since he wasn't going to pay attention to me until the *Wanderer* floated in the safety of the deep hole in the cove's heart, I focused on my work until I killed the engine, drifted my ship into position, and dropped anchor. "All right, we're good, kid."

"That was *amazing*."

"This is going to be our port for a while. It's a blind cove, so unless you're in the right spot, you're not going to see we're here." I gestured to the cliffs and rugged hills surrounding the calm beaches. "Even in a bad blow, the water here stays calm enough; the reef and rocks protect this island. The downside? It's a tight fit; the *Wanderer* is as large a ship as you're getting in here, and most people aren't brave enough to take such a small boat so far out to sea."

"It didn't seem too bad. Some of those waves sure did get big, though."

"We lucked out. No storms."

Abrahan grimaced. "Right. So. What's the deal?"

"This is my island." With so many islands in the cluster, every member of the crew had had one of their own, usually shared with two or three trusted companions. I alone laid claim on my island and its cove, and my captain had enforced my choice with an iron fist.

I often thought she'd given it to me out of pity, close to the home she'd picked to share with Captain Maritza, but far enough away I didn't have to stare at their beloved manor unless I had wanted to. I hadn't used it to stash my wealth until later—far later—but it'd been my safe haven, a place I had gone when I needed to escape from the burdens of my duties as first mate.

"I don't get it."

"Can you swim?"

"Not well."

"Time to learn, kid. I've something to show you, and you have to swim to get there. I'll help you reach it, but you need to hold your breath."

"I can do that."

Nodding my approval, I left anything the water would ruin in the cabin, ordered Abrahan to do the same, and lowered a rope so we'd be able to scramble back on board without having to climb in the hard way over the engine housing. I splashed in and treaded water until he eased his way into the calm sea.

"This way." I floated on my back so I could keep an eye on my young cabin boy, who swam with the grace of a half-drowned parrot. I'd have to do something about his ineffective flailing, but at least he kept his head above the surface.

When I finished with him, he'd give a dolphin a run for its money and sharks a reason to worry if they shared the sea with him.

In order to reach the entrance to my cave, I'd have to dive thirty feet down, locate the tunnel I'd carved with my teeth as a shark, and ascend to the air pocket, which was fed with clean air through holes I'd chiseled into the cliff. I'd carved the shelves inside with care, and I even had gone as far as digging out several rooms to contain my hoard.

"I'm going to pull you along, kid. Just hold your breath and let me do the work. I'd rather not have to beat the sea water out of your lungs today." I grabbed hold of his hand in a steel grip, waiting for him to take a few deep breaths and nod when he was ready.

I dove, and I dragged him with me. The pressure of the curse built in my chest, and I refused it, focusing on the kid I'd sworn to care for as my crew. I kicked hard, diving deep and fast, aware he'd likely realize something wasn't quite right about how I swam, too strong, too adept for any human.

The water filled my nose and mouth, and my lungs accepted the sea without drowning me.

It didn't take me long to find the tunnel, and despite resisting the need to transform, my eyes penetrated the darkness, evidence of the magic's influence over me. I angled my body so I could pull Abrahan behind me without dragging him over the roughened rocks. Once free of the passage's confines, I surged for the surface, shoving the kid ahead of me so I could buy time to expel the water.

I coughed it out, my head turned away from him.

"It's so dark," he whispered.

I smiled and dragged him to the lowest shelf, where I had left a collection of oil lamps. I even had modern flashlights, but I thought a proper lantern would bring the cavern's magic to life for my cabin boy. I'd cheat and use a lighter to ignite the wick. There'd be time enough to teach the kid the wonders of a good flint box.

I lit two lanterns, and I hung one from a hook embedded in the wall so its light would catch on the mirrors lining the cavern, turning the night to day. Gold gleamed alongside tarnish-blackened silver.

Abrahan sucked in a breath and muttered something in Portuguese, his tone awed.

"X marks the spot, m'boy. X marks the spot. Welcome to my home."

TWENTY-ONE

You're loco, Captain Corona.

"THIS, and the House Lost at Sea, is what Benny desired from me."

When I had organized my hoard by era, I'd done it out of boredom, but with Abrahan beside me, I rejoiced in my compulsive nature. Shelf by shelf, room by room, I could show him my legacy, the evidence of my existence, and promise of his future.

"What is this?"

I knew every last piece of treasure from the *Calico*, the story of every man who'd died with her, and the story of every golden ingot, every silver chain, and every copper coin. I began with Mikel, the cabin boy my captain had stolen from his bed as a babe after watching his father beat his mother. Of them all, Mikel's loss I truly regretted.

Given a chance, he would've grown into a fine pirate and a finer man under my captain's careful tending. The worn rag doll, crudely fashioned in the shape of a shark, was so old I feared it'd crumble apart if I touched it. It reminded me of the lullabies Captain Louisa had sung with the falling of night, a rare moment of quiet the crew respected.

"Mikel was six when the *Calico* sank and his life ended. This was his, made for him by Captain Louisa the day after she took him from his home and claimed him as hers." The British had killed him early in the battle, and it had taken me hours of scouring the waters to find his tiny body and return it to the ship he'd grown up on.

I missed him.

"It's so old."

"Yes, more than three hundred years old." I pointed at Mikel's silver spoon, Captain Louisa's gift to him on his fifth birthday, a symbol of her promise to give him a life beyond the sea, one of wealth and riches only she could provide.

So many broken promises burdened the tiny blackened spoon.

"It's a spoon."

"When Captain Louisa took Mikel, she promised him a better life once he served her at sea. That spoon was a symbol of her promise. She wasn't able to keep it. The British killed him and tossed his body into the sea."

"But it's just a silver spoon. Why a silver spoon?"

"It's a symbol of wealth and prosperity.

Someone born with a silver spoon has an easy life. Superstition. She wanted to give him that life. She had no children of her own, so she took him and made him hers."

I left Mikel's doll and spoon and worked my way up the ranks, introducing each crew member to Abrahan, right up until the shrine to my lost captain, which held her flintlock and her cutlass.

Unlike Captain Maritza's, time hadn't left a single mark on either weapon, a result of me returning year after year to care for them. With mine gone, I would take hers and wear them at my side until the day mine found their way back to me. I lifted the weapons from their displays and buckled them into place around my hips. Her hat, which I had maintained over the years, too, was the same as the one I'd lost, for I had crafted mine in her honor. It went on top of my head, and I swept its feathers back, pressing it down so it wouldn't fall off. "These belonged to Captain Louisa, and I think it's time they saw the world again."

I had one item of Ricardo's in my hoard, a worn whetstone he'd kept for luck.

When I found Lucretta O'Malley, I would make her regret having crossed me. I smiled. Pirates needed rivals as much as they needed victims, and in Lucretta, I would have both.

"Isn't there supposed to be a first mate?"

"Yes."

"There's nothing of hers here. Why is there nothing of hers here? What happened to her?"

The problem with the modern world was its lack of true belief, be it in magic, in a chosen god, or in superstition. The gods I discarded as much as they discarded me, I couldn't dispute magic, for it encompassed my entire life, and I'd learned long ago superstitions only kept people from doing what had been perceived as stupidity. "Catalina de la Corona did not perish with the *Calico*, unlike her captain, unlike the rest of the crew. She did not die to the British bilge scum who took everything from her."

"She must have lived, I guess, for you to have been born."

I shook my head. "No, not quite."

"You're loco, Captain Corona."

His favored phrase amused me. There was only one way to make him believe. I turned to the waters of my cave, took three running steps, and leaped into the air. I shifted and embraced the curse as much as it embraced me, transforming before I touched the sea. I dove beneath the surface.

~

ABRAHAN HANDLED SHARING a cave with a massive tiger shark about as well as I expected, and I watched with amusement as he tried to climb the smooth stone walls. I circled, dipping my dorsal fin beneath the waters, investigating my home cave for any changes or invaders. The wise fish fled, and I let them go.

One thought itself ruler of my sea, so I ate it. Served the little bastard right for encroaching on my turf. Finding no evidence of intruders, I surged out of the water onto the shelf I'd carved for that purpose and fought the curse's hold on me. It took longer than I liked, and by the time I returned to my human form, I panted from the effort.

Climbing walls covered in mirrors and smoothed by my endeavors to make my shelves nice and pretty made for a futile exercise, and while Abrahan had managed to get a few feet up, I was able to grab the back of his neck, pull him down, and set him on his feet. "If I was planning on eating you, I would've done it off the coast of Brazil rather than dragging you all the way out here, kid."

"Plumping me up. You were plumping me up. Too skinny to eat. Need to be too skinny to eat." He continued to babble, sliding into Portuguese, back to English, then descending into a chaotic mix of both.

I could smell his fear.

"I was cursed by my captain's lover, Captain Maritza Ludovici, the Black Scourge. My curse was to serve my captain for an eternity if I must. I was the first mate, and instead of dying with my captain, my ship, and my crew, I lived. They called her the Shark Tamer, for whenever she needed a shark, one would appear—me." I let the kid go, smoothed his shirt over his shoulders, and gave his back a reassuring thump. "I don't eat crew, and I stole you to be my cabin boy."

"You're a real pirate."

"I was. I am."

"Do you have a title, too? Like your captain?" Abrahan straightened and pointed at my captain's shrine.

"I did."

"What is it?"

It hurt, but I'd tell him anyway. "I was First Mate Catalina de la Corona, Pirate Princess of the Seven Seas. I had some other titles, but I've forgotten them. Most only cared because I was the first mate of a pirate queen, so the Pirate Princess stuck. The *Calico* was unusual in having two women openly on board."

"Because sailors had some superstition about women on board ships back then, right?"

"Right."

"And you become a shark."

"A tiger shark."

"Because you're cursed. By your captain's lover."

When he put it that way, my life *did* seem

a bit surreal, and I couldn't blame him at all for the skepticism in his voice. "Correct."

"And your captain was okay with that?"

I grimaced. "Guess so. She didn't shoot me when I gnawed on the *Calico* and the *Terrier,* pissed because I couldn't enter the water without turning into a giant fish with big teeth. I have some control over it now at least. Didn't used to."

The truth refused to leave me be. Now and forever, I'd be a man-eater, a shark who'd preyed on humans, sometimes at my captain's demand. Maybe it'd been a century since I'd killed someone, but the urge to tear into anyone—or anything—in the water remained.

Maybe I *had* killed someone during the times the curse smothered my humanity and memories. I'd never know. Pretending I hadn't made it easier to live with myself.

Some pirate I turned out to be.

"That's how you knew how to fight, isn't it? Because you were a pirate. You killed people for a living."

"Yes."

"But there were four of us. You had no fear."

"All there is to fear is death, and death isn't something I fear. I'm long overdue. Death would be a mercy."

While I gathered coins and ingots to sell later, the kid watched me, his dark eyes troubled. Maybe one day I'd better understand other humans. Why did death always bother them so much?

Mine had been a long time coming, and I would welcome it when it came for me—if it ever did.

~

IT TOOK me three trips to take everything I wanted to the *Wanderer,* and on the fourth trip, I shoved Abrahan through the tunnel as a shark at his insistence. Even with the help of the rope, it took several tries for him to scramble onto the ship. I would have a worse time of it.

In order to make it onboard without falling into the water, I needed to jump, transform, and catch hold of the rope or railings. Back in my days on the *Calico,* I pulled the stunt off one out of every four attempts, which often resulted in the crew dropping a rope ladder to aid my efforts. I chose the engines as my spot to attempt the boarding; even if I missed the railing, I might be able to catch myself on the engine mounts before plunging into the water.

Abrahan leaned over the side of the ship and watched with interest while I circled.

Delaying wouldn't help anything, so I dove, gathered momentum, and breached, concentrating on my human form. The curse broke, and the split-second transformation stripped the air out of my lungs. I smacked into the *Wanderer*, slid towards the waterline, and caught hold of the rail, dangling from my left hand while I shuddered and struggled to breathe without gasping.

Slapping his hands on my arm, Abrahan hauled me the rest of the way onto the ship, grunting from the effort. It took me a moment to remember how to make my feet do what I wanted, and I jammed my toes into the brackets and climbed the rest of the way up.

"We need a rope ladder," I croaked.

"If you say so." As soon as I hit the deck, Abrahan let me go and backed away. "What now?"

"We stay here until dawn. Too dangerous to try to take the ship out until it's light. If the tide's low, we're stuck until it rises. It can get pretty shallow near the reefs at times." I'd seen the corals mere inches below the water's surface. The *Wanderer* would be fine in the deep waters of the cove, although the ship would be stuck until high tide. "Of course, after I rest, I might go to the House Lost at Sea."

"Not without me."

Great. It hadn't taken long for the cabin boy to start talking back, and I wondered if Captain Louisa endured a surge of annoyance every time I'd done it to her. Probably. It explained a lot.

I got to my feet and dusted off my clothes, checking to make certain my captain's cutlass and flintlock were still intact. Both seemed to have survived my collision with the *Wanderer* undamaged. "All right. I don't know what we'll find, so you'll need to stay on your guard. While I don't expect any visitors, the Black Scourge *had* been involved with its construction."

"You're expecting trouble."

I appreciated his no-nonsense tone and ready acceptance of change. If he could handle my curse, I held hope he could handle just about anything. "I don't know what I'm expecting, but with her involved? I expect magic."

"Magic," he echoed, his voice weak. "Do you think I'll be cursed, too?"

I hoped not, but I didn't like making promises I couldn't keep, so I shrugged. "You can stay with the ship if you'd like."

For a moment, I thought he would, but then Abrahan straightened his back, set his shoulders, and lifted his chin. "I'm going."

I prayed for his sake that Captain Maritza's powers had gone to the grave with her. While I'd likely miss him when he died, I wouldn't wish an eternity on anyone.

TWENTY-TWO

This is the only way up?

I WAITED until dawn to take Abrahan to the House Lost at Sea. After leaving the *Wanderer* safely anchored in the cove of my island, I permitted him to cling to my dorsal fin. The swim tired me more than I anticipated; the shifting tides woke swirling currents, and if one ripped my cabin boy into deeper waters, it was a coin toss if I'd be able to chase him down in time to save him from drowning.

The ocean could be a cruel and jealous mistress.

I avoided the shallows where the tides ripped water over the corals and rocks, guaranteeing anyone unfortunate enough to be sucked through the eddies would emerge with their bones broken and the skin flayed from their body. I cut across the waves until I reached the right island, then I angled for shore to the staircase carved into the cliff. The sandy beach lasted a few feet before ending at the rocks, a menacing spot for anyone seeking access to the manor high overhead.

Strangers and wise men would head to the other side of the island, facing a steep slope covered in ivy. They'd find boobytraps, pits, and snares for their trouble, most of them non-lethal with a few nastier surprises tossed in.

After we explored the manor, I'd have to show him the way down the hill to the beach and the sandbar blocking ships from getting too close to the island.

As soon as we reached the surf, Abrahan staggered to shore. I retreated far enough to reach my full speed and surged towards the cliff with the waves, beaching myself before fighting off the curse's hold. It took longer than I liked, and my entire body shook.

"You're gray." Taking hold of my arm, he pulled me to my feet. "You all right?"

"Just need to rest a bit—and stay as a shark for a while after we go back to the *Wanderer,*" I mumbled, straightening in an effort to hide my weakness. "It's a bit of a climb to the house. You'll go first, and I'll be right behind you. I can survive a fall. You can't."

Abrahan gulped. "This is the only way up?"

"Unless you like falling into pits, yes. There are a lot of them on the other slope, and I may have done too good of a job hiding them. I know where they are on the way *down...*"

"And you forgot where they are on the way up. Nice job, captain. That was stupid."

Yep, of all the cabin boys to kidnap, I'd gotten the one with a mouth. After a few moments of introspection, I decided a mouthy cabin boy beat a cringing one. I hated when they whimpered. It made me want to pull out the plank, and I didn't have one on the *Wanderer* yet. I needed to fix that.

At the same time, I needed to get a replacement cabin boy and promote Abrahan to a rank that put his mouthiness to good use. Cook would do.

No wise sailor pissed off the ship's cook—or the surgeon. Or the first mate. Or the captain. Or the navigator. Pissing off Ricardo had been a bad idea, one that usually ended up with the navigator tossing the culprit overboard and letting him scream until relenting and lowering a rope. I'd enjoyed the rare times our ships had been close enough for me to watch my lover educate a wise-mouthed lesser pirate.

The list of folks I could use in my modern-day voyages went on and on, and I chuckled at the thought of building a true pirate crew in the modern world of hulking battleships and polluted seas.

Maybe Bensen's idea of diving to scavenge from shipwrecks held more water than I wanted to give him credit for. I loved the sailing more than the plundering, and the dives would satisfy my life-long desire to hunt down treasures at sea. Maybe plastic and garbage polluted the oceans, but beneath the waters, a rich history waited to be rediscovered.

"You're really telling me we have to climb *that?*"

"Stay close to the rock and you'll be fine. I'll survive a fall. You won't."

"Fallen before?"

"More times than I care to count. I carved the steps, which isn't the safest job. The captains thought it wise to make me do it—only member of either crew who could bounce on down with any expectation of getting back up."

"Shit job."

I stared up at the cliff, easily over a hundred feet tall. Measuring it hadn't occurred to me, and I'd never bothered to count the steps angling up its face. I pointed at one of the large rocks jutting out over the sand. "The steps begin there. It's a long climb, so let's get to it."

Abrahan shot me a dirty look but trudged across the sand and set foot to the first step.

~

THE HOUSE LOST at Sea overlooked the

ocean, its front porch a mere twenty feet from the cliff edge. As it had for over three hundred years, my skin tingled when I approached the proud stone building, which had endured through the centuries without any evidence of its age. The glass windows remained clear, as though even nature feared Captain Maritza's wrath should her home be damaged in any way.

My throat tightened, and I stared at the only place I should have ever called home.

"It's huge," Abrahan whispered. "It's a mansion."

Instead of arguing with him, I shook my head and knelt, slipping off my boot so I could retrieve my captain's key. I had no idea how they fit together, but I suspected Captain Maritza's magic would take care of fusing them so they'd unlock the front door, its wood as polished and clean as the day it'd been hung on its hinges.

I'd never been inside. Captain Maritza's crew—and her slaves and hostages—handled the interior while I had worked on the steps leading up to the manor. With shaking hands, I put my boot back on and retrieved Captain Maritza's key from my bra.

It didn't take much fiddling to figure out how the two halves of the key slid together, clicking into place. "I've waited three hundred years for this."

Instead of triumph, I felt dead and empty,

as though the end of the journey hadn't really taken me anywhere, but I had nowhere else to go except to its conclusion. What could be in the manor?

Betrayal and heartbreak had left it alone for so long. Would I find gold? Treasure? What could possibly be within that I actually wanted?

My captain was gone, and not even her bones remained. I suspected Captain Maritza had shared the same fate, her and her crew's bodies dissolved and broken apart in the sea over the centuries. Despite riding high overhead, the sun's warmth didn't reach me. "It was supposed to be our home."

"But then you were betrayed, and your captain and crew died. Right?"

"Right." I lifted the key and watched it spin on its chains. "Two captains, two crews, one house, one key."

"So we just walk up to the front door and go on in?"

I laughed, and it was a bitter, bitter sound. "Your guess is as good as mine. It's not trapped. I've walked up there hundreds of times."

Maybe my count of hundreds came in a little conservatively; I'd paced every inch of the island, always returning to the House Lost at Sea time and time again, until every stone of the building was branded into my memory. If I closed my eyes, I still remembered everything, right down to where the mortar holding it all together cracked before the timelessness of the place had taken hold. Etchings, names and marks made by my fellow pirates, decorated every window on the first floor.

"Let's go." The first step was the hardest, and I forced one foot in front of the other, my gaze fixed on the plain door that had blocked my passage for three hundred years. How many times had I stood in front of it, my hand pressed to the wood, wondering what waited for me within?

Too many times.

Abrahan recoiled a step, and his movement caught my attention. "Abrahan?"

"There's someone here," he hissed.

I whirled around, scanning the front of the house before directing my attention to the slope leading down to the main beach. While the ivy rustled in the wind, its tendrils encroaching on the manor without ever touching it, I saw no sign of anyone nearby.

"Where?"

He pointed at the hill with its thick vegetation. "There."

I drew my captain's pistol and cocked the hammer. "All right, kid. Stay behind me. I can take a round. You can't. If shots are fired, you find cover, wait it out, and make your way down the staircase to the beach. Got it?"

"Got it."

I jogged to the porch, hopped up the stone steps to the portico, and pressed to the building, gesturing for Abrahan to follow. Once certain he kept close, I crept my way to the edge of the house to peek around the corner. "Keep an eye behind us. You see something, hit the deck."

"Right."

I thought through my options. If someone had reached the island, they had a ship somewhere nearby. Most likely, some adventure seeker had gone astray off the coast of Africa, found the island, somehow dodged the reefs, and located the beach.

Maybe it snowed in hell, too.

I curled my lip in a silent snarl. "Back towards the cliff. We'll come back later."

Had I been alone, I would've gone in with my gun blazing and my sword ready to drink the blood of the intruders. Until I had a chance to arm Abrahan with a weapon more reliable than a knife and teach him how to use it, I couldn't afford to risk it.

A good captain didn't put her crew in unnecessary danger, not for so little reward. I had the key. I could return—I would return.

"We're leaving?"

"We retreat, we figure out who is here and why, and then we get what we want. Good pirates always go in with a plan."

A plan would let me find a way to use Abrahan without putting him in harm's way, allowing me to accomplish my goals without his blood staining my hands. Satisfied with my decision, I nodded in the direction of the staircase. The fifty feet over open ground worried me, but I'd shield him and hope for the best. Once we descended, we'd have cover from the rocks jutting out over the steps, and we'd be safe enough in the water.

As a shark, I could drag Abrahan to my island and the *Wanderer*, where he'd be safe. Then I could scout and find who had come to the House Lost at Sea, how they'd found it, and why they encroached on my territory.

I herded him towards the cliff, sweeping the flintlock over the rustling ivy, cursing the restless sea wind for making it difficult to spot intruders on the slope. With luck, my pits had captured or delayed my adversaries, minimizing the work I'd need to do to get rid of them. Depending on their number, I could tie them up and leave them on the South African coast to be found later.

If they touched my kid, I'd turn the ocean red with their blood.

Abrahan kept close, and when we drew within ten feet of the steps, he broke into a run.

Metal gleamed in the sunlight, and the barrel of a weapon followed my ward's movement. Spitting a curse, I whipped the flintlock around, picked my target, and squeezed the trigger. The blast of gunfire echoed off the cliffs, and shouts rang out, but my opponent's gun remained steady.

I couldn't let Abrahan get hit. I couldn't. No matter what, I had to protect him. I could take a hit. He couldn't. I couldn't let him get hit.

The barrel flashed.

I couldn't—

TWENTY-THREE

Nothing pissed me off quite as much as someone shooting me in the face.

Why did dying always have to hurt so much?

No, that wasn't right. Dying hadn't hurt at all. I had no recollection of anything other than the flash of the gun discharging. Light traveled faster than sound, and I hadn't heard—or felt—the bullet hit. Every nerve in my body burned, and bitter, long experience warned I'd either taken the round in the head or spine.

Survival came at a price, and mine was pain.

I waited it out, unable to even whimper while aware of my bones and muscles shifting under my battered skin. The cracks and pops of shattered joints fusing and returning to their rightful place was accompanied by a wet tearing.

I must have fallen from the cliff, too, a

blessing, all things considered. Abrahan knew I'd get back up eventually, although I regretted I hadn't given him more details about my inability to die.

The thought of clawing my way free of a coffin didn't enthuse me at all. I'd done that a few times, and it always involved reviving, dying, reviving, and dying in a relentless chain while I worked towards freedom.

Water flowed around me, catching hold of my clothes and dragging me into the deeps. The sea flooded my mouth and lungs, and as my awareness extended beyond my immediate pain, I realized my heart didn't beat nor did I breathe.

As always, the curse bound my spirit to my body when my body could no longer sustain life. I would linger until my heart resumed beating, then if I remained in the water, I would transform and discard my human skin before I sank back into the darkness.

The last time I'd been killed while in the sea, sometime before the age of pirates had come to an end, I'd woken up on the bottom of the ocean several months later, covered in a thick blanket of silt. I'd been shot in the head, although I couldn't remember much of my execution. My deep slumber hadn't helped my human body heal much, and once I had returned to shore, it had taken me months to recover.

It was a coin toss if I'd stay human or shark while I recovered; the curse did what the curse wanted to do, and it disliked gracing me with consistency after my death.

If I succumbed, I would leave Abrahan alone. Had he been shot, too? Had he reached the safety of the steps? Even if he had, how would he have escaped? Without me, there was nowhere for him to go.

I'd embrace life as a shark readily enough, but I couldn't afford to sleep. If Abrahan still lived, I needed to act. I could take him to the *Wanderer*. I could hunt for him, bring him fish, and protect the ship. Anyone who tried to approach without my blessings would die to my teeth.

I would become a leviathan, lurking and waiting for those who would dare threaten the kid I had claimed for my crew. If I couldn't drive them away, I'd get rid of them one way or another. I would rip them to shreds and feed the fish with the torn remains of their lifeless bodies.

Instead of transforming into a shark, I washed up on the shore of my isle. The surf beat at my chilled body, pounding at me in a steady rhythm until a convulsion tore through me. Pressure built in my chest and head.

It burst in a coughing fit so strong I hacked out water and blood. My heart remembered it had a job to do and thudded to frantic life, each of its beats a sharp stab behind my breasts. Flashes of light bubbled and burst in front of my eyes. I blinked away the sand and salt, my vision blurring before focusing on the *Wanderer*, which bobbed in the water where I'd left her, safe in the deepest waters of the cove.

If I could reach my ship, I would be in a far better position to return to the House Lost at Sea and discover Abrahan's fate. If someone had hurt him, I would abandon all pretenses of humanity, hunt them down, and take my time killing them.

The sun set long before I managed to force my battered body into motion, and every movement triggered cascading waves of nausea and pain. I gagged and lurched to my hands and knees, my fingers digging at the night-cool sand.

It took until sunrise to stagger to my feet, swaying. I needed to reach the *Wanderer*, so close yet so far. The surf washed around my boots, its caress an invitation. If I let go, the sea would take away my pain.

It would claim months of my life, too, which I couldn't allow. What would happen to Abrahan if I succumbed to it? How many months would I lose?

Too many. I locked my glare on my ship and took another step forward. I would crawl over broken rocks and coral if needed. I would claw my way up and over the engine onto the deck. Inch by inch, I would drag myself to the cabin and raid the medical supplies on board.

If the marina had done as I had demanded, there'd be something in the kit to either kill the pain or serve as a stimulant in a pinch. If not, I'd make do somehow, even if I needed to eat coffee grinds for a boost.

My captain's cutlass, still sheathed at my side, jabbed me in the ribs, and I shoved its hilt aside. The water reached my hips, and warmth spread from my chest, the sea whispering for me to join it properly, so I might rule my waters as a shark.

I took another step. I would not abandon Abrahan. I would not abandon him as I had been abandoned.

I would not. The water flowed around me, and I recognized the pull of the outgoing tide, guiding me closer to my ship, which bobbed on the gentle waves.

Abrahan.

~

NOTHING PISSED me off quite as much as someone shooting me in the face, not even losing my captain's flintlock or the key to the House Lost at Sea. I could recover those easily enough—and I would, soon. Why couldn't I have been shot a little higher? Taking a round above the hairline still made a mess, requiring years before hair would grow back over the scars, but losing a chunk of my cheek and jaw made for a bad time for everyone involved, including those who'd have to look at my ugly mug until the scars faded.

Not even Ricardo would be able to smile at me with half of my face mangled. Of course, he'd be inclined to abandon his more pacifistic ways when someone he cared about was hurt. It made him an unexpected threat in battle. Nobody expected the pacifist to start beating heads together, running people through, and otherwise murdering without much in the way of remorse.

According to the ship's electronics, five days had gone by. All-in-all, the curse's ability to heal my broken and battered body had outdone itself. I had a jaw, although the tender, too-soft bone hurt when I touched it or tried to speak. I'd lost several teeth to the bullet, which were already growing back, too, adding to my general discomfort. Raw, pink skin stood out against my tan, marking where the white scar tissue would show given time.

For some reason I couldn't understand, the curse had preserved my lips, which I'd be grateful for later. Nothing hurt more than trying to talk through a twisted and scarred mouth.

A few tentative prods at the back of my skull revealed where the bullet had exited, and the bone there, too, gave under pressure and hurt like hell. I'd lost a large chunk of hair, although I'd be able to hide the bald spot with work and some clever styling.

All in all, I resembled a zombie without wearing any makeup. If Abrahan lived, he'd believe in the curse's power. How would he react to my resurrection from the dead? I expected a meltdown, but I'd endure it. If he had survived, I'd deal with it for weeks if necessary.

Eating hurt, but I choked down as much fish and rice as my stomach could hold. My body would need it to heal, and I couldn't afford to take another unexpected nap. After five days, if Abrahan still lived, he was likely a captive of those who had tried to kill me.

There were many people around the world who shot first and asked questions of the bodies, but few had the ability or resources to reach an island far from land. For someone like me, who could survive on the sea's bounty, who knew the waters and the best routes to reach Africa or India, the island posed little challenge.

Four people came to mind when I thought of those who might reach the island and have the ruthlessness required to steal my treasures—or try to: Benny, Bensen, Captain Naidoo, and Lucretta O'Malley, descendant of the pirate queen Grace O'Malley, who had walked the Earth before the dawn of the Golden Age of Piracy.

If Benny or Bensen were involved, I didn't know what I'd do. If Lucretta's treachery resulted in a hair on Abrahan's young head being damaged, I'd scuttle her frigate, take her captive, and slowly—*very* slowly—revive every last bit of pirate cruelty I'd witnessed in my long years and make her experience them all.

I'd just eat Captain Naidoo.

My first stop would be my cavern hoard, where I'd climb the walls to the uppermost shelves, a spot I hadn't shown my new cabin boy. The metal, waterproofed boxes stored out of reach held my modern tools, and I'd dig out the high-powered weaponry for my next outing to the House Lost at Sea.

If a flintlock and cutlass couldn't do the job, my ACR would give me the best bang for my buck. I'd also dig out the handguns, of which I'd bring two for certain, a Beretta and a Kahr. I liked the little Kahr the best of them; it packed a big punch in a tiny package. The Beretta earned top points for reliability, capable of handling a beating without becoming a piece of scrap metal.

Would three guns be enough? I thought about it, shrugged, and decided I'd go in fully armed. Maybe something a little safer would prove useful, especially considering I needed to recover Abrahan alive. My ARWEN 37 would do the trick, and I'd bring the ammunition box containing my anti-riot rounds.

I'd also toss in a few grenades modified to fit the gun just in case.

A giggle built in my chest, and I adjusted my captain's sword on my hips. Who was I kidding? I'd take everything I had and turn my visit to the House Lost at Sea into a real party. I was done drawing the short straw.

I wouldn't get mad. I'd get even, and I'd enjoy every last minute of it.

TWENTY-FOUR

Just sinking her wouldn't be enough.

IT TOOK me three hours to do a full weapons check, and I savored every minute of it. When I went to the House Lost at Sea, I'd be ready. I even wore a bullet-proof vest underneath my clothes, choosing a t-shirt, jeans, and leather jacket as my war attire. I took rope and cloth to hold my hostages captive, hanging the bundles from my belt for easy access later.

To add a modern flare to my dated methods, I brought along two rolls of duct tape and a handful of plastic zip ties.

I used my boots to stash my knives and a pair of single-round derringers. If I ever made it back to the United States, I'd have to buy a second pair. They were *wonderful*. So much fit into them. I needed to see what other wonders the modern world had to offer.

Excepting pants, as I'd yet to find a good

pair of women's jeans that had proper pockets.

Before I left, I sat on the lowest shelf and meditated, reminding myself over and over I had a job I needed to do and could not afford to nap at the bottom of the ocean for any period of time. The curse would serve *me,* and I'd fight it fin and tooth to complete my mission.

Becoming a shark would be easy. Wrestling back my humanity would be the real challenge.

I dove into the water, and the curse grabbed me with eager hands, ripping away my human shape before I touched the surface. Lashing my tail, I slid my way through the tunnel and angled towards the open ocean so I could circle around to the main island.

High on its cliff, lights gleamed within the windows of the House Lost at Sea, and my fury crested. Someone dared enter *my* domain?

Death would be far too merciful a fate for them. To shoot me in the face was one thing, but to take my key, my cabin boy, and my home? I scouted the island in search for their ship, and I found it anchored a hundred feet from shore near one of the sandbars.

The modernized frigate infuriated me even more than the invasion. I slinked closer, my dorsal fin cutting through the waves. A rope ladder dangled from her polished side, close enough to the sandbar anyone with any skill at swimming could reach the vessel.

The gold plate on her bow informed me her name was the *Serendipity*.

I dove beneath her and went to work chewing on her wooden rudder. It wouldn't sink her, but I wished the captain luck trying to go anywhere without the power to steer the ship. A cursory examination of her engines satisfied me; without the rudder, the *Serendipity* would surely crash into something and sink without any extra help from me.

I'd take the time to sabotage the rest of the ship, however. Just sinking her wouldn't be enough. The frigate would crumble around Lucretta O'Malley's ears, and I'd stalk her through the waters and enjoy every moment of it. Once the *Serendipity* sank, I'd toy with my brunette captive, drag her to one of the difficult-to-reach caverns dotting the island chain, and take my time with her.

It took me several hours of leaping from the surface and attempting to shed the influence of my curse before I managed to transform and catch hold of the rope ladder instead of thumping into the frigate's side as a shark. The effort left my head pounding, and I scrambled onto the deck, bent under the burden of so many weapons. Taking shelter behind one of the large coils of spare rope, I set aside most of my weapons to retrieve later and began my exploration of the ship.

Lucretta O'Malley had taken a great deal of care with the *Serendipity,* and I pulled out one of my knives and went to work, fraying the rigging, shredding the thick canvas sails, and otherwise ensuring chaos when she attempted to leave my islands. I found sleeping quarters for twenty-five, a small number for such a large vessel. Then again, a skeleton crew of ten *could* keep a frigate of the *Serendipity's* size afloat. The engines would make it easier for fewer men to keep her floating.

One, ten, twenty—they'd all suffer by the time I finished with them.

I took savage joy in dismantling the captain's quarters, shredding her clothes, and breaking every little trinket I could get my hands on. I pilfered her golden compass, a piece far too lovely and old to destroy, and I left her captain's log intact, smiling as I added an entry foreseeing the sinking of the *Serendipity*.

It took the entire night to finish my work, reclaim my weapons, and dive from the deck, transforming before I hit the water. I couldn't smile as a shark, so I breached and splashed around in my pleasure at having completed the first step of my revenge.

I also left a few bite marks on the *Serendipity's* hull.

O'Malley would only wish she could tame my striped ass when she found out what I'd done.

Before I assaulted the House Lost at Sea, I would rest. I beached myself where the surf met the shore, deep enough for the water to wash over my gills, but close enough to land I wouldn't sleep and forget I was human.

I DOZED until the sun rode high in the sky, and I hunted to satisfy my hunger before beaching myself and fighting the curse's influence. It took longer than I liked, but I didn't mind braving the staircase in the light of the setting sun.

The shadows hid me, and the moon illuminated my path.

Next time I planned my equipment for an assault, I needed to remember how much my guns weighed. Add in the ammunition, my cutlass, and the bulletproof vest, and I regretted my decision to bring it all. Grumbling curses every last step of the way, I reached the top, unbuckling several of the holsters and easing the weapons into the grasses skirting the cliff.

Candlelight flickered in the windows of the House Lost at Sea, and someone had left the front door open. From what I could tell, there was no damage done to the manor, so I assumed someone had either taken the key from me after I'd been shot or it'd fallen before I'd tumbled into the ocean.

I crawled my way through the grasses to the stone path leading to the front door, dragging my weapons along with me. The murmur of voices warned me of those inside, although I couldn't tell how many or how close to the door they were.

Of Abrahan, I saw no sign.

Since killing my victims wouldn't drag out their suffering, I prepared my ARWEN 37, loaded it with anti-riot rounds, grabbed extra ammunition, and slung my assault rifle across my back so I could grab it if needed. I kept my Kahr and ditched the rest of the weight in the bushes surrounding the manor.

I crept up the stairs, keeping low and easing my feet down so creaking wood wouldn't betray my presence. Before I entered, I needed a good look inside, which meant taking a position beside the door so I could peek around the corner.

A teenager in a rumpled, dirty shirt and bloodstained jeans slumped in a chair inside the foyer, and his snores accompanied the murmur of conversation deeper within the house. Lazy sentries made my job so easy. After a second check to ensure no one else lurked in the entry, I slipped inside the House Lost at Sea.

Silver mirrors reflected my image back at

me into infinity, and I wrinkled my nose in disgust. Maybe if things had been different, if Captain Maritza's loyalty had run deeper, then the two pirate queens would have had an eternity to spend together.

I pulled off a strip of duct tape, cut it with a knife, and held it between my teeth while I uncoiled a length of rope from my belt. First, I needed to ensure the boy's silence. Once I ensured his silence, I would secure him to the chair. I didn't want to kill him—murder wouldn't serve my purposes yet—but I needed to get inside undetected.

Clonking the poor kid with the pommel of my cutlass would leave him with a headache he'd never forget and possibly kill him, but I'd take the risk if necessary. If I hurt the boy, I could take him to shore in the *Wanderer*.

I'd try the gag and tie method first, and if he put up too much of a fight, then I'd smack him around. Palming the tape, I slapped it to his mouth and pressed hard. His eyes flew open, and before he could cry out, I pinched his nose. "Quiet. Make a sound, and I'll teach you how much it hurts to have a cutlass run through your gut."

The kid's face paled to a sickly gray-green, and he froze in place. His eyes focused on my cheek and jaw, and he whimpered. I glanced at my reflection.

Ah. Somehow, the gunshot wound had

opened, and to add to the horror show that was my face, I'd split my lip enough to show the gaps where I'd lost my teeth. I blamed ramming the *Serendipity* in my effort to shift so I could board her.

I'd give him nightmares for a long time to come. Too bad.

It didn't take long to secure him to his chair. I patted his head. "Good boy. You just sit there and wait for a while. That'll teach you to nap while on watch."

On the *Calico,* Captain Louisa would've had the guilty boy walk the plank and play with me for a while before relenting and allowing him back on board. When she was in a truly foul mood, she left the ones who couldn't swim in the water the longest, punishing me for allowing someone irresponsible to stand guard by forcing me to keep him alive in the water.

I'd have to revive the practice if I decided to get a proper ship or fully man the *Wanderer* and return to a life at sea. Abrahan could use some company around his age, too.

My captive whimpered again.

"Shh, little baby. It'll be all right. You're too cute to kill." I wasn't lying, not really. Once he was cleaned up, he'd decorate my ship well enough. Hopefully he'd prove at least a quarter as clever as Abrahan. Nothing annoyed me more than crew incapable of tying their shoelaces without help.

Either way, I couldn't let him go. He'd seen through me, literally, and I had no way of explaining the state of my face. Oh well. What was another mouth to feed? Killing adults didn't bother me, but I'd only slay the young if necessary. I'd give the boy one chance to redeem himself in my eyes.

I tiptoed my way deeper into the manor, and my captive wisely remained quiet.

TWENTY-FIVE

I told you I was tough to kill.

Beyond the entry, a hallway led deeper into the House Lost at Sea, and I recognized my captain's touch in the wood paneling, a match for the *Calico*'s interior when she'd been new. Compasses, sextants, and trinkets plundered from our prey hung from hooks, and behind glass cases, old captain logs waited, intact despite the long centuries.

I bet Ricardo had played his part in the choice of display pieces. He'd loved collecting compasses and sextants, and I'd found ways to add to his collection despite being barred from seeing him.

The memories hurt.

With one look, I could easily understand why someone like Benny would betray me. He loved history far more than he had liked me, and each treasure was marked by a plaque engraved with the date, the plundered ship, and where she'd sunk. The right side of the hallway showcased Captain Maritza and her crew, and the left side tore at my soul.

From the day my captain set sail for the first time to the sinking of the *Calico*, everything was documented. Someone had even sketched portraits of everyone, and the faces of those lost to me so long ago stared at me from behind clear panes of glass, somehow untouched by time.

The artist had captured Ricardo perfectly, and I touched the glass barring me from reaching his portrait.

I'd been right; Lucretta had found someone just like my Ricardo, and I considered going back to her ship and lighting it on fire.

Even I had a place among my captain's treasures, and anyone who had met me would look upon my portrait and know the truth. Whoever had captured my likeness had done it well, right down to the way my hair frizzed when out at sea, the style of my clothing, and the way I stood, eyes narrowed and scowl fixed firmly in place.

I'd scowled a lot after losing Ricardo.

Who had drawn the picture, and how had they done it without my knowing?

I couldn't afford to linger long, and I swallowed to ease the tightness in my throat. Those who had invaded my islands hadn't damaged the delicate frames or sought to disturb the hall and its treasures.

The hallway left me with one question: what had gone wrong?

I'd never know.

Halfway down, the displays from both ships ended, leaving empty cases and frames waiting to be filled. The sounds of conversation grew louder, and I spotted light shining beneath a door at the hall's end. I tiptoed my way closer, straining to listen, but the voices were muffled enough to mask the words.

I didn't notice the intersection until I stumbled across it, hidden behind empty cases. Doorways lined each hallway, and several had light streaming beneath the doors. Only one glow came from the left, while I counted at least six down the other hall.

My captain's side interested me far more than Captain Maritza's, and one-to-one odds appealed to me far more than one-to-six. Then again, if I screwed up, everyone in the manor would know of my presence.

I could subdue the occupants of a single room fast enough to buy myself time until reinforcements arrived, and without any memories decorating the walls, the hallway would make an excellent place to lob teargas canisters and flash-bangs.

The door into the lit room startled me, barred from the outside to prevent those inside from escaping easily. I frowned, turning to examine the other doors. None of them had the mounts present. Why bar only one door?

With my luck, it'd probably been meant to be *my* room, the bar present to give Captain Maritza's crew a false sense of security.

The only way I'd find out would be by going inside. The wood, polished smooth and heavy as stone, ground against the blackened iron brackets. With a grunt, I set it down and leaned it against the wall, careful to make no noise.

I waited and listened for any changes in the sounds from the other parts of the manor. Satisfied no one had noticed me, I grabbed hold of the knob and twisted. It opened with a click, and the wood and hinges creaked. The sounds of cloth on cloth warned me someone was in the room, but they otherwise remained quiet.

I peeked inside, grip tight on the knob in case I needed to shut the door in a hurry. Movement came from a bed pressed against the wall, and a lump under a pale pile of blankets shifted around.

Why did everyone use the pretending to be asleep trick? Sometimes it worked, if I or my captain just wanted the crew to settle down and stop annoying us. When we were really annoyed, we knocked the men from their hammocks and gave them a stern reminder of why we had rules.

I stepped inside the room, closed the door

behind me, and decided to see the trick through to the end. Blankets and sheets made a convenient tool for capturing the unwary. I set my ARWEN 37 on the room's antique writing desk, counted to ten, and pounced.

Thumping onto the bed and my prey, I used my weight and the fabric to hamper my victim's struggles. It didn't take long for me to work my hand under the blankets and grab the back of a slender neck. It took a single warning squeeze to put an end to any resistance.

With my free hand, I peeled away the covers.

Abrahan. A laugh bubbled out of me, and loosening my grip, I gave the kid's hair a ruffle. "Shh," I warned.

He sucked in a breath. "Corona?"

"Aye, aye."

"But they shot you. In the face. You fell." Abrahan's voice wavered.

"I told you I was tough to kill. That explains the barred door at least. I tied the sentry in the foyer up and gagged him, but someone'll find him eventually. How many are in the house?"

"Twenty-three I've seen," he answered, wiggling to sit up. He stared at me with wide eyes, and he paled at the sight of my cheek. I kept still, and he lifted his hand to touch me. "You have a hole in your face."

"I may have smacked my face into a ship a

few times. It'll heal. You all right? Did they do anything to you?"

Abrahan nodded. "They caught me before I could get down the steps."

"Know which one shot me? I have some words for that one." By words I meant a beating and death, but I'd spare the kid from reality for a little while longer. He didn't need to see me get a violent and messy revenge.

"He's dead."

I stared. "What?"

"They killed him for shooting you. Instant they learned your name, the woman in charge pulled her gun, but one of her fellows beat her to the chase, and he shot him. They stripped him and tossed his body off the cliff, and they made me watch while they did it. She… she said it was as much justice as I was going to get. The fellow who'd done the killing just grunted and didn't seem all that impressed. Skeptical, really, like he figured you'd somehow get up to cause them problems. Not sure if he liked the idea or not."

"The woman's name happen to be Lucretta O'Malley?"

With wide eyes, he nodded. "That's her. That guy who wanted me to take your stuff is here, too—that Benny guy. He brought an old man with him. Them two are madder 'n hell. They kept questioning me, and all I told them was that I was with you, and they could stuff it."

"Crew," I corrected. "You're crew."

"That. They asked that. I said yes. They asked what I did on the ship. I told 'em I did whatever you told me and liked it. The woman thought that was funny. I told 'em if I did well, you were gonna let me cook."

The way Abrahan spoke in a rush of words made me think he was worried I'd be upset with him for saying anything at all. I nodded, gave his hair another ruffle, and pulled one of my knives from my boot, offering it to him. "Good job, kid. The first rule is to stay alive, and you did what you needed to do. I'm gonna take that kid on watch in the entrance as loot. You all right with that?"

"Can I boss him around?"

"Sure can. I'll even let you make him walk the plank a few times if he gets rebellious, but no killing him. I'll get a plank just for that purpose. For the moment, we'll use him as leverage. If I keep him around, he'll be the cabin boy, and you'll be above him in the crew."

Twenty-three—twenty-two after I took the watch—versus two were odds I didn't like, and until I had Abrahan stashed somewhere safe, I couldn't risk a more direct approach. They'd taken him from me once, and I wouldn't allow it again. "Time to get out of here, make a plan, and come back later."

Abrahan nodded, dove to the end of the bed, and reached for something on the floor.

With a startled laugh, I recognized my captain's hat, although some of the feathers had dark stains marring them. "Your hat, Captain."

"They let you keep it?"

Flashing me a grin, he hopped to his feet, stood on his toes, and set it on top of my head. "They're suckers. Sniffled a few times, and they stopped trying to take it. Wasn't gonna let them dirty your hat. They took your gun, though."

"We'll get it back," I swore. I would, too, and I'd be charging them all a lot of interest for it. For the moment, I had bigger fish to fry and more problems than I cared to think about.

What *would* I do about Benny and Bensen? Trashing O'Malley's ship satisfied me, but I needed to figure out what to do about them and find out why they were so interested in the legacy the pirate queens had left behind.

We crept down the hall in silence and took the kid on watch with us when we left the manor.

TWENTY-SIX

Well, maybe if your friend hadn't shot me in the face, parts of it wouldn't be missing.

The fastest way to the *Wanderer* involved swimming, and if I wanted to get Abrahan and my hostage there alive, I needed to transform again. The thought of another stint as a shark was enough to exhaust me, but I accepted the inevitable.

I could whine later. In fact, I fully intended on indulging in at least an hour of complaining, forcing my audience of two to suffer until I was satisfied. I figured there had to be something cathartic about a good whine session, or my captain wouldn't have subjected me to them. At the very least, I'd have a new experience.

"Are you going to..." Abrahan gestured to the surf, which beat the shore and inched its way closer to the cliffs as the tides shifted.

"I sure am." With a smug smile, I yanked the duct tape off my hostage's mouth. He yelped and struggled to free his wrists from the ropes binding them behind his back. "Here's the way this is going to work, swabby. We're going for a swim. If you scream, I might decide to change my mind about keeping you alive and eat you. Got it?"

Abrahan slapped his palm to his forehead. "You can't eat him."

"Why not?"

"It's rude."

"So is shooting me in the face. That's really rude."

My hostage whimpered. "Part of your face is missing."

"Well, maybe if your friend hadn't shot me in the face, parts of it wouldn't be missing. I wasn't pretty before, now look at me! I'm going to make infants cry."

"Adults, too," Abrahan muttered.

I planted my boot on his ass and shoved him into the water. "I'm getting a plank just so I can make you walk it, kid."

My intimidation skills needed work; Abrahan laughed at me.

"How can you possibly be alive? You were killed, I saw it," my hostage whispered.

"Get used to it, kid. I'm tough to kill. My name is Catalina de la Corona. You're mine, now, so get used to the idea. If I like you, I'll keep you on board, pay you a fair wage, and keep you fed and clothed. If I don't, I'm going to dump you in the rattiest port I can find, and if I hear you've told a soul about me, I'll hunt you down and eat your liver."

Abrahan splashed his way out of the water and grabbed hold of my hostage's hands. "How do we get him to the ship, captain?"

I glared at my hostage. "Can you swim?"

He nodded.

"Good. You're going to go where I order, or you're going to find out just how effective a peg leg at sea really is. Got it?"

He nodded again.

"Untie him, Abrahan. Let's see if the kid has a single grain of common sense, or if I get lunch."

Maybe Abrahan had the sense to call my bluff, grinning at me whenever our captive wasn't looking, but the kid trembled, and I could smell his fear even with my human nose. "Into the water." I pointed in the direction of my island. "We're going that way."

"We're going to die, aren't we?" my victim whispered, staring at Abrahan.

He laughed long and hard. "You might, but I won't. She likes me. If you think this is bad, give it five minutes. It gets so much worse."

I headed down the beach for a rock I could use to dive from so I could transform before entering the water. It wouldn't do to damage my nice guns and the plunder I'd rightfully taken from the *Serendipity*.

I GAVE my hostage a love bite, and Abrahan balled his hand into a fist and clobbered me over the head in retaliation. My teeth didn't scare him at all, and when I thrashed a bit to express my displeasure at his rebuke, he bonked me again.

I bit him, too, just hard enough to let him know I meant business.

Apparently, I'd done a little too well in teaching him his proper place, as Abrahan hit me like he meant business, too, giving me a headache I'd remember in the morning. I herded them both to the *Wanderer* and boosted them to the deck.

Abrahan leaned over the railing and lowered a rope for me. "I tied it off."

Taking a long nap near the beach seemed like a much better time than breaching, smacking into the *Wanderer,* dropping into the water, and trying over and over to transform without getting drenched. The weight of the guns and equipment would drag me down to the bottom if I missed, and while I hadn't been worried with the sandbar so close to the *Serendipity,* I'd end up a shark again if I screwed it up.

Snagging the rope in my teeth, I dragged it to the stern, tugging it into place over the engine mounts so I had extra handholds if I missed.

It took me five tries to throw off the

curse's influence, and I ended up drinking half the ocean before I snagged the rope and hauled myself up to the deck. I coughed and spit water, grimacing at the throb in my cheek, jaw, and the back of my head.

Flopping on the *Wanderer's* deck, I considered the pros and cons of sleeping beneath the stars. Footsteps approached, and Abrahan nudged me with his bare toes. "You can't sleep there."

"Lies," I croaked.

"I took that guy to the spare bunk and promised to feed him dinner if he didn't cry or scream."

"No screaming is a good start. My head hurts too much for screaming. He can cry all he wants, as long as he does so quietly."

Abrahan crouched beside me and went to work unbuckling my holsters, setting my weapons aside. "Do I want to know where you got so many guns on such short notice?"

"Hoard. Hidden cache."

Instead of the anger I expected for having kept secrets from him, he chuckled. "I should have guessed. I saw you had the first aid kit out. Got everything you needed? If not, they have one in that house. We can raid it and take it from them after you've gotten a chance to rest, right? They seemed pretty determined to keep me healthy."

"If they'd hurt you, I would've done more than scrap their ship."

"You scrapped their ship?"

"Ate the rudder. Tore the inside to shreds. Payback for what they did to my house. Ripped all her clothes to shreds, too." A weak laugh escaped me. "They were going to shoot you. Couldn't let them."

Abrahan took off my hat, set it aside, and started examining my head, his fingers tangling in my hair as he tried to move the frizzy mess out of the way. "You have a bald spot, and your hair's all tangled."

Why was he so concerned over my hair? "Don't worry about it. It'll grow back."

"Want anything? Coffee? Tea? Something to eat?"

Right. If I didn't give the kid something to do, I'd be willing to wager the entire *Wanderer* he'd lose his mind within ten minutes. "Coffee, and if you're up for it, dinner. I'll crawl along in a few minutes."

"I've done nothing ever since they dragged me into that house." Abrahan bounced to his feet and ran across the deck, his bare feet slapping against the wood. Stifling a groan, I lurched upright and began the tedious process of gathering my weapons so I could lock them in the storage box out of our hostage's reach.

By the time I made my way into the cabin, Abrahan was working over the stove, watching a bubbling pot while a large chunk of tuna thawed on the counter, already sprinkled with spices. “Want me to catch you a fresh one, kid?”

“No. I want you to sit down and drink your coffee.”

Someone had taught my kid some bad habits, and I was too tired to do anything about it, so I sat. Scowling made my entire face ache. “You’re sure they didn’t hurt you any? You said they had a first aid kit out.”

“Not their fault I fought back. I earned my lickin’.”

“Abrahan.”

“What?”

“How badly were you hurt?”

“Couple of scratches, a few bruises. Nothing serious.”

I got up, headed deeper into the cabin, and hunted down my hostage, who, true to Abrahan’s words, cowered on the spare bunk in the smallest nook in an out of the way corner. “Hey, you. Is it true my kid only got banged up a little?”

My hostage gulped and nodded, squirming in his effort to back away from me.

“Got a name?”

“Lester.”

“This is how this is going to work, Lester. Abrahan’s going to cook something. You’re going to go sit your ass down at the table, and we’re going to take a stab at this being civilized thing. I’m going to ask you questions. You’re going to answer them. If I think you’re giving me answers I want to hear rather than the truth, you're not going to like what'll happen, so let's cut through the bullshit." Talking hurt, and I clasped my hands behind my back so I wouldn't poke at my cheek. Without waiting for an answer, I headed into the kitchen and sat.

Drinking coffee with a busted mouth proved an exercise in patience and pain, but I managed. Abrahan sighed, shook his head, and rummaged through the pantry, returning with jars of spices.

It took Lester almost ten minutes to work up the nerve to emerge from the safety of his bunk, and he picked the chair across from me, the farthest away he could get.

"No one is going to believe you if you tell them a woman missing half her face turned into a shark and kidnapped you, you know. It'd be wise if you just kept that to yourself." I fought another battle with my coffee and declared myself the winner; more ended up down my throat than on me.

Abrahan sighed, grabbed a dish cloth, and tossed it to me. "I'd give you a straw, but I don't think it'd help. Maybe a funnel?"

"Don't you get smart with me, boy."

"She's all talk, very little bite," he informed our hostage. "Usually."

While it never would have occurred to me to cook tuna from frozen, my cabin boy turned chef went to work to make it happen.

Any other day, I would've watched with interest, but I forced my attention to Lester and kept it on him. "The *Serendipity's* captain is Lucretta O'Malley, correct?"

Lester swallowed, his gaze sliding to the door behind me, and I was willing to bet my entire hoard he calculated his chances of making an escape. The moment his hope of dodging an interrogation faded, his expression dulled and turned lifeless. "Yes, ma'am."

"Why did she come here?"

"It's hers by right!"

Both of my eyebrows took a hike. "Excuse me?"

"It belongs to her. She is the direct descendant of the Black Scourge. It is hers by right!"

Deep in my bones, ice formed, spread, and chilled my entire body. Captain Maritza had had a child? A child with someone descended from Captain Grace O'Malley? Life had gone on after the sinking of the *Calico*, but it had never crossed my mind the Black Scourge would ever have a child of her own. I could've seen *my* captain having a child, had she lived long enough, but not the Black Scourge.

She had never had a use for men, and had, like my captain, preferred the attentions of other women. In that, we differed, and I suspected my unwillingness to pursue anyone other than Ricardo had factored in my downfall from my captain's favor.

It explained so much. If Benny and

Bensen consorted with Lucretta O'Malley, who could prove her lineage to the Black Scourge, their interest in my items made sense. To them, she would have been their rightful owner.

"The house isn't hers by right. It is mine." I lifted my chin and stared down my nose at Lester, fighting my desire to clack my teeth together and scowl. "My name is Catalina de la Corona, and I was once known as the Pirate Princess of the Seven Seas. I was the first mate of the *Calico*. Before the Black Scourge betrayed us, it was to be *our* house. She has no claim."

Lester sucked in a breath. "That's impossible."

Could he truly be so stupid? I pointed at my face. "Do you not remember how this happened?"

"Naidoo shot you. It must have grazed."

Him again? It was well enough he was dead; it saved me the effort of having to kill him myself. Rising to my feet, I turned around, parted my hair, and showed him the back of my skull. "Yes, it grazed right through and exited here."

Of all the things I expected, Lester lurching to his feet, running out of the cabin, and throwing up over the rail wasn't one of them. At least he hadn't thrown himself overboard. I followed, grabbed the back of his shirt, and waited for him to finish retching his guts out. "So, Naidoo was the one who pulled the trigger, huh? Where's the *Lady of the Lake*?"

I gave Naidoo credit; he talked the talk with the best of them, and I hadn't pegged him as the ruthless type, although I was more than willing to view him as greedy and happy to dirty his hands for a profit. He had lacked the edge I associated with most coldblooded killers.

Lester gasped for air, and once he regained control of his stomach, he slumped over the rail. "The captain scuttled her."

That explained Naidoo's willingness to pull the trigger. Abrahan likely hadn't been the target at all; if *my* ship had been scuttled and the reason for it stood in front of me, I'd likely shoot, too. "Know why?"

"The captain was pissed. Hired him to do a job, and he botched it."

I dragged my hostage back into the cabin and sat him down before fetching him a glass of water. "He didn't botch it. I merely decided I didn't like being set adrift on a life raft in the middle of the ocean, so I left. Shame about the ship. The *Lady of the Lake* was lovely."

If Lester's eyes widened any more, they'd pop out of his head. "You're the one my captain wanted?"

"I suspect that was only because Benny and Bensen recognized the design of my pocket watch, cutlass, and flintlock, told your captain, and wanted to get their hands on it badly enough to trash my home to do it. Makes a sick amount of sense, if their loyalty was to her before they had met me. It was probably your crew who did the actual deed. Benny wouldn't condone it, neither would Bensen. They would have tried to find some other way to sucker me out of my property."

The betrayal still stung, but I accepted it with a shrug. I'd done far worse for my captain. How could I blame either one of them?

I *would* remain rather unhappy over their involvement in my home's destruction and the loss of my possessions, but I'd move on as always. I'd have to think long and hard on how best to handle the situation.

When I got my revenge, it'd have to cost them, but I didn't want to hurt them too much. Before they had shown their true colors, I'd appreciated their friendship well enough, even when they had annoyed me.

I really did make a terrible pirate at times.

Abrahan shoved the tuna into the oven and parked on the chair beside me. "Those two men seemed pretty upset when they realized you'd been shot. And the one who'd shot Naidoo, too. They weren't happy I'd lied to them, either. Then they realized you were the one giving me the orders, and they got a little too interested in me for my liking. That's how I ended up locked in that room. They were trying to figure out what to do with me, since I'm part of your crew."

Our hostage flinched and stared down at his glass of water. "The one who shot Captain Naidoo is our navigator."

I hated history. Why did history always have to repeat itself? I didn't want anything to do with a rival crew's navigator. I'd walked that path once, and I refused to subject myself to such loss again.

"Lester, did they tell you what they were looking for in the house?"

"They weren't looking for anything—it's a part of my captain's heritage. She calls it her family's legacy."

Why did history have to repeat itself so often? Why couldn't the dead sleep? Why did time have to march, steady and relentless? In a way, Lucretta did have a partial claim on the House Lost at Sea, but I was in no mood to offer her any concessions.

She had taken too much from me, just as her ancestor had. It was so easy to hate them both for it.

"What does she intend to do with the manor?"

"Keep it, I think? She was talking about setting up docks to better protect the ship while here and building a proper path up the hill. They weren't expecting the museum, and I think it bothered them—especially the picture of your ancestor."

I hoped it had cost them a lot of pain and time finding a way up to the manor. I snorted at the fact Lester could accept the hole in my face and my cursed form, but he couldn't believe the truth of my past. "No, the picture of me. Not my ancestor. That's me."

"That was three hundred years ago. Impossible."

Abrahan pinched the bridge of his nose and shook his head.

"Hey, kid? Please tell me she has smarter men on her crew. I think I want to return this one and get a different one. I'm not sure I can deal with this level of stupidity an entire voyage."

"If that doesn't teach you to think a little further ahead, nothing will."

"Don't you get smart with me, Abrahan."

"Someone has to."

When glaring didn't inspire fear or bring forth an apology of any sort, I reached over, grabbed the kid's ear, and twisted until he begged for mercy. "Do you want to be swabbing the decks for the next month?"

"No, ma'am."

I released him. "So, Lester. Why do you serve O'Malley?"

"She's my aunt."

I smiled despite the pain. "Well, well, well. This just got really interesting."

TWENTY-SEVEN

There was no room on my ship for even more damned ghosts.

I LOOKED FORWARD to making Lucretta O'Malley regret her efforts to take what was mine, and I'd use her nephew to accomplish my goals. And, in a nod to Abrahan's cleverness, I'd do it his way and take my time with it.

For a few moments, I would allow the rival captain and her crew to think they'd won. In reality, I moved my pieces into place, held them captive to my whims, and bided my time. When I acted, I would make it clear they all belonged to me.

The tides would shift in my favor, and when they did, I would take everything back. I would have my flintlock, my watch, and my cutlass, and I would take the loyalties of O'Malley's crew and make them my own.

I had a problem with navigators, though, so I'd probably send that one on his way.

There was no room on my ship for even more damned ghosts.

The first step of my plan involved the *Serendipity*. If I left the ship intact, the marooned crew might escape my islands and return to civilization. I couldn't allow that. Until I finished with them, the House Lost at Sea would become their home, their prison, and the grounds for the perfect revenge.

I would use Captain Maritza's ambitions against her, and since I couldn't reach the dead, I'd enjoy ensnaring her descendant. I would turn the tables, and while history would repeat itself, the story wouldn't end the same way, not this time.

There'd be no love lost. There'd be no love. There wouldn't be two crews. There'd be one: mine. I would destroy Lucretta O'Malley and her ambitions, and I'd make the woman lick my feet for the mess she'd made of my life.

But first, I needed to pry every bit of information I could out of O'Malley's nephew, especially in terms of his lineage. While some pirates didn't care, others took matters of family seriously, and I numbered among them, as had my captain—and Captain Maritza. "You're going to do three things for me, Lester O'Malley. Should you do as ordered, you'll return to your captain safe and sound, with only that one nip to show for your trouble. Understand?"

The boy gulped and nodded.

"Good. First, I need to know her—your—lineage. All of it. Your family obviously takes such matters seriously. Start talking, and begin with Grace O'Malley."

"Grace O'Malley's youngest son, Hubert, married Almira, the daughter of a prideful family of merchants. They had a son, Thaddeus. Captain Maritza took Thaddeus as part of a raid on Ireland several years before the sinking of the *Terrier.* She liked his looks and decided she wanted a daughter to inherit her legacy, so she used him for that purpose."

Damn it. That matched the story I'd heard already, with the exception of Captain Maritza securing a daughter for herself.

That made sense, as Captain Maritza hadn't valued men as highly as she'd valued women.

Many legends and speculations surrounded Grace O'Malley and her ventures as a pirate, and one of them included some raunchier tales of her dalliances. I had paid it no mind; I didn't hold faith in the superstitions about women on board ships, although I found it interesting two people from the same crew had had children who had gone on to get married.

It didn't surprise me in the slightest Captain Maritza would take a man of her choosing to secure a daughter. "And Thaddeus?"

"Their first child was a son, and unsatisfied she didn't have a daughter, she decided to try again." Lester scowled, and I couldn't blame him for disliking that portion of his family history.

"With Thaddeus?"

Lester shrugged. "Doesn't matter. The Black Scourge and her crew disappeared when the *Terrier* sank. Thaddeus O'Malley, by that point, had returned to his home with their son. My aunt intends to find every part of our heritage and reclaim it."

Lucretta must have been a child born from that son.

"Except the *Terrier* is in a museum."

"Permitted by our family, of course."

I wanted a pin so I could pop Lester's egotistical little bubble. A few minutes talking to him erased any guilt I'd have over marooning him, his crew, and his captain on my islands. I'd have to make certain to block access to my hoard in case any of them decided to go for a swim.

A few minutes as a shark and some rocks would bar the entry enough for my needs.

"Of course. For your second task, you will deliver a message to your captain and her crew." I got up, dug through the drawers in the cabin until I found some paper and a pen, and went to work writing a little letter informing Lucretta O'Malley she would be a guest along with her crew at *my* home until I saw fit to allow them to leave.

I signed it, smirking at the thought of Benny and Bensen recognizing my handwriting. I would have fun with them all. It took me a few minutes to locate an envelope, and after stuffing my letter inside, I sealed it and slapped it onto the table. "Your third task is to torch the *Serendipity.* Leave nothing but smoldering planks when you're finished. I'll even provide you with enough gasoline to make certain she burns."

Lester paled. "You mean to maroon us."

Clapping slow and loud, I smiled at my hostage. He blanched. "You figured it out. Well done. Since I'm not a complete monster—yet—I'll even be nice enough to return and bring you supplies. It wouldn't be very nice of me if I left you here on your own to die on this tiny little island so, so far away from civilization. If you're lucky, I'll only leave you here for a month or two in time out. Accidents do happen, you know. And sometimes, some nice, loyal friend who hears a few people she knows were lost at sea might go out searching. Serendipitous fortune isn't unheard of. It'll make such a lovely story for a dull news day, won't it?"

Abrahan laughed and got up to check on dinner. "You're a terrible person, Corona."

"Revenge is like a fine wine. It tastes better once it has aged."

FEAR DID funny things to people, and I used Lester's against him, forcing him to do my bidding. With haunted eyes, O'Malley's nephew set the *Serendipity* ablaze, and I left him on the sandbar to find his own way to shore, watching from the bow of the *Wanderer,* a safe distance from the embers swirling up on the winds to rain down on the surf.

It took her a long time to burn down to nothing and sink, and long before the flames died away, I spotted those on shore watching their hope of escape creak and break apart.

Abrahan watched with me, leaning on the rail. "Now what, Captain?"

"We're going to go on a little voyage. I think we'll come up with a good cover story about how I was kidnapped, left for dead, and was helped by a nice Brazilian-American lad who found me—an orphan, as far as he knows. You'll come with me back to America, and we'll deal with the fallout of my horrible luck on a much-needed vacation. Since I quit my old job, I'll even make it look like I'm looking for something new. My boss even said she'd try to give me a better offer. Maybe I'll humor her. It'll be a pain in my ass dealing with all the paperwork if Benny reported me as dead, but we'll see. I don't know what he'll have done with my phone."

"You can do that?"

"I fully intend to. We'll have to play it by ear; it all depends on what Benny told people —if he told anyone anything. He might not have. It would look bad for him if he was too involved with my potential disappearance. If he was wise, he'd file a missing person report with my last known location as somewhere in Brazil. I won't know until we reach the United States. We have time to figure something out and make some plans. As long as our story stays straight, it'll be fine. When we can, we should stick to the truth as much as possible."

"And what about them? And that house? And your pistol. They're all important to you, aren't they?"

I stepped away from the railing and went to work preparing to unfurl the sails. The jolly roger, improvised with shreds of cloth sewn together, already flew high and proud on the mast, large enough for those on shore to see.

The next time they saw it, it'd be a much different flag. Unlike my captain or O'Malley's distant ancestor, my skull and crossed bones wouldn't feature a mermaid or a sea serpent, but a shark.

My curse would become my symbol, and

when I set sail for new waters, it would be as a true pirate, complete with a crew of my own, built of men and a woman who had tried to best me at my own game. My day would come, and soon.

TWENTY-EIGHT

Who else was brave enough to beat sense into me?

THREE DAYS after leaving the House Lost at Sea, we reached a port with an embassy, and I was regretting my decision to maroon Benny and Bensen with Captain Lucretta O'Malley and her crew. While I enjoyed the thought of Lucretta trapped where she'd no hope of escape, I worried for the pair I'd once held in high esteem. Their treachery had cost me greatly, but my traitorous heart hurt.

I loved neither as I had loved Ricardo, my crew, or my captain, but I couldn't deny the truth anymore. I did love them.

Damn it. I'd crossed the line I'd sworn I'd never cross again. I'd crossed it with them, and I had crossed it with Abrahan, too. I'd wielded my need for wit and intellect as a shield and sword to defend myself, too high a standard for most to overcome, but the three of them had slipped through my defenses.

With shore in sight, I'd run out of time to

change my plans and second-guess myself. For better or worse, I needed to return to civilization, undo the damage O'Malley and her crew had done to my life, and come up with a better plan for dealing with the rival crew—and the two men I'd been foolish enough to trust.

I turned to Abrahan, lifting my chin and staring down my nose at him. "How's my face?"

My cabin boy turned cook and First Mate snorted. "Your lip's split, but it's a normal split now, rather than that jaw-displaying monstrosity of a hole. You're bruised, but it's not too bad. For the hundredth time, you fit your part, Captain. Stop your bellyaching already. I know what to do, so go bunk up and look sickly or something. I've got this."

How had the brat I'd kidnapped in Brazil gone from a mewling weakling to bossy in such a short period? I couldn't tell if I was to blame—or if I wanted him to change. No, on second thought, I didn't want him to change. I wanted to keep him.

Who else was brave enough to beat sense into me?

I was in too deep again, and I began to understand, a little, why Captain Maritza had created so many problems for me—and taken Ricardo. I'd served a different purpose to her, and the fault had been with me. Abrahan now stood in my shoes, but I had one thing my captain hadn't.

Abrahan didn't love me, not like a man loved a woman. No, he'd found a different mistress, a new love, and one I swore I would help him chase. I'd seen him staring out over the rolling waves with his soul in his eyes.

Captain Maritza had resented I'd stolen her navigator's attentions from her and the sea.

Abrahan's heart now belonged to the sea, for which I was grateful. It happened from time to time. All it took was the first real storm, the first real glimpse of the ocean's fury, and the damage was done. The thrill of the chase, the lure of the sea-whipped wind, and the whispers of waves would forever mark my young companion's heart, a curse as deep and robust as mine.

I would be content coming a close second in his affections, for it would bind me to him far more than wealth, prestige, or the promise of adventure. With me, he'd see the world and all her seas.

It would change my plans and force me to the water more than I'd intended, but it was a small price to pay. I'd already lost that war. For as long as he breathed, I would take him where he wished to go. But first, there was the matter of revenge.

Grumbling curses, most of them in rusty, antiquated Spanish, I headed into the cabin so

Abrahan could sail into port and begin the next phase of our plan, our game against Lucretta O'Malley and her crew. Everything hinged on him. From my mugging, which had been reported as lethal, to my disappearance at sea, Abrahan had concocted a simple story to explain it all.

Instead of being one of the muggers, he had witnessed the attack, saved my life, and at my urging, taken me out to sea on a ship I'd been in the process of purchasing. A hurried sale later, we had escaped the port city. Then, everything had gone wrong.

Equipment had failed, damaged during a storm I'd confirmed had moved through the area. We'd been swept off course, lost at sea with little hope of finding shore.

Only good planning on my part, the *Wanderer's* water purification system, and some luck fishing had kept us alive long enough for the winds and currents to drag us to the Cape of Good Hope.

If everything went according to plan, he would head straight to the United States Embassy. In any other port, we would have been fine, but I worried the police would remember me, adding complexity to our already complex con.

It took Abrahan less than five minutes to reach the dock, secure the ship, and disembark, setting our plans into motion. I hated waiting without knowing if he needed my help. For our plan to work, I had one job to do, and that was to maintain the ruse I was injured but healing. Between being shot and my fall from the cliff, I had plenty of injuries to pull off my role.

While still tender, my skull had fused, the bone hardened enough to escape notice from most. My head injury was our riskiest gamble. If any x-rays were taken, I didn't know if the holes would show. The images could potentially betray the bullet holes, resulting in a lot of unwanted questions I couldn't truthfully answer.

It took Abrahan two hours, but when he returned, he brought Americans accompanied by two dark-skinned South Africans, both of whom seemed less than thrilled with their assignment. I had expected two from the embassy and had gotten four, but the number of Americans present wouldn't change any of my plans or our cover story.

And so, beneath the blazing South African sun, the game began.

~

THE UNITED STATES EMBASSY didn't have an on-staff doctor, and I counted my blessings. I refused care, drawing on American stereotypes to play the role of a stubborn, headstrong woman who wouldn't accept anything other than the best, even if it meant crossing an ocean to get it. Claiming I'd survived so far worked, although the gullible embassy employees annoyed me almost as much as the betrayals I tried to ignore but couldn't.

The Americans wanted to question Abrahan, but I refused to let him out of my sight, claiming I owed him my life for his courage and quick thinking. His passport smoothed his way, buying me the time needed to establish my identity so I could get a replacement passport. A few phone calls to my ex-boss confirmed most of my story, and when the government couldn't find Benny or Bensen to question, we played stupid—and concerned.

It was easy to feign being concerned. I didn't know what supplies they had on my islands, and although there were fish and fuel for fires, would they be able to harvest the ocean's bounty without a ship? I wasn't sure. I didn't know enough about Lucretta O'Malley and her crew.

I did my best to ignore my misgivings, and within forty-eight hours, I was on my way back to the United States with Abrahan, preparing for the nightmare of paperwork waiting for me. Fortunately, I hadn't been believed dead long enough to lose any of my belongings, which would have made the next phase of my revenge difficult.

It was petty of me to engage in psychological warfare with mortal men and a woman I probably would have liked if she hadn't crossed swords with me. In a few years, they'd grow old and die, and I'd have the greatest satisfaction of all, watching their temporary empires crumble around them while I endured.

In turn, they would get the ultimate revenge against me, as the sands of time fell away and they could move on to the next life, if there was anything beyond death. I'd stopped wondering long ago. No, my revenge would be simple.

I would wait them all out, and when death came calling for them, I would watch them wrestle with their regrets until they became just another bad memory among many. But first, I would make them indebted to me for rescuing them from the House Lost at Sea —*my* house.

Sometimes, I truly wasn't a nice person.

With Abrahan at my side, I returned to the ruins of my landlocked home to discover someone—Benny and Bensen, most likely—had moved ahead with the construction of a new house. A foundation had already been poured for a much larger building than the one Lucretta O'Malley had destroyed in her eagerness to take my pistol and cutlass. My Rolls-Royce was in the old garage, waiting to be moved into the new one, and my motorcycle waited with it.

I wasn't sure what to think. Had Benny and Bensen been attempting to preserve evidence of my existence? Why else do it? I should have hated them for everything that had happened, but I didn't.

I couldn't.

I had changed, and I didn't like it. Abrahan hovered at my side, a silent sentinel, until I grunted a curse and stalked to my Rolls-Royce. I tossed him the keys, hoping to introduce him to the third love of his life.

Within five minutes, the car had worked her magic on the kid and put him under her spell. I directed him to a nicer hotel in New York, booked us into a room with two beds, and began planning my return to the House Lost at Sea. First, I needed to reclaim my cutlass and pistol from the insurance company, which would cost me a week unless I was either lucky or persuasive.

A week would do. The instant we were settled in the room, I got on the phone and went to work while Abrahan hovered, his expression thoughtful. When I hung up, satisfied with the agent's promise to have my prized items returned in four days, Abrahan planted his hands on his hips and glared down his nose at me.

"What?"

"What are you up to?"

"Why do you think I'm up to something?"

"You're always up to something."

For someone so young, he had too much insight. "Fine. We're going back."

"Why?"

Cursing myself for teaching the boy to ask questions, I got to my feet, headed to my bag, and dug through it to inventory what I'd need to make a properly dramatic entrance—of the non-pirate variety. "We're going to parley with them."

"Why would we do something like that? Aren't they right where you want them?"

Guilt had a way of ruining the best of plans, even mine. Hundreds of years hadn't cured me of having a conscience, although I'd done a good job of smothering it most of the time. When I'd left Benny and Bensen at the House Lost at Sea, I'd been content enough with their chances of survival *if* they were wise.

Modern humans were so soft compared to those born and raised in the Golden Age of Piracy. They lived longer, however—as long as they kept close to civilization.

The island's water supply would keep them alive for about a month, assuming they were incapable of fending for themselves.

I scowled, angry at myself for worrying about their fate. "Killing someone is the least satisfying form of revenge."

Amusement lit Abrahan's eyes, and I rather disliked his playful smile. "You're feeling guilty."

"No, I just have a bad feeling."

"Most of us call that guilt, Corona."

I'd really have to make the damned brat my first mate, as he had a smart mouth on him, and I waggled my finger. "Have I told you that you're a smart ass today?"

He grinned. "Five times since noon. Yesterday, nineteen times before you threatened to ground me for the rest of my life. I'm hoping for twenty today."

What a smart ass. I rolled my eyes and shook my head. "Fine. I feel guilty."

"Why?"

"Abrahan," I growled in warning.

"It's not my fault your statements require elaboration."

Why had I insisted on expanding the brat's vocabulary during our voyage back to the Cape of Good Hope? Oh, right. I couldn't stand ignorant idiots incapable of using words longer than three syllables. Damn it. I'd served myself a serious dish of just desserts. "Smart ass, smart ass, smart ass."

Good behavior should be rewarded, even when it annoyed me.

"Eight," he reported cheerfully.

What had I done to deserve such a mouthy kid as my crew? Ah, right. I'd kidnapped him. Next time, I needed to screen my victims for smart-ass tendencies *before* grabbing them and setting sail. I'd save myself a lot of trouble.

Still, he was using his head, no matter how much I disliked having to face the consequences of my actions. "I let them get too close to me," I confessed.

It wouldn't take him long to figure out who I meant.

Abrahan's smile softened, and he sat on the edge of the bed he'd claimed as his. "You're worried they don't have the supplies they need. You're also worried about the storm brewing at sea—and don't think I hadn't noticed you mumbling about the weather. Believe it or not, it's a rather human reaction."

"If you already knew why, why ask me?"

"I wanted to know if you knew."

Someone must have cursed me again, saddling me with a brat prone to the same tricks I'd pulled once upon a time. I shook my head, went through my bags again, and grudgingly admitted I'd have to go shopping *and* do some sewing before I could set sail. "Who died and made you my shrink? Make yourself useful and check on the *Wanderer*."

"She's in the marina where I left her, and her storage fee's good for another week. I checked this morning."

Of course he had. He tended to wake up before I did, which gave him plenty of time to cause trouble—or be responsible without my supervision. "I'll be booking a flight for South Africa for five days from now. I want you to make your lists and plan for sufficient supplies for them for a month. Get two medical kits set up; if you need help, ask me. I'm going to be watching the weather, but I wouldn't be surprised if we run into a storm on the way. It's getting to be that time of year."

"Are you going to leave them marooned there? The *Wanderer* isn't large enough for their entire crew."

I shot him a glare. "I'll start with Benny and Bensen and see how I feel after that."

My cabin boy turned cook and gunning for his place as my first mate arched a brow, crossed his arms over his chest, and leveled a glare worthy of a captain in my direction. "How many times are we going to return to that island to ferry people off?"

Damn it. "I didn't say we were."

"I don't believe that for a second, Corona."

We would, and he'd hold it over my head until I admitted I'd grown soft. "I don't care about the others on the island."

"Sure you don't. That's why you went through so much effort to maroon them there rather than killing them. You're really bad at this revenge thing, aren't you? You should work on that. If you want revenge, take over that woman's crew. Make her your slave or something."

"Why would I want her as my slave? I have the feeling you're the one after a little revenge. What am I going to do with her if I take her as a slave?"

While I doubted he meant a literal slave,

I'd lived when people had been property, but I'd shelter him from that reality as much as I could. I wouldn't take anyone, even her, as a slave. I hadn't condoned slavery during my mortal life, and I wouldn't participate in it now, hundreds of years later.

Captain Maritza had dipped her hands in the slave market too much for my liking.

"She's kinda hot, Corona. I'd totally have sex with her."

I choked on my own spit, coughed, and glared at him. "No, Abrahan. You're not taking Lucretta O'Malley as a sex slave—or as a cabin girl."

"Spoilsport. Sell her to one of her enemies, then. She's got to have them. Take those men you want, find out who else holds a grudge against her, and let *them* deal with her. That would turn the tables on her, wouldn't it?"

We'd only committed one act of piracy, and he was already thinking like a hardened pirate. Next, he'd be asking me if we could make her walk the plank. I wouldn't tell him I'd enjoy it so I could tease her as a shark.

A little fear wouldn't kill her, and toying with the Black Scourge's descendant seemed like a good time to me.

"Enemy of my enemy is my friend," I muttered, considering if I wanted to take that route with the woman. It could work—and keep her off my back for a while. Such a plan could also backfire spectacularly.

"Exactly. Taking her two accomplices isn't enough. She almost killed you."

"I don't blame her for what Naidoo did, Abrahan."

"You should. He was part of her crew."

The thirst for revenge did strange things to people; I'd have to nip his desire for payback in the bud before we reached the House Lost at Sea. I sighed. "I'll think about it."

TWENTY-NINE

Are all pirates so crude?

LONG AFTER I should have made plans and booked our flight to South Africa, I obsessed over Lucretta O'Malley, her crew, and the circumstances that led to our clash. The Black Scourge and my captain had started as rivals, that much I remembered. Then, somewhere along the way, they'd become lovers. I remembered that, too, as I'd resented how my captain's focus had shifted too much in favor of a rival pirate.

History had a bad habit of repeating itself, and I wondered what would become of us and our crews. Somehow, I'd come full circle, trapped in a tangled web of emotions I'd thought long abandoned.

Lucretta O'Malley wasn't the Black Scourge. I needed to remember that. I needed to remember she had nothing to do with my captain's death. Her meddling in my affairs had annoyed me, but I understood her; she chased her family's legacy.

I was woman enough to acknowledge she had no way of knowing who I was, what I had been, and who I was willing to become to hide my cursed past. Her scheming had already involved Abrahan, who would never forget magic lurked in the darkest corners of the world, curses were real, and the sea held more secrets than he had ever imagined possible.

Maybe Lucretta, Benny, and Bensen shared my Abrahan's shoes, too. They'd seen me fall. A real human would've died.

Then I'd come back and reclaimed what was mine, torching their ship and trapping them on my island, surrounded by the evidence of the two pirate queens who had once sailed the seas. I stared out the window without seeing anything, wondering what to do—if I needed to do anything at all.

Lucretta O'Malley likely had enemies. With a little work, I could find those enemies if I wanted. I turned away from the window, pulled out my replacement cell phone, and searched the internet for the woman who had chosen to cross swords with me. As expected, she had enemies, having left a long line of disgruntled collectors in her wake.

Like her ancestor, when Lucretta O'Malley wanted something, she got it. She tried honey first, and when that failed to gain her the results she desired, she coerced, outwitted, and conned her way to victory. Like the Black Scourge, she had a reputation, and it wasn't a good one.

Everyone agreed on one thing: the woman was a silk-wrapped sword, hiding her lethal edge under a sophisticated veneer.

She also hated most men, just like the Black Scourge.

History truly did have a bad habit of repeating itself.

I laughed and spun around in my chair to face my partner-in-crime. "Abrahan?"

Lounging on the bed he had claimed, he lifted his hand to indicate he listened while most of his attention remained focused on his book.

"When you were with Lucretta, did she mention anything about being a lesbian?"

That caught his attention, and Abrahan dog-eared the page he read, set his book aside, and arched a brow. "No. She might be bisexual. Her first mate's a man, and she was definitely banging him at her leisure. She did make one comment, though."

Abrahan's hesitance captured my attention. "Oh?"

"She said she was disappointed she wouldn't be able to give you the spanking you rightfully deserve."

I snorted, cleared my throat, and coughed so I wouldn't break into a fit of hysterical laughter. "She said that to you?"

"Not to me—to those two men of yours. I think she was trying to piss them off, but it didn't work, especially since they both agreed they wouldn't mind a turn. The commentary only pissed off her navigator. Are all pirates so crude?"

"Yes." I cleared my throat again to control my urge to chortle at the thought of that conversation. I'd never considered Benny or Bensen as partners—not like that. Age and gender meant little to me, but my excessive standards kept most at arm's length. "Back in my day, women weren't welcome on board. My captain was one of the rare exceptions, keeping me as part of her crew. She made a point of never engaging with any of the crew, too."

"Well, that Lucretta woman does."

"Good for her." As I had from the day I'd been cursed, I wondered if my life would have been different if my captain had chosen to be a little more promiscuous. I doubted it. My captain's lover probably would have killed me rather than curse me. Competition between pirates rarely ended well, and I found no shame in admitting the truth.

I became jealous and territorial as much as the next pirate. My jealousy and territorial tendencies had only showed through for Ricardo, and my captain's solution to that had been simple.

She'd barred us from seeing each other along with her wretched lover.

Still, I longed to discover what was beyond the curse. Hundreds of years of searching had ended in failure as always. I had returned to the House Lost at Sea and seen its treasures, yet I lived. In the end, revenge didn't matter; I would linger long after Lucretta wasted away to bone and became a memory among many. Revenge would come no matter what I did.

She would live, grow old, and die while I endured.

A smile pulled at my lips. I had her trapped at the House Lost at Sea, and I would take it away from her, enjoying the moment when realization struck her. No matter how long she held my island as hers, she would lose in the end. I would end an era and destroy the evidence of the life I'd once led. I would find a way to make stone burn, and the House Lost at Sea would become rubble and another memory.

I would free myself from the chains of my past, and while still cursed, I would move on.

The Golden Age of Piracy was long over, and it was time I set sail for new seas and different pursuits.

"Corona?"

I grimaced. "I'm woolgathering. I have some things to take care of, so hold down the fort while I'm gone."

First, I needed to make a few phone calls, place an order for new boots and bitch over the high cost of a rush order. Then I'd get the supplies I needed to make two outfits, one for me and one for Abrahan. I would use modern methods, modern fabrics, and old styles to create something new. Instead of pirate, I would aim for a more comfortable explorer, a treasure hunter—something kinder than anything I'd done before.

Later, I would have to thank Lucretta O'-Malley for doing what no one else had ever managed to do for me. It was time for me to move on and make a future for myself and Abrahan. Without her, I wouldn't have taken that final step to casting aside the old and welcoming the new.

Maybe in time, I would do what I had never done before and transform my curse into a blessing.

I snorted at my folly, shook my head, and headed for the door.

~

WHILE I WAITED for the insurance company to return my flintlock and cutlass, I transformed myself from the Pirate Princess of the Seven Seas into a modern day treasure seeker. I borrowed the loose-fitted, billowing blouse I favored as a pirate, ditched the corset in favor of a more comfortable sports bra, and wore new jeans that would fade in time but last years as long as I bothered to wash them every rare now and then. The boots, however, were non-negotiable. Leather, up to my knees with folded tops and laced, water-proofed and treated to survive exposure to saltwater.

Abrahan got a leather fedora. Like my jeans, it would scuff and fade in time. Then, after he finished cooing over his new hat, I indulged in an expensive leather coat for him, one capable of surviving through many adventures, on land or at sea.

I planned to take him off the beaten path, too. I'd seen the world's oceans, but I hadn't delved far onto land, and I meant to change that.

I really would have to thank Lucretta later; without her meddling, I never would've considered expanding my boundaries and hunting trouble for the sake of the excitement and thrill of discovery.

When I wasn't sewing or hunting supplies, I watched the weather. The first storm missed my islands, much to my relief. However, a second storm was brewing, and to reach the

House Lost at Sea, I would have to sail through it. With a bit of luck, the storm would blow itself out by the time we were on the water, but I doubted we'd dodge the squall. While we had encountered choppy waters on the way to the Cape of Good Hope, Abrahan would get his first taste of truly rough seas.

The package from the insurance company arrived by courier as promised, and I tore into the packaging to check over my prized possessions. They had been cleaned and cared for, although I found evidence of wax in the inlays confirming someone had made a mold of both pieces. I curled my lip in a silent snarl.

I had my weapons back, and I'd established my place as their true owner. I wouldn't make the same mistake twice, and if Lucretta tried to take them from me again, I'd shove them both up her ass crosswise. Satisfied, I returned them to their box, taped it closed, and shoved the whole thing in my suitcase. It fit, barely, and I packed the rest of my apparel around it. I left a little note in the suitcase on the box with my address and instructions for return, as well as my permit numbers for international transport and the penalty for confiscation.

Some things I took seriously, and I wasn't about to have some uppity airport employee wrecking my prized possessions without being aware there would be consequences headed their direction for illegal handling. I'd paid through the nose for permits to transport the gun and sword.

Abrahan watched me, his brow creased and frowning. "You're up to something."

"I'm always up to something," I confessed, zippering my suitcase closed, locking it, and situating the travel tags. "You're ready to go?"

"I was ready to go yesterday."

"Got your books?"

"I bought three new ones yesterday while you were cursing your sewing machine."

"There will be a test."

"They're sleazy romances."

I shot him a look. "Romeo and Juliet or Hamlet?"

"Romeo and Juliet. Why on Earth would they commit suicide after knowing each other for three days?"

"Love makes people do stupid shit. It's a rule of the universe."

"I can't believe you're making me read this," Abrahan muttered, waving the book in question at me. "It's so…"

"Dated? Ancient?"

"I was more thinking violent, ridiculous, and kinda cheesy."

I laughed. "I'm making you read it because where we come from is just as important as where we're going, and Shakespeare has a lot of good lessons hidden away in his words.

Mostly, don't do anything in any of his plays, and you might live a long and happy life. His works illustrate just how much times have changed."

Of course, I hadn't learned how to read until after I'd set sail; Captain Louisa had taught me so I could maintain her records. I'd discovered reading for pleasure far later in life, long after my ship had sunk.

"But wouldn't books on navigation and sailing be more useful?"

"We'll get there. I think we'll start with some legends and myths before we dig into practical skills."

"Legends and myths? Why?"

Grinning at him, I shoved my suitcase towards the door. "I think I'm due for a leave of piracy—at least of the ship-based sort. I'm tired, and while I've sailed every last one of the oceans and swum in all the seas, I haven't really explored. Sunken treasures, hidden temples in deep jungles—I want to pick a myth and chase it."

Abrahan looked at me as though I'd lost my mind. "You can take the pirate out of the sea, but you'll still be a pirate, Corona. Even I can tell that much. Don't be crazy."

I leveled my best glare at him. "You've gotten mouthy, boy."

"Just obeying your orders, Captain."

"Smart ass."

He laughed. "That's twelve for today."

"Grab your bag, you brat. We have a flight to catch."

He was right; I'd never stop being a pirate, but I'd at least pretend I could be something else for a little while.

THIRTY

Time would tell. It always did.

ALL GOOD THINGS came to an end, and the weather proved no exception. When we set sail from the Cape of Good Hope, the *Wanderer* burdened with supplies, I prepared for the storm; I watched the forecast with a wary eye, well aware how a little depression could grow teeth and bite.

The ocean refused to bend to another's will. I supposed that was why I'd fallen in love with it in the first place. It persisted despite the floating islands of trash clogging its currents and killing the life that had once teemed beneath the surface.

I had hoped to avoid the inevitable encounter with man's mark on the eternal sea, but the floating debris stretched out as far as I could see with the towering columns of storm clouds churning beyond.

Abrahan gaped, leaning over the rail for a closer look at humanity's blight. "That's vile."

Yes, vile was the perfect word for what mortals had wrought on the planet we all called home. "Lash the sails and tie everything down; it's going to be a rough ride."

We'd hit the storm at nightfall, and I'd have to rely on my cursed nature to ride the waves and keep the ship afloat. If the sea and storm won, I'd be challenged keeping Abrahan alive.

Maybe the ocean remained a constant, but I'd changed. This time, I wouldn't sit idle and watch the slaughter, helpless to change my crew's fate. I would defy the ocean as I did every time I set sail, and it would taste the bitterness of defeat.

Abrahan was mine. While the fear of death remained, for death would come to him as it would for Benny, Bensen, and everyone else I knew, it would not be today, no matter how fierce the storm and monstrous the waves.

I challenged the weather and sea dressed as a modern-day pirate, my old sword and flintlock hanging from my hip, my boots so new the leather creaked when I walked. In time, they'd mold to the shape of my feet, assuming I didn't trash them on their debut voyage, a rather real risk. Salt and leather didn't play nice, even when I'd paid through the nose to protect them.

Time would tell. It always did.

"You're doing it again, Corona."

I twitched. What *would* happen if I marooned my smart ass kid on the mountain of trash? Would it—and he—withstand the storm? Then again, he was exactly what I deserved, and I despaired as much as I rejoiced. He had the right of it, too. I should have been hard at work preparing the engines, setting the lamps, and lashing the few loose items down while he secured the sails before heading into the cabin. Instead, I wondered what I would do once we reached the House Lost at Sea, and how I would deal with Lucretta O'Malley and her crew. "I was strategizing for when we hit that storm."

While I spoke the truth, I also lied, and Abrahan snorted, confirming he'd seen right through me. As far as diversions went, I thought it had been a good one. "Are you going to try to sell me beachfront property in the desert next? That's the dumbest excuse you've come up with yet. That little storm doesn't bother you."

"I should make you walk the plank, kid. You could ride it out with the trash."

"You wouldn't do that. You like me too much, and I follow orders. See? This is me following orders, securing the rigging while you wax poetic over heaping mounds of garbage and a few clouds."

"You're going to be eating your words about those few clouds soon," I warned.

"I'll wear my life vest. I do value my life."

"That's the smartest thing you've said all day."

"So, what has your sharky tail in a kink? The last storm, you eyed the clouds, cackled, and told the weather to bring it on. You're looking at that junk like you think it's going to bite you."

"Have I told you you're a smart ass today?"

"Seven times," he reported.

"I'm trying to figure out how I will deal with O'Malley."

"That's easy. Make her your bitch."

I sighed, closed my eyes, and prayed for patience. "Why would I do that?"

"It would be satisfying for you. It would be all the payback you need, and you'd be happy after you conquered her. Then you can suggest she sleep with me, as making me happy would make you happy, and I'm pretty sure sleeping with her would make me very happy."

I scowled, but as I kept insisting he think things through, I went through the motions and counted the ways the woman had thwarted me—and how she might be a suitable partner for him if I found her tolerable after getting my revenge. Perspective mattered. Lucretta O'Malley was the product of a long, proud history. It had begun before I'd been born with a scorned woman out for revenge. Grace O'Malley had kickstarted the wheels of fate. Through her son and my captain's lover, life had continued on until Lucretta's birth.

I wouldn't count her heritage as a black mark against her. Our past shaped our futures, but it didn't dictate.

We all made our choices.

The first mark against Lucretta was her decision to take what was mine believing it belonged to her by the right of her heritage. She had outwitted me, not in intellect, but in her unfailing determination. I could—did—respect that.

We were a lot alike, although the years had worn away at me until I only clung to a few things and let the rest slide away like a wave retreating over the sands. Grunting an acknowledgment of Abrahan's point might keep him quiet for a few minutes.

He went back to work on the rigging with a smug smile.

"As there will be no unwilling partners in my crew, if you can convince her to romp with you in your bed, you're certainly old enough to do what you want. I won't tell you no. That said, I don't think she's worthy of your company, and you should have higher standards."

"But she's *hot*."

"She's also the kind to stab you in the back, she's probably old enough to be your mother, and you deserve better."

"Ew. I didn't need to think about her being old enough to be my mother."

"And thus, your lust dies, a tragedy."

"You're mean," he complained before giving his tasks his complete attention.

I ducked into the cabin and pulled out the battery-operated lamp I'd lash to the mast to serve as my main spotlight for wave watching when night fell and the ocean raged. I tested to make certain it still worked, nodding my satisfaction at the bright beam. I coiled rope around my arm, shimmied my way up the mast, and lashed it into place. The battery would last twelve hours once I turned it on, which would get us through the night. I tested the angle to ensure it would illuminate where I'd need it most.

My cursed inhuman eyes would do the rest of the work.

The waves rolled, and the *Wanderer* rocked, riding them with the surety of a far larger vessel. I'd chosen well, and I smiled at the thought.

I climbed back down, thumping to the deck and dusting myself off, leaning back to recheck my work. Assuming nothing collided with the lamp, it'd hold. Nodding my satisfaction, I busied myself with the engine, going through my checks on autopilot.

Lucretta's first true accomplishment was her scheming with Captain Naidoo; had I not been cursed, she would have won her opening gambit, although I still wasn't sure why she'd targeted me in the first place. I'd make certain to ask her once I finished turning the tables on her. Lucretta's second accomplishment was in her successful theft of my property, although I'd come out ahead of the game in the guilt factor and the acquisition of a new, better home—upgraded on the dime of her crew, from what I could tell from the construction work done on the foundation.

Her recruitment of Benny and Bensen counted as her third achievement. I had underestimated them both and had paid for my error. In turn, she had underestimated Naidoo, and had I been human, the final victory would have belonged to him.

My first victory was my survival, my second was the sinking of her ship, and my third would be my return to the House Lost at Sea, where I would even the scales. But how?

What could I do that would hit her as close to the heart as I'd been hit?

Maybe the Black Scourge had taken my beloved captain away from me, but I'd prevented history from repeating itself. When the damned woman's descendant had tried to pull the same devilish trick, I had reclaimed what was mine. Abrahan still lived. In that, I had already won.

His loyalty belonged to me. It occurred to

me I could do to her as had been done to me, whittling away at Benny and Bensen until their loyalty shifted to me. I had time and patience.

But then I'd be no better than the Black Scourge. No, I needed something else, something better.

"So she's smart," I growled, startling Abrahan, who yelped and whirled in my direction. "She tried to take what was mine, so by rights, I should try to take what is hers. I just haven't decided what or how yet."

"You already took her ship."

"Ships can be replaced."

"So, take her crew."

"I could, but no. I won't. I won't do as was done to me. Not this time."

I would escape it all, and perhaps, with time, I'd put Ricardo's memory to rest.

"What do you want, then?" Abrahan leaned against the rail, tipping his head back to watch me with an arched brow. "If you're not interested in making her yours, you're not interested in her crew, you're not interested in her ship, you have to want *something*."

Perhaps the hardest part was acknowledging what I couldn't have. "If I could, I would have the Black Scourge feel the despair of watching her world fall apart around her as mine had fallen apart around me, cursed to live forever while she, coward that she was, enjoys the peace of death."

"But you won't do that to Lucretta, will you?"

"I won't, however much I'd like to make her regret following in her ancestor's footsteps."

"So, if you can't make her an enemy, make her an ally instead. That way, you win. Think about it. If that rival captain hated you enough to curse you, having her descendant dancing to your tune would be the ultimate payback. It just proves you're the better pirate."

"And what exactly am I supposed to do with her as an ally? It's not like I need her or her crew."

"I'm sure you'll think of something. You're smart like that." Abrahan shoved away from the rail and headed for the cabin. "I'll be making sure everything's tied down as proper while you do whatever it is annoyed pirate queens do when their crew get mouthy."

"Smart ass," I muttered.

"Eight!" he chirped, waving before he ducked through the doorway to resume his work.

He gave me a lot to think about. If I didn't accept her as an enemy, what would she become? A friend?

I snorted at the thought, shook my head, and prepared the *Wanderer* for the storm.

THIRTY-ONE

I was wrong.

STORMS HAD a way of taking people by surprise, even the most experienced of sailors.

I didn't laugh at Abrahan when the rolling seas got the better of him. At my suggestion, he fled below decks to endure—and avoid—the ocean's wrath. The bucking of a ship bothered most sane people, but for him, it was the realization of his mortality in the face of waves larger than the *Wanderer,* which hadn't been built to withstand the abuse I was putting her through.

Waves broke over the ship, flooding the deck and draining out the stern. The wind hissed its impotent fury over my defiance, and I laughed at the sting of the salt on my face and the crash of thunder as lightning split the heavens. Each white-capped crest could be our last, but my ship faced them down with indomitable spirit. She creaked beneath my feet, cutting into the rifts between the waves for her wake to be devoured by the hungering waters.

No matter how badly humans wrecked her, the ocean persisted. Each lurch of the deck beneath my feet reminded me, the howl of the gale called me home, and in the moments the *Wanderer* launched over the crests and took flight, the rest of the world dropped away into an abyss, lost to the first true love of my life.

The sea had taught me what it was to truly love something unobtainable, and it had cursed me as much as the Black Scourge had. We fought, and often, but I always returned and always would.

Soaked to the skin and chilled by wind and wave, I found the answer to my dilemma, a purpose for Captain Lucretta O'Malley and her crew, and a goal I could chase without regret. First, I would set Abrahan on the path to a fulfilling life, with or without me.

Then I would use her as she'd tried to use me. I wouldn't take wealth, fame, or power. No, I'd recruit her, swearing to haunt her line until its extinction, unless she helped break what her ancestor had inflicted upon me. It was simple, it was obvious, but it was perfect.

My freedom for hers was an equivalent exchange. It would absolve me of guilt and put an end to the endless cycle. Maybe it would work, maybe it wouldn't, but she was the one thing I hadn't yet tried: a direct descendant of the one who'd turned her love for my captain into my living nightmare, one without an end in sight.

It had occurred to me to hunt down a descendant of the Black Scourge, but she hadn't been someone I ever thought would have children of her own. I'd reasoned away the possibility, and worse, I'd made assumptions—wrong ones. I'd thought the Black Scourge would have shared one thing with me, loyalty to the woman we had both loved, albeit in different ways.

On the other side of the storm, I would acknowledge my mistake, learn from it, and see what new waters waited for me. Turning an enemy into an ally was the one thing I hadn't tried, and the excitement prickling beneath my skin wasn't just from the storm's charge in the air, the adrenaline of denying the ocean its chance to claim another soul, and my love of challenging the weather and tides.

I sailed through the night, and the thundering storm tattered and broke apart in the dawn light. It took several hours for the waves to settle, and when they did, leaving the sea glassy and still, I checked our location and charted our course for the House Lost at Sea. After a fond pat of the *Wanderer's* mast, I peeked into the cabin.

Another time, I would ask Abrahan why

he'd thought climbing under the table was a good idea. He wore his red and yellow life vest and clung to a table leg. Leaning over, I braced my hands on my knees and arched a brow. "Comfortable?"

"Very."

"The storm's over. You can come out." I straightened, taking a closer look at the pantry and our bunks. He'd done a good job securing everything, and while some cans and sacks had gotten tossed around, nothing had spilled. "You did a good job in here. I've corrected our course, and it should be clear sailing for the rest of the trip. I need to do a once over of the ship and check the keel, so you're on duty for a while."

"Are we leaking?"

"I really doubt it. She's not listing, and she feels normal."

"You're really sure the storm's gone?"

I grinned and leaned over to meet his gaze again. "And here I thought you weren't worried because it was a tiny little storm."

"I was wrong."

"You'll get used to it, don't worry. The first ride is always rough, but next time, I'll have you out on deck."

"You look like a drowned rat."

"It was a bit wet out there. Come on out, kid. The water's calm. I had an idea."

Abrahan scowled, his eyes narrowing from suspicion. "What sort of idea?"

"I think I have a use for Lucretta O'Malley."

"Are you seriously telling me you were on deck during the storm thinking about her?" Crawling out from beneath the table, he peeled off his life vest, hung it up, and shot several glares at me before peeking out the door. "How could you?"

People reacted to fear in different ways, and Abrahan's flabbergasted accusation amused me. "What else was I supposed to be doing?"

"You could have sunk the ship!"

In time, he'd grow to become as insane as I was, and I looked forward to it. Until then, I would enjoy his discomfort and prod him along until he conquered his apprehension over the sea at her worst. "I didn't, did I?"

"Oh. Yeah, I guess that's true." The realization seemed to startle him, and he took a second look outside. "It's so calm. Are you sure we're not dead and this is heaven?"

I laughed, headed to the railing, and leaned over to point at a few wayward pieces of plastic floating in the water. "Heaven's pretty polluted."

Joining me, Abrahan peered over the railing. "It really is. That's sad."

"I remember the ocean when plastics didn't exist, the waters were clear, and life teemed beneath the surface. The reefs were brilliant, colored, and marvels to behold, and the water was clear—so clear you could see to the heart of the world in places. Anyway, I have the perfect use for her."

"What?"

"I'll make it her responsibility to break my curse. If the history of the past is so important to her, then I will remind her that it is thus her duty to undo what her ancestor did to me. It's fair."

"But what will happen to you?"

It was the nature of humans—and even myself at times—to worry about what the future held. "I expect I'll die. How I'll die, I don't know. Maybe the years will catch up to me in an instant, or maybe I'll begin to age like a mortal should. Until the curse is broken, there's no way to know."

"Have you aged at all since you were cursed?"

"No. I always revert to how I was the day the Black Scourge cursed me. Even my hair regrows to the same length, and I carry the scars of my youth."

"It's like you're frozen in time, then?"

Yes, that was a good way to think of it. I was frozen, trapped in a body that should have long since withered away. "That sounds right to me."

"So maybe you'll keep living after the curse is broken."

Understanding struck hard. People like Abrahan, young but no stranger to death, feared what I didn't—my death. I crossed my arms over the railing and stared out over the glassy water. There was only one thing I could give him with any certainty, a promise I'd likely regret in the future. "I'll be careful should we find a way to break the curse. I'm rather looking forward to dragging you to every dark, shadowy corner of the Earth before I hang up my hat."

"I can live with that."

So could I, and with a nod, I returned to my work, leaving Abrahan to stare over the ocean with a thoughtful expression on his face. My inspection of the keel could wait until Abrahan found his feet again and wasn't quite so engaged with the reality of mortality.

A few more years for his peace of mind was a small price for me to pay.

THIRTY-TWO

I didn't think that through all the way.

The House Lost at Sea was as I remembered, perched on its cliff as proud as the sea it overlooked. Another storm was brewing in the distance, and I expected it would wash over the islands within a few hours, churning the waters and ensuring no one was going anywhere, not if they valued their lives.

I valued Abrahan's life far more than my own, so I eased the *Wanderer* into my cove, anchored her, and left her in the safety of the natural harbor no storm had hope of destroying. Instead of swimming, we'd take the pair of canoes Abrahan had cleverly ordered for our voyage. I burdened one with supplies, anchored a rope to it, and dove into the water so I could do my fair share of the work and tow it to the main island.

What would be the best approach for dealing with Lucretta O'Malley? I'd handled many a parley, browbeating superstitious men while my captain watched with smug bemusement as I turned their lives upside down on her behalf. Despite belief, parleys hadn't always been peaceful, especially when superstitious men thought they could take what they wanted. Time and time again, I'd waited for them to make the first move and break the code, which gave me the excuse I needed to wipe the deck with their unconscious bodies. More often than not, I battered three or four men at one time until the other side learned my captain was to be feared and respected.

Back then, people had an easier time accepting a woman could become a shark, as superstitions were one short step from the belief in magic. As for Lucretta and her crew, I'd already planted the seeds of belief in my survival, I'd reclaimed some of my pride in the burning of their ship, and I would win the war with words instead of violence.

I glided through the waters, pulling my canoe while Abrahan paddled behind me. Sane men wouldn't have left the safety of the cove, but I supposed I'd numbed him to the dangers of the shoreline after our rather violent voyage. I'd have to work on that; respect for the ocean was equally as important as courage.

Lucretta O'Malley stood on the shore near the charred ruins of her ship, and Abrahan slid his canoe onto the sand, splashed into the water, and retrieved the rope from my mouth, dragging the supplies closer so they wouldn't return to sea on a rogue wave. "O'-Malley," he greeted, and his wary regard and obvious dislike in his tone amused me.

"Have you come to parley, then?"

"I haven't. She has." Abrahan pointed at me without turning his attention from the rival captain.

Later, I would reward him well for his wisdom. A gun of his own, a sword he could be proud of, and the parrot he desired would be the first signs of my favor—assuming he demonstrated he could take care of the long-lived bird. I slipped into deeper waters so I could gain speed for my leap to shore.

The transition from shark to woman finished in the blink of an eye, and it took a single step to traverse the boundary between the sea and land. I allowed my disdain to show in my frown, looking the woman over from head to toe. Her time marooned on the island hadn't done her clothes any favors, but her proud stance and narrowed eyes promised she hadn't been worn down quite yet.

If she found my transformation startling, she did a good job hiding it, which I acknowledged with a slight inclination of my head. She had bested me once, and it was my turn to shine.

"Lucretta." My use of her name counted as an insult, as I stripped her of rank and heritage, my tone colder than the unforgiving sea. "Will you parley?"

I savored her scowl, the tension in her body, and the corner I'd put her in. The tables could turn in the next few minutes, but for the moment, I stood as the victor, and we both knew it.

"I'll parley."

The hatred in her tone wouldn't work in my favor; I knew all about hate, loathing, and the desire for revenge. I'd put mine aside and test her mettle. We could work together. I had something she wanted, she had something I wanted, although she didn't know that yet.

Tossing Lucretta a bone would serve me during negotiations. "We've more supplies with my ship. Abrahan will serve as my voice while I bring them."

Without waiting for her acknowledgment or agreement, I grabbed the spare rope from my canoe, rigged it to Abrahan's, and began unloading. He joined me, and within five minutes, both were emptied. I shoved the crafts into the surf and dove in. Shifting in the shallows meant I had to plow my way out to sea, far less graceful than I liked, but it gave me a chance to show off my other form and ensure Lucretta understood what she faced.

I snagged both canoes by their ropes and

towed them to the *Wanderer*. The supplies would protect Abrahan, and as a shark, I could maroon us all on the island together, preventing the stranded crew from succumbing to the temptation the small vessels offered. While the ploy was underhanded, I'd rely on the traditions of the past, where even in parley, the enemy wasn't to be trusted.

If she harmed Abrahan while I was gone, she would learn how cruel a pirate could truly be.

Loading both canoes took time, but with the storm on the horizon, I emptied my ship of the necessities and a few luxuries to keep the stranded happy—or at least a little more comfortable. Well aware the marooned likely hadn't enjoyed much fresh food, I also took the time to hunt, sliding through the waters until I found a young tuna. It fought well, but not well enough, and I dragged it to shore to discover the supplies gone and Lucretta waiting with Abrahan, Benny, and Bensen. I surged up the surf, twisted, and flung my prize at their feet.

The tuna flopped several times before the life fled its body, and I thought it an appropriate omen.

"That's awful," Abrahan muttered, shaking his head and kicking water at me.

I showed him my teeth, and he laughed.

Maybe I would get him two parrots, one

for each shoulder, and I'd make certain they were as smart mouthed as him.

Twisting around, I returned to the sea and fetched the canoes, towing them to the beach one at a time. When Abrahan emptied them, I returned them to the *Wanderer,* lashed them into place, and checked my ship was ready to ride out the storm without me. By the time I had finished, Lucretta's crew had ferried everything off the beach. Abrahan waited alone.

I shifted and stepped out of the water, grunting at the ache of hard-used muscles. "I didn't think that through all the way."

"Which part? Showing off your magic or serving as a pack mule?"

"Pack mule. I want her to know I'll eat her if she crosses me."

"It's safe to say the message was received. Your two friends were particularly startled. All three of them clued into the nature of the Shark Tamer about five minutes after you dragged the canoes off. I think they've got you figured out. That navigator showed up, caught one look at their expressions, and started laughing. Then he wandered off, still laughing. I think that one is out of his right mind."

Well, maybe one of her crew might be worth getting to know, if his reaction to the whole mess was to laugh. Then again, no.

No more damned navigators.

"I think they had me figured out from our last encounter, Abrahan."

"No, not really. I think O'Malley believed you're like her—an enthusiastic, dedicated descendant. She didn't believe you were the real deal. I think she does now."

Interesting. "They took the supplies up to the house?"

"Yes. O'Malley said she would prepare the meeting hall for the parley and requested her crew be in attendance. I didn't think you'd have a problem with that, but I told her she was the only one who could show up armed. She agreed to my terms. I've got a knife in my boot, but I'm going to give it to you when we go inside."

"Good. Her crew's mood?"

"Better than I expected. She has them on a tight leash."

It would do. I straightened, lifted my chin, and returned to the House Lost at Sea to take back what was mine and so much more.

THIRTY-THREE

Pirates shouldn't return to where they've marooned enemy crews.

NO MATTER how many times I returned to the House Lost at Sea, I doubted the sense of loss and regret would ever fade. On the outside, nothing had changed. I went first; in the old days, I'd gone first to a parley, too, as a show of strength and often an underhanded insult to those my captain wished to negotiate with.

Then, I took the risks out of loyalty and love at my captain's request. I'd been both a weapon and a shield, and it had been an honor to defend her and the crew. I'd also understood I was expendable but important enough to toe the line of parley. If the rival side stooped to treachery, my life was of little importance compared to my captain's.

Now, I took those risks because I had nothing left to fear. What was death? For me, it would be a mercy. I would take another bullet for Abrahan, even if it meant I would begin the cycle of life and death all over again. Perhaps Lucretta O'Malley hadn't wanted Naidoo to fire, but he had. My life had cost him his, although only Abrahan had known some of the truth.

I wondered if Lucretta would have fired if she'd known I couldn't die.

Either because someone understood I wouldn't knock or worried I'd kick the door down, a definite possibility all things considered, the door was open, the foyer empty, and lanterns illuminated the entry hall. The mementos of years long lost still decorated the walls, but I ignored them in favor of the woman waiting in the intersection beyond.

"Pirates shouldn't return to where they've marooned enemy crews," O'Malley declared, her hands on her hips, her body stiff in defiance.

Was she serious? I laughed long and hard, shaking my head at her misconception of the past—or her belief in rules that didn't exist. "A pirate does exactly what she wishes to do. There is no such thing as honor among pirates or thieves, and even parley is a dangerous endeavor. But you have no way of knowing that, do you? History often misses the details, and families often sweep the undesirables beneath the rug. It happens. The little things, like an ancestor's treachery, get lost over the years. Let me educate you. When you parley, expect betrayal and treachery. Some of us had honor, but the Black Scourge did not. She did what ensured her victory, and that was that. My captain wasn't much different. Pirates could be trusted for one thing: if the pay was high and the captain well versed in the issuing of threats, they'd remain loyal—not truly dedicated in many cases, but loyal enough."

In many ways, my captain had chosen poorly, but I kept my opinion to myself. Unless Lucretta aimed another jab in my direction, I'd keep feelings about the Black Scourge and my personal experiences sheathed.

"Parley is sacred."

"Who fed you that load of dung? The good captains would honor it, but there were as many bad as there were good, and a wise pirate never expects the rules of parley to hold. That's a good way to get a crew killed. Pirates broke laws more often than they kept them, and parley was just another rule to be broken. I've never understood the modern desire to romanticize an era of violence and treachery. And make no mistake, O'Malley, it was very violent and very treacherous. I'm proof of that."

"I confess I doubt you are *that* Catalina. A twin, perhaps?"

I laughed again. "You watched me transform from shark to woman and back again, yet still you doubt?"

"Hallucinations happen."

"There are no hallucinogens on this island unless you were diving for puffers and sampled the wares. But had you, I'd expect you'd be dying soon enough. I suppose you could have caught some tainted seafood. I thought the tuna would have been sufficient evidence. A shark doesn't give up a tuna like that. But, if you need more evidence, come here." Turning to Abrahan, I gave him my flintlock. "If she tries anything questionable, shoot her. I recommend aiming for the head. That tends to be lethal."

"Yes, ma'am," he replied, taking my weapon and holding it with the care of someone who'd handled a gun before. "Cock the hammer, pull the trigger?"

"Exactly so." Facing Lucretta, I removed my hat, tucked it under my arm, and swept my hair up to present the back of my head. "Touch."

"What, exactly, am I looking for?"

I chuckled. "You'll know when you feel it."

Time had helped, but bone took longer to regenerate, and a depression remained where the bullet had torn through my skull. At first, her touch was uncertain, but she patted my head, located the spot, and rubbed several times before sucking in a breath. "There's a hole."

"Not quite a hole; the bone is thinner there right now. It'll grow back in time." She'd learn soon enough that was the entire problem. Releasing my hair and shoving my hat back onto my head, I spun and looked down my nose at her. "I'll make this clear, Lucretta O'Malley. Your ancestor cursed me, and I hold you responsible. Undo what your blood has done. This is why I'm here to parley with you. I am as I was hundreds of years ago, when the Black Scourge sailed the seas and robbed me of the death I had earned and deserved at my captain's side. I hold you responsible, and only when the curse is broken or the blood of your line has vanished from the Earth, will I let it go."

"You were quick to start with the threats."

"And you were quick to open fire."

"Point," she conceded. "His actions were against my wishes."

"And your wishes were to have me conveniently removed by setting me adrift off the shores of the Cape of Good Hope for what reason?"

"At the time, I viewed you as a potentially valuable acquisition. There are those who think highly of you, claiming you're a woman of rare intellect, insight, and skill."

"Several hundred years of experience does tend to give me an advantage."

"We didn't know that. We'd assumed you were like me, a descendant with a rich heritage."

"My line ended with me."

"You're alive."

"I'm also barren, and there are no others. I was an only child." The way her eyes narrowed led me to believe she understood the repercussions of an only child during an era where most families lost many children to illness, disease, and war. "Curse or nature, I'll never know, but I suspect a bit of both. So, knowing that, Lucretta O'Malley, will you parley?"

"I'll parley, on one condition."

"Ask it."

"Your true name, the one of your birth."

"It is as I told you from the beginning. I am as I was, Catalina de la Corona, the Pirate Princess of the Seven Seas, and the reason Captain Louisa carried the name of Shark Tamer. I've other names, but I've forgotten them. That is the only one that matters."

"And your family's name?"

I shrugged. "If I had one beyond that, I don't know it anymore and haven't for over a hundred years. Some things are better left forgotten and undisturbed within their graves."

PER ABRAHAN'S CONDITIONS, Lucretta and I were the only ones armed, and the sole member of my crew made a show of returning my flintlock and digging his knife from his boot. After his knife came several other weapons, including a pair of kitchen knives, wire cutters that'd make a mess if he tried to snip an artery, and a box cutter.

I needed to have a talk with him about excessive yet ineffective weaponry, especially since he pulled a multi-tool card from his wallet, one with a rather sharp edge. If he got creative, he'd be able to do some damage, but I'd have to teach him the wonders of concealed carry. A knife could be dangerous even in a gun fight, if the shooter wasn't fast on the draw. I'd seen plenty of swords kill gunmen before a single shot was fired, but times had changed.

Most of Abrahan's weapons went into my pockets or boots, and the rest I lined up on the table within easy reach. Modern-day pirates wouldn't recognize the lethal force I put on display, as the items I kept in the open seemed safe compared to the ones I hid away. Should one of them try something, I'd enjoy showing them what the sharpened edge of a metal credit-card sized tool could do. It'd be bloody, painful, and potentially lethal—if I went all out.

I wouldn't, not without just cause, but I enjoyed thinking about it.

I tried to ignore Lucretta's crew in the room, especially Benny and Bensen, who stared without bothering to disguise their curiosity and interest. The man with a striking resemblance to my Ricardo annoyed me, and

I was tempted to have him sent away so I wouldn't have to remember my past. Instead, I scowled, made a point of refusing to look at him at all, and focused on the rival captain. Her crew annoyed me, their gazes prickling the back of my neck, but I endured without acknowledging them.

Soon enough, I would discover if this ending led to new beginnings or closed another chapter in my life. I wanted the whole damned book shut with a definitive clap, but I'd try to balance my desire for rest with Abrahan's sensitivity on the subject of my death. I wasn't certain how to factor in Benny or Bensen—or that damned man who dared to look like my Ricardo and insisted on staring at me.

I hoped Benny and Bensen had enough years behind them to understand death should come to all things in time, and I was long overdue.

But I could have a little fun first, couldn't I? Perhaps at their expense, but I *was* a pirate.

We did things like that.

Lucretta took her place on the opposite end of the long table; as the victor, it was my right to sit first. I nodded to the seat at my right, and Abrahan sank onto the tall-backed chair. I never sat during parley, not even during my captain's days, so I perched on the table's edge and used the chair as a boot rest. Grace O'Malley's distant descendant could handle cleaning the upholstery, and I preferred leaning back, one arm behind me keeping me somewhat upright while I kept a hand free to reach for one of my many weapons.

I sacrificed comfort for mobility, and if I needed to act, I would long before anyone else could rise from their chairs.

Lucretta sat, rested her forearms against the table's edge, and pressed her palms together. Some might view it as a gesture of prayer, contemplation, or humility, but I saw it as a declaration of wary peace.

She could still act, but she left herself open to attack, trusting me to adhere to the rules of parley and refrain from violence. I supposed my position sent a similar message, seeming relaxed for those who weren't perched on a hard table without the benefit of a cushion. Ah, style, the inflictor of agony for hundreds of years and counting.

"All right, Corona. You extended the offer to parley. Let's parley."

I smiled, leaning my head back and lifting my free hand to adjust my hat so it wouldn't fall to the floor. "You have something I want, and I mean to have it in any way possible. I prefer using honey, but I will use force if needed."

"How pleasant, beginning a parley with threats."

"It's a parley, not a cocktail party. You

should be pleased I didn't begin the parley by offering you a wicker basket containing the decapitated head of one of your crew. That was one of your ancestor's tricks, did you know that? If she knew a parley was coming, she'd send one of her scourge out late at night, snatch a member of the rival crew, relieve him of his head, and open negotiations with a gift—a very bloody gift. Personally, I found the Black Scourge's methods a bit repulsive. Captain Louisa preferred to open her negotiations with live hostages. It built better goodwill than an open slaughter."

Lucretta scowled. "I don't appreciate you insulting my family."

"It's not an insult if it's the truth. She wasn't a nice lady. By definition, she wasn't a lady at all. She was a pirate. She was a pirate who, after her treachery sank my captain, our crew, and ship, went on to join the O'Malley bloodline through one of Grace O'Malley's descendants. That's the problem with history; I'm not going to pretty up the reality so you can cling to the romanticized bullshit of the Golden Age of Piracy. And it's just that nowadays, romanticized. The sea is a cruel, harsh mistress, and pirates were as cruel as the ones they served. There were good pirates, yes, but they were few and far between. The Black Scourge wasn't one of them. She was aptly named. Parley was broken as often as not, and wise captains came prepared to face treachery and were grateful if things remained calm."

"I have no intention of breaking parley."

"It doesn't serve me to break the rules of parley with you."

"That's something, I suppose. Very well. What do you want?"

"I want the agreement that you and your crew will work to break the curse your ancestor, the Black Scourge, inflicted on me on behalf of her lover and my former captain. This existence was not my choice, and I hold you and your line responsible."

Someone from her crew grunted, a displeased sound I opted to ignore.

"I see no reason to accept punishment for another's crime."

"I see several reasons. First, you wrongly believed yourself the sole inheritor of *my* property. Second, you attempted to have me kidnapped, murdered, and otherwise inconvenienced. Third, I'm the one running this show, and you're stuck on this island until I decide to help you leave. I'm quite happy to turn my home into your prison—and don't think for an instant this place belongs to you. It's not your captain who built it, it's not your crew who decorated these halls, and it's not your hands that helped carve the steps and turn this island into a habitable space. Who do you think brought the plants, cultivated the fruit trees, and turned a stagnant pool into a potable spring? Not you."

To drive home my point, I held up my hand and waggled my fingers at her. "For days, weeks, and months, *my* hands carved the steps and shaped this island. For years, *my* ships came to these uncharted shores to see if the House Lost at Sea withstood the sands of time the same as I. For centuries, we've waited. You wouldn't be within these walls at all, had I not gone to my captain's final resting place to retrieve the key that is mine as the sole survivor. That was the deal, Lucretta O'Malley. First came crew, and only when the last of us died, would this home pass down to the descendants."

Lucretta's gaze locked on my hand, and her eyes narrowed. "What proof do you have?"

"You are not owed any proof at all. If anything, *you* should be proving yourself to *me.* You're the one lacking proof. I was old long before your grandmother was born, girl. I want the rest I've been denied. I've lived far beyond my time, and I have witnessed the world change. You can defy me, but should you, it'll be the rest of your family line I'll haunt until I get what I desire, and until I do, I have an immortal life to plan, to wait, and to act. If your shoulders don't carry the burden, another's will. Perhaps a child of yours, or a cousin, an aunt, or anyone else with even a trace of the Black Scourge's blood left in their veins. You will find me a patient hunter, and time is on my side."

"She's the real deal," a sickeningly familiar voice stated, his tone a mix of amused and resigned, something Ricardo had mastered after long years of dealing with Captain Maritza and her lover, my captain.

A bone-deep chill crept through me. If I turned my head, I'd identify the source of the voice, and he wore my lost lover's face.

Lucretta O'Malley shot a glare at the speaker. "And how would you know?"

"I told you, O'Malley. I have my secrets. I showed you the *Terrier's* location. I knew that location for the same reason Catalina knew the final resting place of her captain's beloved ship. Those were, and still are, my waters, and I led you to that ship for my own purposes. Then, it had been freedom in death. But such freedoms have lost some of their appeal now."

"Ricardo," Lucretta warned.

"Won't you look at me, Catalina?" Ricardo asked, and his tone turned inquisitive—with a side-dish of seductive. "It's been a while."

"Some three hundred years now, I suppose," I replied, the bitter bite of betrayal digging even deeper. "Did you enjoy destroying everything I own?"

"I played no part in that, and I advised her against toying with you. She didn't believe me. I encouraged her to wear your stolen goods to that gala so you would know who had crossed your path. I had not expected your attachments to them to be so strong you'd choose to leave immediately. I'd intended to pull you aside and resolve the matter there, but you had other plans, and I knew better to interfere when your temper ran so hot."

I would need a lot more time than I had to process what he told me—and consider the one thing I hadn't considered before.

His captain hadn't cursed just me. The bitch had cursed us both.

Hundreds of years broke around me, shattering under the weight of reality and having carried so much grief, alone when the one person I'd missed the most had wandered the world without me. I clacked my teeth together, inhaling to control my turbulent emotions. "They were all I had left."

"Well, I was certainly surprised when I realized I'd crossed paths with you after all this time, so that is perfectly reasonable. I'd had suspicions, but I knew for certain when I saw she'd taken your items."

I wanted to leave, set sail, and leave him to sort his own crew out. "I see."

"Are you two finished?" Lucretta demanded.

"Oh, no," Ricardo announced, and I tensed at the sound of footsteps drawing closer. "I've only begun. You can't ignore me forever, Catalina."

"I most certainly can. You always picked the shitty crew. I have matters to discuss with your captain."

He chuckled at my jab. "O'Malley has served her purpose, and unlike Captain Maritza, she is not holding the threat of your death over my head. We're beyond that worry, aren't we? Of course, I had not known that, not then. Not until the day the *Terrier* sank beneath the waves, and I'd died for the first time."

I understood that; I'd been pretty shocked the first time I'd died and come back from the dead. If Ricardo hadn't known he'd been cursed, he wouldn't have had any reason to believe I still lived. As I hadn't realized his captain had cursed him, as well, I hadn't had any reason to believe he still lived.

My captain had done her best to erase him from my life and my heart. She had failed.

I wondered if she'd known of his curse, and bitch she could be, had hidden it from me to prevent me from having hope of a future.

Ricardo joined me on the table, perching nearby so I'd either have to acknowledge him, close my eyes, or turn around to avoid him. I considered taking the coward's route, but I lifted my chin and glared at the man.

He hadn't changed much since he'd been my lover, although he carried a few new scars on his cheek. My hand moved of its own accord, and I traced one of the marks with the tips of my fingers.

He turned his head and kissed my palm, one of those little displays of his affection he'd enjoyed showering me with in the days I'd stolen with him between voyages. I should have done something other than freeze, unable to think of anything other than his living warmth.

"Ricardo," Lucretta warned again.

Ricardo gave my palm another kiss. "Catalina isn't the only one cursed by your ancestor, although I find the circumstances of my curse a great deal more tolerable considering the changed circumstances. You no longer have anything I want, and Catalina told you nothing but the truth. Pirates were not valiant figures, the rules of parley were rarely followed, and your ancestor enjoyed severing heads and using them as gifts to start negotiations. Her negotiations usually ended with someone's death. You're not stupid. You saw my portrait, and you recognized my likeness. You read my name. You suspected me, although you said nothing. You now understand why I insisted you don't hurt her boy. She has always taken matters of crew seriously, and had you done more than bruise him in the first scuffle, you would have signed our death warrants. Well, yours. I'm rather difficult to kill."

So he was. As was I. What had been a curse for so long had become a blessing—assuming the curse wouldn't break now that I had discovered there could be a world with both Ricardo and I still in it.

But then again, I remembered the curse and the words Captain Maritza had used.

I was so cursed to serve my captain for an eternity if I must.

My curse wasn't tied to the man I had believed forever lost to me.

Lucretta's mouth dropped open, and she spluttered.

"Well, this explains a lot," Bensen muttered. "Little Cathy, spending hundreds of years love sick for Ricardo, of all people."

I bristled at that, but Ricardo laughed. "You're just upset because you see her value. I saw her first, and we both know she never had eyes for either one of you."

That was the Ricardo I knew, confident to the bitter end. I sighed and settled in to watch my plans blow up in my face, leaving me with zero idea of how to proceed.

Ricardo had, like he had hundreds of years ago, changed everything at his whim.

"Captain?" Abrahan asked.

Well, I did have one idea of what I would do. I freed my hand from Ricardo's clutches so I could point at him. "This one comes with us, Abrahan."

"Understood."

"Kidnapping me again, my little princess?"

I could either break down into an emotional mess or wear the old shoes I'd walked in when we'd had a life together. "And you will enjoy it, Ricardo."

"Of course."

Of course. I straightened my shoulders, focused on Lucretta O'Malley, and lifted my chin. "I've changed my mind. The only thing I want is this man, and I will take him. In exchange for safe passage from my island, you will owe me a single favor. I expect it will involve something like unburying a lost treasure, and as I'm a generous captain, I'll even permit you to have your fair cut of the booty. I'll even give you a gift to make such an alliance worth your while. I'll tell you what you want to know about your ancestor."

"I can accept those terms. Tell me about the Black Scourge."

I frowned, lowered my foot from the chair cushion, and turned so I could stare across the table, tucking one knee up while I let my other foot dangle. It made ignoring Ricardo's presence easier, when every instinct demanded I haul him away and hold him safe aboard the *Wanderer*. "What do you want to know? I'll be honest with you, Lucretta. I hated her then, and I hate her now. She viewed men as a plague, one she enjoyed wiping from the Earth. I sometimes think she cursed me so she would have an easy way to get rid of the bodies she didn't want found. When someone annoyed her, she would have my captain, her lover, bring her ship closer and have me dispose of the unwanted cargo. She rarely killed them before forcing them to walk the plank. Then, I had no control over the curse, and humans made easy, filling prey."

Everyone at the table, even Abrahan, blanched. After thinking about what I'd said, I grimaced at my ineloquent and accidental confession of having eaten pirates while a shark. I shrugged, since it was the truth.

"You ate people."

"I'm a shark, O'Malley. What were you expecting? A picnic? To a shark, a human is nothing more than an unusually shaped meal. It took many years to learn to be a human in a shark's skin. It's called a curse for a reason." I waved my hand to dismiss the subject. "I haven't eaten anyone in decades."

"You sound proud of that," the rival captain muttered.

I wondered if I would go a day in my long life without someone judging me for who and what I'd been. Probably not. People struggled to accept what they couldn't understand, and then they sought to change what they couldn't understand so it would be easier for them to bear. "Well, you would be, too, if you went into a frenzy whenever there was blood in the water. And no, I didn't eat anyone from my crew when the British sank our ship and took our lives. I drowned a few Brits, though, for which I'm not sorry. I may have taken a few bites. Deserved, if you ask me."

Ricardo sighed at that. "I, too, am guilty of taking a few bites, and I definitely ate a few Brits after they sank the *Terrier.* I went out of my way to find Brits to eat. Revenge, for your death and for the death of my crew. I should have known you had been likewise cursed."

We'd proven to be our worst enemies. "What did she curse you with?"

"That I would remain cursed until she released me from her service."

He, too, had earned an eternity.

For the first time in hundreds of years, eternity didn't loom in front of me, a torture to be endured. Did I even want the curse to be broken? I regarded Ricardo with a furrowed brow.

"Knowing how to break the curse, if it can be broken, isn't a bad thing."

I shrugged. "We can look into it while we look for treasures."

"More treasures?" Abrahan complained. "Don't you already have enough?"

I regarded the brat with a raised brow. "A pirate never has enough treasure. This is a sacred rule."

"And if I find a way to break your curse?" Lucretta asked.

"I've hundreds of years of treasure stored

here and there. Should you discover a way to break the curse and we find eternity distasteful, we won't have much use for that treasure, now will we? But make no mistake. I will not willingly share the location of my treasure with you. But, with your cooperation, I can share a treasure with you now."

"What treasure?" Lucretta demanded.

I could appease the woman's greed—and buy her favor at the same time I kept her busy for years to come. "The *Calico's* final resting place, of course. Is that not part of what you desire? To reclaim your ancestral legacy? Your Black Scourge was nothing without my captain, and the *Terrier* is no prize without the *Calico*. But I warn you, she rests in deep, treacherous waters, and I wish you the best of luck raising her from her watery grave. Some things are best left undisturbed. As for the rest, there is only one person who knew your ancestor better than I, and it is her navigator."

Ricardo grunted his displeasure. "You have said all that there needs to be said about Captain Maritza. She was named the Black Scourge for a reason, and you would be happier not knowing the truth. It is far darker a reality than you would like."

THIRTY-FOUR

Somehow, my nightmare had become a dream.

Hindsight was ever perfect. Had I thought ahead, I would have come prepared with a list of ways Lucretta O'Malley and her crew could help me break my curse—or help me find some lost treasure. She'd given me a lost treasure, one I valued above all others.

I struggled to believe Ricardo was real, but the bastard kept capturing my hand when I least expected it and kissing my palm. If I ignored him, he scraped his teeth against my skin.

The *Wanderer* was not nearly large enough for him, me, my libido, and the brat, who would discover I had a wild side when the right man came into the room. Or into my bed. In fact, I needed a bigger ship, one that allowed for proper, separate cabins.

I almost regretted sinking the *Serendipity*. Almost.

Lucretta had no idea where to start, her

crew left as soon as a chance appeared, and when the dust had settled, Abrahan, Ricardo, and I remained in the dining hall with Lucretta, Benny, and Bensen.

The pair I'd worked with for so long kept quiet, and I recognized their blend of shock, doubt, and guilt. Of the two, Benny seemed the most disturbed, which made sense. Bensen was older, and age made a difference when coping with the unexpected oddities of life.

Answers wouldn't be found at the long table once meant to unify two crews, especially not after having successfully stolen Lucretta's navigator. All I could do was make a proposal I hoped I wouldn't regret. Abrahan would like it.

If Lucretta O'Malley accepted my proposal without modification, I expected it would take most of her lifetime to come anywhere close to discovering a way to break my curse. She would be old, and death wouldn't be the enemy it was for her now. With Ricardo, I could wait another three hundred years before earning my rest.

I'd be happy to settle with even one full lifetime with him.

Somehow, my nightmare had become a dream, a blessing in careful disguise for the right moment.

I had a future with Ricardo in it.

"As I don't expect you to have a method to

break my curse, and my circumstances have changed, I would like to propose a period of one year for you to research your family line in more detail, looking through your historic records for any interesting information. Once a month, you'll contact me with any updates. You'll also provide me with all the information you have on the Black Scourge, a genealogy of the family line, and any stories passed down over the years—especially those that seem more farfetched than the others."

Lucretta grimaced. "There are a few of those. And understanding your situation, I'm inclined to believe they're more fact than fiction now. While I'm willing to share this information with you, there's something I want from you as well."

"What do you want?"

"A complete accounting of my ancestor's career as a pirate."

Ricardo cackled, and I shushed him with an elbow to the ribs. "Easily done. I'm not responsible if you don't like what we tell you, and I don't know everything, as I wasn't part of her crew, but I'll tell you what I remember. Ricardo can tell you what he knows, as he was part of her crew. What I know isn't as much as you want, however. I've forgotten a great deal."

"Would you be willing to subject yourself to hypnotism?"

"I'll entertain most methods of gaining

knowledge, but I won't allow any hypnosis without Ricardo supervising. I can even tell you what I know doesn't work. That list is rather extensive."

"Well, shooting you in the head and tossing you off a cliff should be on the list of unsuccessful methods," my rival captain replied, her tone wry.

"Or trying to drown me."

"Have you tried burning at the stake yet?"

"Lucretta, that's taking it too far," Benny burst out, slapping the table with his palm.

I laughed, and Ricardo jabbed me with his elbow. "Hardly, Benny. Really, relax. It's a valid question. I haven't tried a stake, but I've been in several fires. I've been in a ship fire over water, so that would technically count as a witch burning, especially since it was a rather effective attempt to get rid of me for a while." I hummed, wondering how many times I'd been killed over the years—too many to easily remember. Later, I'd make a list. "Car accidents don't work either. All the severity of the injury does is change how long it takes for me to get back up. If I'm in water, I might be down for a few years, so it's an effective way to get rid of me temporarily, but I always come back."

"I've been burned at the stake. It doesn't work. It did take a rather long time to come back from that, however. The more extensive the injury, the longer it takes to recover from it," Ricardo announced.

"Plane crash?" Lucretta asked.

"That's one I haven't tried, but mainly because I haven't felt like throwing a few million at trashing a bird and polluting the environment. I doubt it'll work—planes didn't exist when the Black Scourge cursed me. If there's a way to break it, I suspect it'll be something that was viable back then." I hesitated, shrugged, and added, "If the curse can be broken at all."

"So, you're open to experimenting."

"I think it'll be mandatory, although I find I'll limit my experimentations somewhat, considering the changed circumstances."

"Damned straight you'll be limiting your experimentations," Ricardo muttered.

I'd missed his possessiveness, second only to mine.

"I can work with that. And while my ancestor may be the one responsible for your cursed state, I don't work for free."

I smiled. If money was what Lucretta wanted, I had it. "I think we can come up with an agreement. I can scavenge small items from any shipwreck you can find from almost any depth. Ricardo can help with that. I probably know a few wrecks no one has found. The *Calico* remains where she is, untouched. But if you want the *Calico,* you'll have to earn her—and you will be respectful of my dead."

My dead had crumbled away with nothing, but their spirits remained with the ship, and that counted.

"I accept that condition. I solemnly swear to treat her dead well and raise her to sit with her sister ship on display."

I shook my head. "Even if you find her, she's likely beyond restoring. Should you touch her, I believe she'll crumble, and no amount of resin will save her."

"That's a fair claim. The *Terrier* was in remarkably good condition when we found her, which was a big factor in her restoration."

If she wanted a *Calico*, I could buy her loyalty to my cause simply enough. I slid off the table. "Wait here. I'll return shortly."

My cave included more than just monetary treasure, and I had one thing she didn't: the plans for both ships, right down to their figureheads. My captain had kept copies of both. The Black Scourge probably had as well.

I'd taken care of them over the years, preserved in the darkness in sealed tubes to ensure they survived the ages—and they had. Strolling out of the House Lost at Sea, I paused by my captain's portrait long enough to trail my fingers along her cheek. No matter how many centuries went by, goodbyes remained hard, the pain didn't fade, and

I wondered what could have been if fate hadn't dealt us such a cruel hand.

Ricardo followed me, and he stood at my side while I regarded my captain's portrait. My stubborn streak was several hundred years wide; for the first time since my captain's death, I'd let go of one of her treasures without regret, the one promising and binding her to the Black Scourge.

If Lucretta's ambition was great enough, maybe the sister ships would set sail one last time, though I didn't know who—if anyone—would captain them.

It wouldn't be me. I'd chart a new course with a new ship.

The storm was building outside, and I halted on the steps to watch the dark clouds roll in and listen to the wind wail as it hit shore. The first drops of cold rain fell, and I smiled. I'd done the cliffside steps more times than I could remember when the seas churned and the gale screamed its fury over my repeated escapes.

"I will be very displeased if you fall and lose us more days," Ricardo announced.

I'd be pretty displeased, too. "You're my booty from this venture, so don't you go falling and costing us more days, either."

"I find your terms acceptable."

While the surf slammed the shore, I ignored the ocean's temper and slipped into the water, shifting and swimming for the comforts of the old cave hidden from human eyes. Like me, Ricardo transformed into a tiger shark, and he nipped at my fins whenever I ignored him for too long.

Somehow, we made it to my cave without attacking each other—or indulging in more base instincts. The cave remained as I'd left it, as always, and I gathered the pair of scrolls, and to prove I could do as I claimed, I gathered gold, silver, and the odd weapon or two from the Black Scourge's day to entice Lucretta into forging an uneasy alliance with me.

Ricardo waited until I'd made a pile of loot before he pinned me to the wall, using his body to hold mine hostage. "We need to talk."

We needed to do anything other than talk, and I scowled at his declaration. "Is it talking about how the bunks on the *Wanderer* are not big enough for two to sleep comfortably? If so, yes. We need to talk, and we will need to acquire a better ship. The brat is mine, I claimed him, and you won't evict him from my crew. He's good at cooking, and I'm spoiled now, Ricardo."

I needed time to think before we could talk about the ruin of our lives—and where we could go moving forward.

"I find this is a very important discussion point, so yes. We definitely need to talk about that."

"I can afford a bigger vessel than the *Wanderer.* I bought her on a whim, although she's a good ship. I'll give her to the brat when he's earned it, and we'll use her for when we're near the coast."

"After interior renovations to allow for a larger bunk."

"Ricardo."

"I had spent the rest of my life believing my captain had been the reason for your death, regretting everything I hadn't done to keep you mine and keep you safe. I will not allow a too small bunk to come between us."

"Well, you'll have little choice in that. It'll be cramped quarters if I lug anyone off this island, and I'll need to. I will do so somewhat resentfully."

"Who do you plan to take off the island?"

"Benny and Bensen, as they will be missed more than that Lucretta bitch."

"Now that she knows we're cursed, she'll try to break it just to get rid of us."

I snorted at that. "I'll just provide her with treasure greater than the joy of ending our lives."

"I doubt you have such a thing."

"I've the original blueprints of the *Calico* and the *Terrier.*"

"I stand corrected. You do have something worth that much to her. Very well. And this treasure hunt?"

"I'm a greedy pirate who likes treasure."

He laughed. "You also did like your treasures, that is true. So, you've picked up a brat, have you?"

"He tried to badly stab me in Brazil, so I decided he could be the cabin boy. But he's got a smart mouth and likes to cook, so I let him cook. He might make a good first mate."

"I will protest, loudly, if you try to prevent me from working as a navigator."

He would, too. "I suppose."

"You suppose?" He pressed closer, until our noses touched. "I see I'm going to have to persuade you."

"And how do you plan on persuading me?"

"As the ship isn't suitable for my conquest, I will pose for you, reminding you of what you're missing, all the way until we reach shore, after which I will use my charms on you until I get my way."

I didn't need any additional persuasion. "Okay, you can attempt such a persuasion. I will not be easy to convince."

He laughed, released me, and picked up half of the bounty I'd selected from my hoard. "Of course not. You like being difficult, and I enjoy when you're difficult."

That he did—or had, three hundred years ago. Amazed at the thought of having a future, I gathered my share of the hoard and jumped into the water, careful to transform before submerging. Ricardo followed me, and he nipped my fins, annoying me until I chased him.

He goaded me into pursuing him around the islands until I tired, which encouraged him to nuzzle and nip at his leisure.

I wanted to take a nap in the safety of the cove, but Ricardo urged me back to shore, much to my dismay.

By the time we returned to the House Lost at Sea, thunder rolled, incessant and deafening, and while being indoors muffled the sound, the building shook. I chuckled at the cracks of lightning, doubting even a direct hit could do anything more than inconvenience the structure, which had withstood the centuries without nature winning a single battle in their long-fought war.

Ricardo smirked, carrying his equal share, with more spring in his step than I found appropriate.

I blamed my still-healing skull, which would reduce me to a tired mess for at least a few more weeks.

I returned to the dining hall and dumped all but the scrolls on the table. "Here's proof I can do as I claim. Consider this a down payment for your future work and tentative alliance—and payment for taking a member of your crew."

Taking a few moments to spread out the pieces, I itemized them in my head, assigned values based on what she could get on the market, and finally said, "This is easily worth two million dollars to the average buyer. However, they may be worth more to you than that. All of these things were taken in joint efforts between my captain and the Black Scourge. Most were my shares, but some were retrieved from the *Calico* after she sank. I think you'll find them in decent enough condition."

Greed lit the woman's eyes. "These were taken by both crews?"

"I thought you'd find them interesting, and it's just a fraction of the treasures I've amassed over the years."

"She's a bit of a dragon," Abrahan announced. "I'm surprised she doesn't pile up those gold coins of hers to sleep on."

"Coins do not make a comfortable bed."

Abrahan crowed his triumph. "So, you've tried it!"

"Who wouldn't? When you've got *that* many coins sitting around, it has to be done at least once. I don't recommend it, but you're welcome to get poked in uncomfortable places by coins if you really want."

Lucretta narrowed her eyes. "How much wealth do you have?"

"Enough to pay you a salary for the rest of your life and not miss a single coin." I held up the pair of metal tubes, each one six inches thick and stuffed full of pages. "This is what you want, and this is why you're going to do as I desire."

"What are those?"

"The original blueprints for the *Terrier* and the *Calico*, right down to the species of wood used for every last plank, the formulas for the tars and sealants, the style of rope, and even the fabrics and coatings used for their sails. Both captains kept a copy of it. I salvaged them when the *Calico* sank, for my captain was wise and stored them in a watertight container. I've cared for them over the centuries, so they're still legible, the paper is sound, and every last one of the ships' secrets are here for your curiosity."

Lucretta's eyes widened, her mouth dropped open, and the color fled from her cheeks. "The original plans for the ships? You have the original plans?"

I bit my tongue so I wouldn't snap at her for something beyond her control, waited until the urge passed, and sighed. "These were among my captain's most prized possessions. I have many of the prized possessions of most of my crew, reclaimed from the sea and kept in my care. These are but two of those things."

Why was letting go so hard? I popped the cap off the tube containing the *Terrier's* design plans and eased the thick sheaves of paper free, yellowed with age but intact and in as good a condition as the day they'd been drawn. Circling the table, I smoothed them out in front of the Black Scourge's descendant one page at a time until every room, every plank, every inch of the once proud ship surrounded her. "You've seen the *Terrier*'s shell. You can confirm the truth of my words."

"We have some sketches of the ship, which helped us identify the wreckage. I'm beginning to believe our sketches are a crude attempt to copy these. My family lost our originals."

"Likely sank with the ship. You might be able to find the case, but if the seals broke, the plans would be ruined. If you take me to where you found the wreckage, I can look for you. I know what I'm looking for." An uneducated eye could easily overlook the box. I doubted it had survived, but it cost me nothing to look.

Ricardo knew what to look for, too, and I cast him a glance.

"They were destroyed in the wreck. The captain burned them so they wouldn't be used."

Of course. I shook my head at the waste. "I would like a copy made for my reference, but the originals can be yours.

"For all this, you just want me to work at unveiling the nature of your curse so you can break it if you please? And go on treasure hunts with you?"

"Yes."

"What guarantee do I have that you're not just trying to trick me?"

My brows shot up, and I wondered just how—or why—Ricardo had put up with such blatant idiocy. "You're joking, right? There's millions on this table, the prints of your ancestor's ship in front of you, and I'm asking for some honest work in exchange. Once a year, we'll have a gathering, you and I—and two of your crew—to discuss your progress. Money is not an obstacle for me in this venture."

"And what will you be doing while I'm trying to break your curse?"

I smiled, stealing a glance at Abrahan and Ricardo. "I'm going to show Abrahan the world and look for treasure, of course. I'll do whatever I please with Ricardo, which is a great deal. I'll keep Abrahan busy and teach him about life outside of the prison of modern civilization, and as for Ricardo, that is none of your business."

"You're going to what?"

"Hunt for treasure." Hunting for treasure sounded like the sort of vacation I needed, conquering a new stretch of the world, one untouched by my past, although I'd drag the most prized part of my history along with me for the ride.

"Are you insane?"

I pointed at myself. "I'm hundreds of years

old, and I transform into a man-eating tiger shark. If you were expecting sanity, you're the one who's crazy."

Ricardo snickered. "I'm as old and as crazy as she is, and I'm in full agreement with her. We came from a different age, Lucretta—one you don't understand for all you're proud of your heritage."

"Very well. Where are you going to search for this treasure?"

"I'll probably look for the myths with a little bit of truth hidden deep in jungles where only the insane or an immortal would go. I'll probably scout it with Ricardo, determine if it's safe for others, and bring Abrahan on the second venture if it seems a conquerable challenge for a mortal."

"Count me in, then you have a deal."

I blinked. "Pardon?"

"Count me in on those treasure finding expeditions. I'll bring two of my crew, we'll handle our yearly meeting on one of these ventures. You find us treasure, we'll split the risk of the second venture, equal shares. We'll work on the curse at the same time. If there's more than one venture a year, very well—we have more than one meeting a year. I'll even pitch in on possible expedition targets."

The Black Scourge's descendant wanted to go treasure hunting in potentially lethal locations? I frowned and turned to Abrahan. He held his hands up in a gesture of surrender. "Don't look at me, Captain. I signed up when you started talking about exploring hidden jungles. I can't blame her for wanting to catch that kind of crazy."

I drummed my fingers on the tube containing the *Calico's* plans, shook my head, and set it in front of Lucretta. "Very well. Should I find some interesting hidden treasure in some inaccessible and potentially lethal remote location, I'll make certain to let you know."

"Then we have a deal."

I pulled Abrahan's knife from my pocket and drew a thin scratch across my palm to seal the deal and saw Lucretta had done the same. A slow laugh built in my chest, and I clasped hands with her, shaking my head over the ludicrousness of sealing a deal with a woman I should have considered a living devil and my enemy.

But then again, thanks to her greed and ambition, she'd given me a gift I could never repay. She wouldn't get Ricardo back; I'd fight her to the death over him, and I would not repeat the mistakes that had cost me so much. In the meantime, I would focus my attention on what mattered, reclaiming what I'd thought gone forever. "We have a deal. We'll see you in a year, Lucretta O'Malley, after I bring you a vessel capable of taking you all from this island."

Judging from her expression, she'd hate me for life, but I didn't care.

I'd already claimed everything I needed from her, although I'd keep my word should I be unable to avoid the siren's call of treasure and adventure.

About R.J. Blain

Want to hear from the author when a new book releases? You can sign up at her website (thesneakykittycritic.com). Please note this newsletter is operated by the Furred & Frond Management. Expect to be sassed by a cat. (With guest features of other animals, including dogs.)

A complete list of books written by RJ and her various pen names is available at https://books2read.com/rl/The-Fantasy-Worlds-of-RJ-Blain.

RJ Blain suffers from a Moleskine journal obsession, a pen fixation, and a terrible tendency to pun without warning.

When she isn't playing pretend, she likes to think she's a cartographer and a sumi-e painter.

In her spare time, she daydreams about being a spy. Should that fail, her contingency plan involves tying her best of enemies to spinning wheels and quoting James Bond villains until she is satisfied.

RJ also writes as Susan Copperfield and Bernadette Franklin. Visit RJ and her pets (the Management) at thesneakykittycritic.com.

Follow RJ & her alter egos on Bookbub:
RJ Blain
Susan Copperfield
Bernadette Franklin

www.ingramcontent.com/pod-product-compliance
Lightning Source LLC
LaVergne TN
LVHW090345140125
801169LV00004B/75

9781649640451